Praise for *Let Us March On*

"Shara Moon bursts onto the historica[l] ... Lizzie McDuffie, who finds herself a [p...] through four Roosevelt presidential [...] comes FDR's personal valet. From the [...] ... grappling with marital difficulties and racial strife, Lizzie fearlessly advises the president as his 'self-appointed secretary on colored people's affairs,' forever asking herself 'Am I doing enough? Can I do more?' A quietly compelling portrait of a woman in the shadows, at last stepping into the light. *Let Us March On* is a story that will linger long in the memory!"

—Kate Quinn, *New York Times* bestselling author of
The Briar Club

"*Let Us March On* is a wonderful debut about Lizzie McDuffie, a woman whose passion and strength shine throughout the novel. A true warrior, she uses her position as personal maid to FDR to advocate for the civil rights movement. Shara Moon delivers a moving story that is both beautifully told and powerful."

—Madeline Martin, *New York Times* bestselling author of
The Booklover's Library

"*Let Us March On* is an immersive, elegantly crafted novel that brings to life an unforgettable American hero, Lizzie McDuffie, and her commitment to social justice and the early civil rights movement. Moon's storytelling will engage, delight, and educate readers about a unique woman and the significance of her contributions to Black American history. Inspired by actual events, *Let Us March On* is a must-read."

—Denny S. Bryce, bestselling author of
The Trial of Mrs. Rhinelander and *The Other Princess*

"Wonderfully crafted, *Let Us March On* transports us to the FDR White House in this engaging portrayal of the remarkable Lizzie McDuffie, maid and confidante to President Roosevelt. Her love for her president, her husband, and her determination to be a voice for those who had no voice earn her a well-deserved place in our history and in our hearts."

—Shelley Noble, *New York Times* bestselling author of
The Tiffany Girls and *The Colony Club*

"Shara Moon's debut *Let Us March On* is a story about a quiet woman who used her voice in a big way: to influence the most powerful man in the country. Moon guides us through a behind-the-scenes glimpse of the FDR White House through the eyes of housekeeper Elizabeth McDuffie. Spanning from the 1906 Atlanta race riot to that sad day in April 1945 in Warm Springs, Georgia, that changed everything, this is a story of a woman's resilience and compassion that readers will find hard to put down."

—Kaia Alderson, author of *Sisters in Arms* and
In a League of Her Own

"*Let Us March On* by Shara Moon is a stellar example of returning a forgotten, unsung heroine to us in bold strokes. The engaging narrative will have you turning pages to figure out how Lizzie McDuffie, a White House maid, became a civil rights crusader, one who boldly proclaimed herself FDR's 'secretary on colored people's affairs.' This compelling novel, framed by the epistolary style using powerful, intimate correspondence, invites readers to discover Lizzie, her journey, and her pivotal role in history."

—Vanessa Riley, award-winning author of *Island Queen*
and *Sister Mother Warrior*

"*Let Us March On* is a heartfelt glimpse into life below stairs in FDR's White House, told from the unique vantage point of his personal maid, whose friendship with the forward-thinking president placed her in a position of real influence to advance the cause of Black Americans. With vivid historical detail and memorable cameos, Moon deftly portrays Lizzie McDuffie's transformation from maid to advocate, capturing the voices of the burgeoning civil rights movement and those working behind the scenes to make change. An inspiring and uplifting must-read."

—Stephanie Dray, *New York Times* bestselling author of
Becoming Madam Secretary

"Shara Moon's debut historical fiction, *Let Us March On*, is a moving and poignant novel that brings to life the people who worked tirelessly behind the scenes during the multiple terms of President Franklin D. Roosevelt, and also the deep friendships developed. Not only does Moon shed light on very important relationships FDR had with Lizzie, his self-appointed 'secretary on colored people's affairs,' and her husband, Mac, the best valet and companion FDR ever had, but more importantly, the struggles to make the president and his cabinet aware of the needs of the people, and civil rights movement that the president was keen to fight for."

—Eliza Knight, *USA Today* and internationally bestselling
author of *Can't We Be Friends*

"*Let Us March On* highlights the remarkable true story of Elizabeth "Lizzie" McDuffie, a domestic servant in the White House during FDR's presidency. Although initially his maid, Lizzie soon becomes FDR's friend and trusted advisor, shining a light on the terrible injustices facing Black Americans. Moon paints an engaging portrait of a courageous woman who used her unique influence to smooth the path toward civil rights. A gem of a book!"

—Elizabeth Langston, author of *Once You Were Mine*

"In *Let us March On*, Moon introduces readers to an unsung American hero, Lizzie McDuffie. Written from her perspective, we are invited into an intimate portrait of Lizzie's life, love, mission, and activism as she becomes one of FDR's most trusted advocates and a courageous voice for the civil rights movement of her time. Beautifully written and impeccably researched, I highly recommend!"

—Katherine Reay, bestselling author of *The London House* and *The Berlin Letters*

"Moon's storytelling masterfully brings to life Elizabeth McDuffie's challenges and achievements within a world struggling with racism and hate, as well as her personal fears and frustrations with the sluggish tides of change. *Let Us March On* is an amazing read that will leave you with a desire to know more about this remarkable woman."

—Monica Chenault-Kilgore, author of *Long Gone, Come Home*

Let
Us
March
On

Let Us March On

A NOVEL

SHARA MOON

WILLIAM MORROW
An Imprint of HarperCollinsPublishers

LET US MARCH ON. Copyright © 2025 by Shara Moon. All rights reserved. Printed in the United States of America. No part of this book may be used or reproduced in any manner whatsoever without written permission except in the case of brief quotations embodied in critical articles and reviews. For information, address HarperCollins Publishers, 195 Broadway, New York, NY 10007.

HarperCollins books may be purchased for educational, business, or sales promotional use. For information, please email the Special Markets Department at SPsales@harpercollins.com.

FIRST EDITION

Interior text design by Diahann Sturge-Campbell

Library of Congress Cataloging-in-Publication Data has been applied for.

ISBN 978-0-06-321342-5

24 25 26 27 28 LBC 5 4 3 2 1

To Mrs. Elizabeth McDuffie.
Thank you for writing your story.
You've earned your place in history.
I'm honored to be sharing a part of it.

Sing a song full of the faith that the dark past has taught us,
Sing a song full of the hope that the present has brought us.
Facing the rising sun of our new day begun,
Let us march on till victory is won.

—JAMES WELDON JOHNSON

Let
Us
March
On

Prologue

April 11, 1966
Atlanta, GA

O h, darling boy!"
I wrapped my tired arms around the handsome Franklin Delano Roosevelt Jr. and gave him a tight squeeze. He was careful as he gingerly wrapped his arms around me in a gentle embrace. At eighty-five, I wasn't the stout and limber Lizzie I once was.

"It warms my heart to see you." I pulled back and studied him closely. "Let me take a good look at you."

I had on my Sunday best, even though it was a Monday, and he had on a sharp suit. It was still jarring to see how much he favored his late father. And it wasn't just in name and looks that he took after him. He clearly had picked up his political ambitions as well.

"You look as handsome as ever, Franklin Jr. All that campaigning hasn't yet taken its toll, I see."

He laughed. "I have a good team of people behind me. They keep me together."

"No one would ever be as good as I was, I'm sure."

"No one," he agreed. "As a matter of fact, there's an open spot just for you, if you're interested."

"No, thank you, honey." I patted his hand. "Besides, you couldn't afford me now, anyway."

He threw his head back and laughed deeply. That laugh reminded me so much of his father that I couldn't help but share in his mirth.

"You're probably right, Duffie."

I took his hand and guided him to the sitting room. "Here, come sit. They can wait a little while for us to visit first."

Franklin Jr. helped me down into my seat before taking the chair beside me.

"Your mother sent me a very sweet letter right before her passing."

Franklin Jr. nodded. "I know you two kept in touch a lot over the years. She would always mention you and how you were faring."

"She was such a lovely woman."

"Yes, she was." The sorrow in his voice was quite vivid.

I could understand his pain. No matter how much older one gets, it was never easy losing one's mother.

"By the way, thank you for agreeing to all this, Duffie. I know how it might look, but my campaign manager thought it would make for a good story."

I smiled at the face that so much resembled his father's. Franklin Jr. wasn't the youthful man that I remembered, yet the way his eyes sparkled made me think of another lifetime ago, when he was a more rowdy young man.

"Well, he's not stupid. If a visit with me will help you secure more Negro votes at the polls, then I'd happily sit with you and a room full of newsmen."

A look of relief flashed across his face and I patted his arm in reassurance again. This meeting had been planned for months, yet it still filled me with joy to see one of my favorite Roosevelts again. I have always been a friend of the family, even after so many years had stretched between us. I knew their heart was in the right place when it came to the country and its citizens. Yet as much as Franklin Jr. had my support for his bid for the New York governorship and tomorrow was the anniversary of his father's death—a solemn day for us all—I still felt it important to remind him of his responsibilities.

"You know, I see so much of your father in you. I'm almost not surprised that you decided to run. But do you know why your father was a four-term president?"

"Because the people didn't know how to let go."

I heard the slight bitterness in his words and could understand where they came from. No one, particularly those of us at Warm Springs, would ever forget April 12, 1945.

Franklin Jr., however, along with the rest of the Roosevelt children, had needed a father. Instead they'd had to share him with millions of Americans who needed him just as much.

"I think it's because the country needed him as much as he needed to lead us. No other man could have done what your father did. He managed to heal and unite our nation while suffering through his own burdens. The people saw that. They valued and respected his commitment to making our country the strongest it could be."

"So what are you getting at, Duffie? You don't think I'm ready for the commitment?"

"I didn't say that. But what I don't want you to do is rely solely on your family name to win that election. I also don't want you to rely on my name to pick up the Negro vote."

"I wasn't—"

"I know, honey. Your heart's in the right place, but it wouldn't be the first time a Roosevelt wanted to use what little influence I had to win an election. And I'm okay with that, so long as the Negro isn't forgotten in the process."

"Of course they won't be. The civil rights movement is gaining traction, and as New York's next governor, I look forward to working with civil rights leaders like Reverend King to make strides in the Negro's advancement and fair treatment."

Spoken like a true politician . . .

I studied him carefully, trying to find hope and assurance in his words. Except I couldn't help but feel the emptiness of his words. I had seen so much ugliness these past few decades . . . Have seen too many social justice warriors slain in the search for basic human and civil rights.

"Are you familiar with Malcolm X, Franklin Jr.?"

"Yes, I've heard of him . . ." He shifted in his seat, appearing uncomfortable at admitting to such. That's what the man Malcolm X had been known to do—make people uncomfortable. At least that was the case before he was brutally gunned down last year.

"Well, I met him once. When he was just a high-spirited little boy, much like how you were. I watched how tragedy and hate turned little Malcolm into the man so many have come to fear. But while some saw an angry Negro, others saw a hero. What I saw was a young man who never got a fair chance at life."

"I understand . . . But you can't expect change by promoting anger and violence."

"Anger and violence are powerless when met with kindness. Do you know who said that?"

Of course he didn't.

Though I took liberties with what Malcolm had actually said,

I could tell from Franklin Jr.'s confused expression that he had never really bothered to listen to what the slain activist had been saying all along.

"Men like Dr. King are making strides in the civil rights movement, and he's doing so peacefully."

"My dear boy, you have to accept the fact that some people believe in the 'eye for an eye' doctrine."

"Doesn't the Bible teach against the 'eye for an eye, tooth for a tooth' philosophy?"

"Absolutely. But after what I've seen in my eighty-plus years, how can you blame them?"

I knew from his pensive gaze and the way he shifted in his seat that I truly had his attention.

"You have to understand, Franklin Jr., that the Negro people have been fighting for civil rights long before today. We have marched and protested without violence, we have turned the other cheek in the name of peace and equality. But has it truly gotten us far? A nation that has ignored the basic human rights of *all* its citizens for this long can't be shocked when they are ultimately confronted by men like Malcolm X."

I tried to control the earnestness in my tone. I didn't want him to feel as if I was preaching to him, but I needed him to understand that we still had a long way to go if we wanted to see real change in this country.

Franklin Jr. glanced down at his hands before looking back up at me. "I sympathize with the plight of the Negro, Duffie. I really do. Even with the anti-lynching bill . . ."

"I know you tried your best, dear," I assured him. I had followed his career closely enough to know the effort he had put into fulfilling his mother's legacy in getting an anti-lynching bill passed into law.

Unfortunately, lynchings still remained an unholy, yet lawful, act of terror against Negroes.

"I just feel this issue is much bigger than me," he murmured.

"It doesn't have to be." I took his hand in mine. "This country makes it next to impossible for humans to meet in America and not be conscious of their color differences. I remember when your father would make his speeches. When he addressed the country, he never singled out the Negro. This made some resentful. But I, like many, understood why he did this. He was trying to unite us as one nation, for we are all American citizens. What we're fighting for isn't a Negro problem, it's an *American* problem."

Franklin Jr. squeezed my hand. "My purpose for running is to ultimately serve the American people. I can only hope to be as great a man and leader as my father."

I knew he meant that. Franklin Jr. carried the legacy and challenge of a great name.

"Well, I will pray for your success and safety," I said, and I left it at that.

For the next few minutes, we shared a pleasant visit before his entourage, along with the reporter who had traveled with him, was allowed into the room. The interview was short and brief, for which I was grateful. It had been a while since I'd had to entertain and I could already feel the weariness seeping into my bones.

"So, Mrs. McDuffie," the reporter called out. "There've been rumors that you are working on a memoir about your life in the White House. Is this true?"

A small smile tugged at the corner of my lips as I thought of the letter from Margaret Mitchell so many years ago.

Write your story, Lizzie, the popular author had written. *Write it in your own words and write it soon.*

That had been all the encouragement I needed.

"Yes," I answered, suddenly feeling shy about it. "It's still a work in progress, but in it I write about the twelve years I spent working for and with the Roosevelts."

"I'm sure there will be plenty who will be eager to get their hands on it."

Suddenly the reporter reached into his breast pocket and handed me a business card.

"When you're ready with it, give me a ring. I might know an editor in New York who would be interested in it."

I took the card. I waited until they had all left my home before I pulled open the drawer to my desk and placed the card inside.

It lay right on top of the rumpled pages of my unfinished manuscript.

I grabbed the stack of sheets of my unfinished memoir and sat in front of the old typewriter. It was a project I had put off long enough, and now that I had genuine interest in my story, I felt rejuvenated about it again.

I remembered the first day I reported for work at the White House and the feeling that swept over me when I stood in the room where Abraham Lincoln had signed the Emancipation Proclamation.

I remembered meeting with Marie Dressler and Amelia Earhart and Marian Anderson at the White House for the first time. I remembered Katharine Hepburn and Shirley Temple's not so secret visits to Hyde Park. I even remembered my audition for the part of "Mammy" in *Gone with the Wind*.

Those memories flooded me with a wave of deep nostalgia. I wasn't prepared for the sudden emotion that rocked me, but I couldn't help but revel in the memories.

While we should have been mere servants to the Roosevelts, for so many Afro Americans Mac and I had been seen as much more.

They had come to us desperate for justice, hungry for salvation. As valet and maid to the most powerful man in America, Mac and I had tried our best to make a difference. I couldn't remember the number of calls or letters we had received during those twelve years, but I do remember the one thing they all desired: a moment of the president's time.

But not everyone had found the deliverance they sought.

For my part, there were more failed attempts than there were successes—and so many moments I wanted to quit this new role in which I had found myself.

Of course, I didn't.

And I didn't let Mac stop either.

Win or lose, we continued to march on.

As I flipped through the browning pages of my old manuscript, my eyes landed on some of my most interesting tales. A small, quick smile tugged at the corner of my lips from the memories.

It wasn't the greatest thing I had ever written, but it was still my story . . .

PART 1:

Our New Day Begun
(1932)

Chapter 1

San Francisco, Sept. 25, 1932:

I had heard that there was not much prejudice against the Blacks in the West, but this is the first city where it seems to be true. Here we can get an even break, but I have been told that it is not so in Los Angeles. If Negroes expect to leave the South for equal rights in the West, they might as well stay in Dixie. I believe FDR will win by a landslide. Everybody is wild over him, and our crusade has been great!

—Your Loving Husband

November 8, 1932
Atlanta, GA

Mac was right.

Franklin Delano Roosevelt was about to win the election in a landslide.

The unassuming, suspiciously liberal New York Democrat was

about to become the next president of the United States. So much would change—not just in my life, but for the country.

The thought was both exhilarating and terrifying.

"Lizzie, is that tea ready yet?"

"Yes, Mama."

I brought over the two teacups to the sitting room where my spunky, near seventy-year-old mother sat in her night dress, listening to the radio broadcast of the night's election results. She straightened on her favorite high-back navy-blue chair as I handed her the steaming cup of peppermint tea.

Her hair was already wrapped and in curlers, and she was very much ready for bed. But like everyone else around the country, we both waited eagerly to hear the final election results.

"Any new updates?" I asked, taking the seat across from her.

Before she could answer, the broadcaster's excited words came piercing through the radio speakers.

"Votes are continuing to be counted as more polling stations report in. It appears there will be a clear winner tonight, folks."

My stomach tightened and I took a quick sip of my tea. I was good at letting my emotions get the best of me. The idea to make the herbal tea came from the rising anxiety that had been twisting in my gut all night.

So far, it didn't seem to be helping.

As I continued to sip my tea, I couldn't help but think back to that moment nearly two years ago when Mac had informed me of his boss's intentions to run for president of the United States. At first we had laughed at the idea. No way would the country vote for a feeble man like Franklin Delano Roosevelt. Where his cousin, former president Theodore Roosevelt—God rest his soul—had been the embodiment of strength and vitality, Mr. Franklin Roosevelt was a Northern Democrat stricken with polio. That didn't necessarily paint him in the best light.

Even in the beginning Mac had doubted his boss's chances.

"Lizzie, the man's got polio, for crying out loud," he had said after I voiced my concerns over the New York governor's intentions. *"He'd never get past the primaries."*

I had to admit that had helped to ease my worries some. I even chuckled at the thought of the governor's political aspirations going very far. Despite Hoover's failing presidency, support for a Democrat in the White House seemed tentative at best and practically unlikely.

"Besides, what would it look like for a good Republican such as myself to be working for a Democratic president."

I had scoffed then, reminding my husband that he was already working for the Democrat politico. But even as I spoke the words, I knew Mac had not had any choice in it. The recession had hit everyone hard around the country. President Hoover was proving to be a depressing and dour leader. He maintained his position that the economy had little to do with his leadership and everything to do with "external forces." He didn't even bother to address the plight of the Negro.

Still, Franklin D. Roosevelt was no "Teddy" Roosevelt, and the idea of this New York Democrat as president was practically laughable.

Until it stopped being funny and started becoming a reality.

It was then that Mac's attitude over the possibility began to shift.

Ever since Mr. Roosevelt had been nominated as the Democratic candidate for the presidency, the atmosphere around the country had been one of hope. And that had evidently invigorated

Mac. Many of his letters as of late centered around the governor and his campaign for the White House. It was clear from those letters that Mac was becoming very interested in getting his boss to Washington.

This game of politics is great! he had written in one of his earlier letters. *We are drawing big crowds everywhere! If that's any indication, we're in!*

His thrill over the idea practically jumped off the page. Like many others, Mac believed a win for Mr. Roosevelt may be just what the country needed. But I wondered if he truly believed that.

At first, I couldn't understand it. Mac loved his home, his community. He was a deacon at the Liberty Baptist Church. He sang in the choir. He was active in his Masonic lodge.

Why would he possibly want to move to Washington DC?

The more I reflected on it, the more I believed it was the notoriety of becoming the personal valet to the president of the United States that truly excited him.

"Have you spoken to Mac at all today?"

Pushing my thoughts aside, I shook my head and took another sip of my tea. "No. We haven't spoken in days. Apparently, Mr. Roosevelt keeps him very busy."

Still, my husband could find two minutes to call me.

But I kept those bitter words to myself. I didn't want to get into another long discussion with my means-well, yet overly meddling mother about Mac's possible move to the White House. It was no secret that Mama was also excited by the prospect of Mr. Roosevelt's win. To have her eldest daughter and son-in-law working for the most important family in the country would be just the kind of prestige a former slave girl could have in this country. Which is why I couldn't fault her for her high hopes and wishful thinking.

I just wanted her inflated expectations to be centered around reality.

Just because Mac's position with Mr. Roosevelt would extend from nearby Warm Springs and the remote grounds of Hyde Park to the bustling halls of the White House didn't mean I would be allowed to join him.

In fact, I wasn't even certain we would be able to live together once the Roosevelts moved to Washington.

That thought only added to my anxiety.

I took another sip of my tea.

"You know, you can always call him," Mama said pointedly. "You both need to start planning your next move once Mr. Roosevelt becomes president."

Once again, I reminded my mother, "Even if he does become president, Mama, that doesn't mean I get an automatic position in the White House."

"Oh, nonsense. I'm sure Mac will have no problems securing you a job there. He's pretty chummy with Mr. Roosevelt, and I'm sure they'll need the help."

I shrugged. Though we both knew Mac cared very much for his boss, it didn't mean the sentiment was returned. Mac worried over Mr. Roosevelt in a way I'd never seen him do over another man, much less a white one. He laughed with him, doted over him. Perhaps he even idolized him a little. I didn't quite understand it, but somehow my husband had managed to form a strong bond with the white Democrat.

"I don't know, Mama. They might very well move in with their current staff. They may not need to hire any more help."

"Well, you're a smart, hardworking woman. If you don't get a position with them, I'm sure you won't have trouble finding work somewhere. Washington is filled with possibilities."

"And so is Atlanta."

I recognized the lie the moment it left my lips. Mama did as well, but she didn't bother to argue with me. We both knew that since the recession, work and opportunities everywhere were few and far between. Especially for the Negro. I was lucky the Inmans hadn't let me go what with business not doing so well for them these days.

As one of the wealthiest and most affluent families in Atlanta, they had also felt the strains of a heavily stressed economy. Despite my twenty-plus years of service with them, I wasn't spared from their new financial restraints. Although Mrs. Emily Inman had assured me the change was temporary, there were no signs of things returning to normal anytime soon. But I couldn't complain. I was lucky to still have a job, even with shorter hours and a lower wage.

Besides, I had gone through two generations of caretaking and service with the Inmans. They had become like my extended family and Swan House had become almost like my second home. I enjoyed working for them and I especially enjoyed being around the children.

But Mama was right.

There were more opportunities elsewhere. If Mac moved into the White House, there was no question I would follow him. Four years was a long time, and I don't think I was prepared to be away from my husband again for that long. I had never lived anywhere else outside of Georgia, and I couldn't be certain I was ready for the move, but the thought of us being apart for that long became almost unbearable to consider.

With a small sigh, I settled back in my seat and took a look around at what I had considered home since Mac had taken on the job with Mr. Roosevelt. I would be leaving this familiar space . . .

leaving Atlanta and those precious Inman children . . . leaving my family and friends . . . leaving Mama.

But there was a season, and a reason, for everything. And right now, my season was to be with and to support my husband.

"Okay, Mama, you win. Tomorrow I'll call Mac and—"

"Shhh." She waved a hand at me as the radio announcer's excited voice once again came through the box. "Quiet, now. I think this is it."

"I was just—"

Mama shushed me again and leaned toward the radio, her attention fully focused on the small box.

"Reports are in, folks, and America has spoken."

I scooted to the edge of my seat, my breath lodged in the back of my throat.

"The Democratic New York governor Franklin D. Roosevelt has defeated Republican incumbent President Herbert Hoover in a landslide victory!"

"Hallelujah!" Mama exclaimed.

I released the breath that I held.

"Roosevelt has taken the seat with over four hundred electoral votes. His remarkable victory is the first by a Democratic candidate since President Woodrow—"

Mama shut off the radio and slowly got to her feet, a wide grin creasing the corners of her round, cocoa-brown cheeks. "I knew he was gonna win. But sometimes it's better to hear it out loud, you know?"

I silently nodded, not protesting as she gathered our empty teacups and headed to the kitchen.

She hadn't been alone in her thinking. The whole country, especially Mac, had anticipated this win. But there was nothing like having it made official. If what Mr. Roosevelt promised during his campaign was true—that the country would be getting a "New Deal" and that even Negroes wouldn't be forgotten in these programs—then it was no surprise that he had won.

And I was still trying to wrap my mind around it . . .

Mr. Roosevelt, Mac's boss, was going to be the thirty-second president of the United States.

Now that the election results were in and the victory was confirmed, I needed to start planning. I would write to Mrs. Roosevelt, asking for a job in the White House. Any job. And if the Roosevelts didn't see fit to hire me, then I would find another job somewhere in the city.

Because no matter how I felt about it, one thing was certain: If Mac was moving to Washington, so was I.

We wouldn't be spending these next four years apart.

I would make sure of it.

"DUFFIE, DO YOU think this Christmas we can put on a play for Mommy and Daddy?"

"Of course, honey."

Little Sam Inman knew I could never pass up a chance to put on a play. There was something about taking a character from the page and bringing them to life before others that I found irresistible.

But just the mere mention of Christmas made me realize just how fast time was flying. Even now I couldn't keep my thoughts from returning to the election—or Mac. Just a few weeks had passed since the results were announced, and the atmosphere around the country was one of great hope.

And something akin to relief.

Change was just a season away, and that made the upcoming holidays feel much more special. Evidently, Mr. Roosevelt's win was just what the country needed to bring about some much needed good cheer.

"What play did you have in mind, honey?"

The six-year-old little urchin smiled up at me mischievously. "*A Christmas Carol.*"

I laughed and sat on the edge of his bed. He should have already been asleep, but it was customary for him to keep me talking a little while longer. Tonight, I decided to indulge him.

"We did that one last year. Remember?"

"I know. But this year I want to play Scrooge. Mimi can play Marley's ghost."

"Hmm, I don't know if Mimi will like that very much." His downward face tugged at me, and I realized it meant a lot to him to play the lead this year. "But we can ask her."

In a flash, his cherubic little face lit up. "Can we ask her now?"

I should have known that question was coming. "It's late and, unlike you, your sister's probably asleep now," I said simply. "Let's wait until tomorrow. We can bring it up at breakfast."

"Okay," he groaned.

I bit back a smile at his pouty face. "*Okayyy*," I mocked dramatically, brushing back his wispy blond curls.

He let out a big yawn and I rose from the bed.

"All right, now time to get some sleep."

Just as I finished tucking him into bed, his mother walked into the bedroom. Miss Mildred looked a bit surprised to see me, but she quickly hid it behind a small smile.

"Duffie, you didn't have to put Sammy to bed tonight. I was coming up to do so."

"It's no problem, Miss Mildred," I assured her. "I never tire of putting my favorite little dumpling to bed."

Very soon there wouldn't be many more nights like this, and

that thought was in the forefront of my mind as of late. Twenty-three years was a long time to work with one family. Even before the Roosevelts, when Mac had just been part owner of the McDuffie and Herndon sixteen-chair barbershop, he had been grooming Miss Mildred's husband, Hugh Inman. Mr. Hugh had been one of Mac's regular customers, until the unfortunate accident to Mac's leg had forced him to pursue a new career path.

Thinking on the years I'd spent with them, I couldn't shake the sadness and guilt I felt at leaving them, especially the children. I knew it was a conversation I would soon need to have with Miss Emily, the matriarch of the family, so they could secure a replacement. But truth be told, I wasn't ready to have that conversation with them yet.

The moment I did, I knew it would become all too real.

"Well, thank you for handling that," Miss Mildred said as she came closer to the bed. She was dressed in a green and yellow plaid day dress that complemented her curly blond hair. Hair that resembled her young son's.

"How are you feeling tonight, darling?"

"I'm feeling great, Mommy!" He stifled back another yawn. "I'm not tired at all!"

I tsked. "Little Sam Inman, it's too close to Sunday for you to be lying to your mother."

He hung his head and looked rightfully chagrined. "Yes, ma'am," he muttered, then just as quickly moved on to his preferred topic. "Guess what, Mommy? I'm going to play Scrooge in our play for Christmas this year!"

"Is that right?"

Miss Mildred glanced over at me and I met her quick gaze with a smile. I couldn't be certain if that look was because she didn't want her young, sweet son playing such a grouchy character or if she was just weary of the children's plays in general.

"We can talk about that more tomorrow," she told her son, brushing her hand across his cheek. "It's time you got some sleep."

To my surprise, little Sam did not protest when Miss Mildred and I made our way out of his room. I waited until we got to the end of the hall to broach the subject about the play. I had found a nice escape in my performances with the Inman children, and I think they felt the same way as well. It had also become another area where we could bond. No matter what their mother felt about them, I still wanted it to be something we continued together.

"Miss Mildred, if you're concerned that little Sam will have a hard time remembering his lines, you have nothing to worry about," I assured her. "I modify the play so they won't be tripped up by the lengthy passages."

"Well, it is a mother's job to worry."

"I understand."

Although I knew her comment wasn't a slight against me, I still couldn't help but feel a bit miffed by her words. Why God hadn't seen fit to bless me and Mac with a little one of our own I will never understand. Sometimes I felt that if we had a child together, perhaps his absence wouldn't feel so stark. But I have had a lot of time to get over my sense of inadequacy, and I had long ago made peace with the fact that I would never bear my husband a child of our own. And since Mac had been blessed with a son from his first marriage, this never caused a rift between us.

But there were moments, like now, where I had to remind myself that motherhood didn't define who I was.

"It's not their performance that worries me, Duffie. It's the play itself."

I wasn't surprised to hear this. As employers went, Miss Emily and her daughter-in-law, Mildred, were some of the kindest and approachable women to work with. When Miss Emily had invited her oldest son, Hugh, and his young family to move into Swan House after the passing of her husband, I initially had my reservations about the younger woman. But despite Miss Mildred's very reserved appearance, she was surprisingly a very pleasant woman. She just tended to live in a state of constant worry, particularly when it came to her children. And I couldn't fault her. I couldn't imagine having two young children to rear with a husband who spent more days out of the home than in.

"As much as I love the little performances you and the children put on for us each year, we can't have them performing *that* particular story."

"But Miss Mildred, little Sam loves that story. He is excited to play the lead this year."

Miss Mildred waved her hand dismissively. "He's just a child. He doesn't understand the story as well as you and I. It's not very appropriate. And considering we will be entertaining guests this Christmas, I would not want my children embarrassing themselves speaking on matters they know nothing about."

From the woman's pinched expression, I knew that now wasn't the time to inform her that her children understood the story better than she realized. I had made sure of that. They understood that it was about greed and redemption, and about the power of love and compassion. I honestly couldn't quite understand why anyone wouldn't want their children to learn and express those basic ideals.

"The children are going to be heartbroken if I tell them they can't perform this year. What harm would it do to let them put on the play this one last time?"

"Duffie, this matter is not up for discussion. I will not have my children prancing around making insinuations about how the rich should treat the poor and causing our guests to be uncomfortable over unnecessary moralistic judgments."

Now I understood.

It wasn't about her children's moral compass, but more about how her family and friends—those surrounded by power and privilege—would view them. Though I didn't quite agree with her thinking, I knew from her rigid tone that her decision was final.

"All right, Miss Mildred. Would you like to break the news to him or should I?"

Though I knew it wouldn't matter. Little Sam would be disappointed no matter what, and my heart broke at the thought. Over the years, I had come to accept that the children I was hired to care for, whom I helped raise, were like my own. I had spent just as much time and invested a lot of my heart loving, caring, and worrying for each and every one of them. I felt like I was more godmother than caregiver to them all, and no one could take that away from me.

"I'm sure you can find the words to let him know gently. Besides, let's keep the holidays festive. Maybe they can recite that Christmas poem I heard you read to them once."

"'A Visit from St. Nicholas'?"

She cocked her head to the side. "How does it go again?"

I smiled and began reciting, going by memory, which was not difficult at all. "'Twas the night before Christmas, when all through the house not a creature was stirring, not even a mouse. The stockings were hung—"

"Yes, that one!" Miss Mildred burst out. "That's a very sweet rhyme that I think everyone would enjoy."

And with that, the decision was made.

I couldn't dwell further on it. The end of the year was fast approaching and soon I would be starting a new life, in a new city.

That thought was jarring, but it didn't compare to my one overwhelmingly nagging emotion . . .

That I missed my husband.

I missed the life that we had once shared here in Atlanta. Despite the tension between us these past few months, I still missed him. He'd sent photos and lots of letters, but it wasn't the same as being able to see and touch him.

I tried to occupy my time with work and other interests, but it wasn't the same. There were times I wanted to take a stroll around the city or go to the picture show, but the thought of going on my own was depressing.

On the other hand, pining for something I couldn't change didn't make things any better.

So the next few months I kept myself busy. I was about to embark on a new chapter in my life, and with so much change happening all at once, keeping busy wasn't hard. Day after day, the idea of leaving Atlanta, leaving my family and friends, became easier. In fact, I began to look at it as an adventure, and suddenly I gained a new outlook.

I may have been leaving my home, but *home* had always been a relative word in my life. Home had always meant memories, love, comfort, safety.

And I realized now that my home was wherever Mac was.

Chapter 2

March 4, 1933
Washington DC

I t was weather like this that made me miss Atlanta.

It had been just a few weeks since I had made the move to Washington DC, and although I didn't feel the overwhelming sadness I thought I would feel after leaving Georgia, I couldn't seem to get comfortable—or warm—in this new bustling city.

Today was Mr. Roosevelt's inauguration and unfortunately the weather was cold and bleak. But it in no way matched the energy or spirit of the crowd that had gathered to witness the monumental occasion. I was one of the lucky few to receive the coveted privilege of attending his inauguration with the Roosevelt servants.

Mac, who had secured me a seat close up in the yard of the White House, had unfortunately been the only one not able to attend.

I stood huddled together with the White House servants, some hailing from Albany and Hyde Park. My teeth chattered as much from excitement as from the cold. Just as I had anticipated, the

Roosevelts had brought on many of their current staff to come work at the White House. I may have been the only nonemployed guest among them. It was only because I was Mac's wife that I received this honor of standing among them.

"Excuse me, miss. Are you McDuffie's wife?"

I turned to the woman who posed me the question. She stood directly behind me, bundled in a thick coat against the frigid air. She was a petite young thing who looked just as chilly as I felt, but her dark eyes were kind and filled with a spark that said she wasn't too bothered by the weather.

"Yes, I am."

She smiled and held out a gloved hand. "It's a pleasure to meet you. I'm Kathuran Brooks, but everyone calls me Kathy."

I took her hand, wondering if she was newly employed with the Roosevelts or if she had been one of the few servants they had brought from their residences in New York.

"Nice to meet you, Kathy. I've gotten used to being called Duffie at work, though my friends call me Lizzie."

She smiled. "Well, I'm hoping we will be fast friends."

"I don't see why not."

"I hear that you'll be joining us as one of the maids here. Are you excited?"

I didn't know how to answer that. Because, truth be told, I was still waiting for Mrs. Roosevelt to respond to my inquiry. I had written her back in December—and again in February—about a possible position among her staff, but I had yet to hear back. I tried not to push the matter, but rumors where already spreading in the press that I was joining my husband as part of the many Negroes the Roosevelts would employ in the White House. This left me feeling awkward and very much like a fraud, since none of it was true. Or at least nothing had been confirmed.

But I understood that Mrs. Roosevelt was extremely busy in preparing for her family's big transition to Washington. I told myself I would wait until after the inauguration to reach out to her again. Until then, I had no definitive answer as to where I stood in this great house.

"I arrived just a few days ago, but I'm excited to be here," I replied instead. "Are you one of the new maids hired?"

Kathy nodded. "I used to work at the Whitelaw Hotel, but a friend of Mrs. Roosevelt's personally referred me and I secured a position here not too long ago. I can't believe how excited I am to be working for a Democrat!"

I laughed. "Mac and I said the same thing not too long ago."

"Well, so far I've met with some of the other maids and doormen and it looks like we have a solid group. Except for Fluffy, all the rest of us are colored."

"Fluffy?"

Kathy chuckled. "Oh, sorry. I mean Mrs. Nesbitt, the head housekeeper. We call her Fluffy, but of course not to her face."

Suddenly, music began playing and we knew that was the signal that the ceremony was starting. Never in my wildest dreams could I have imagined myself in this moment. It was exhilarating to know that I was witnessing a part of history. It was safe to say that I no longer regretted my decision to leave the Inmans and move to DC.

During the past six years while Mac had been in his boss's employ, I got to see the Roosevelts through my husband's eyes. I'd never had the opportunity to meet Mr. Roosevelt myself, but over the years, I had been able to learn a lot about him through Mac's letters.

From what Mac had told me, Mr. Roosevelt was a cheerful man who never complained. He liked to do everything he could for himself. He never wanted people to help him out of a car or to hold his arm when he walked, unless absolutely necessary. He insisted on shaving himself and liked selecting his own clothes.

So far, I liked what I heard.

The rest of the day passed in a whirlwind. Mr. Roosevelt's speech had been captivating and inspiring. He was a great orator, and I could see why Mac was taken with him. I could also see why he didn't think twice about following his boss to the White House. If I could only secure a position in this great house, then maybe leaving our home, our beloved family and friends, behind would make this move to Washington worth it.

After the inauguration, the servants went off to begin preparing for the day's many ceremonies. Mac had hinted at the fact that I would be alone today, as he would be highly occupied with the president-elect.

Now *the* president of the United States.

I managed to avoid Kathy and the other servants and ducked into the living quarters provided to Mac and me until permanent assignments were made. To my surprise, Mac was inside. Though I was happy to see him, I couldn't say he felt the same. He was clearly frazzled and completely oblivious to my presence.

"Mac, did you hear me?"

He finally glanced over at me before turning his attention back to his task of tucking his shirt into his pants.

"Sorry, Lizzie, honey. What did you say?"

I bit the inside of my cheek to tamper down my annoyance. "I asked how you were doing."

"I'm running very late."

"You can still take two seconds to ask me how I'm doing."

He grabbed his jacket and came to stand in front of me. For the first time, I could clearly see the fatigue in his mocha-brown eyes.

"Sorry, dear. How did you enjoy the inauguration?"

"I—"

A sudden knock came at the door.

"Mac?" a deep male voice called out. "Are you ready? The president is asking for you."

Mac quickly shrugged on his dark suit jacket, which complemented his high-yellow complexion. With his short salt-and-pepper strands combed neatly back, he looked every part a refined valet. He planted a quick kiss on my cheek before rushing to the door.

"I've gotta go, honey. I'll be back to get you when we break for dinner."

"All right." I barely got those words out before he was out the door. I sat on the edge of the bed and glanced around the small room. What had started off as a hopeful, exciting day was quickly becoming as bleak as the weather.

This was the first time in all my adult life that I felt out of place and of no use. And never in my twenty-three years of serving others did I feel more invisible than I did today.

THE MORNING AFTER the ceremony, Mrs. Eleanor Roosevelt finally sent for me.

Mac had returned to our room well after I had gone to bed last night and had risen earlier to begin his day with the president. It baffled me how we could be under the same roof again, yet still barely see each other.

But I didn't have time to think about us right now. I hurried across the fine red carpets and through the corridors of high white walls, passing by paintings and antiques that were about two centuries older than I was. My stomach was twisted in nerves as I was quietly ushered into the large office of the First Lady.

Behind the large mahogany desk sat Mrs. Eleanor Roosevelt. I don't know what I expected when I entered the office, but I hadn't expected to be in awe of the woman. She had a prominent and elegant presence about her that exuded warmth, confidence, and grace.

When I stepped fully into her office, she rose from behind her desk, a friendly smile gracing her lips.

"Mrs. McDuffie, it's a pleasure to finally meet you."

She held out her hand to me and I shook it, a bit surprised by how much she towered over me. She was an attractively tall woman, and I could understand now why her presence was so striking. She was also very homely, but her blue eyes were kind and her calm, poised demeanor was very approachable.

"The pleasure is all mine, Mrs. Roosevelt."

"Please, have a seat." She gestured toward the chair beside me before resuming her place behind her desk. "I apologize for not addressing your inquiry for possible employment with us sooner, but as you can imagine it's been quite a circus the past few months."

"That's quite all right." Usually I was a bit more engaging than this, but my nerves couldn't quite settle enough for me to relax around her. "I'm grateful you've found the time to meet with me."

She nodded. "Well, I was hoping Mrs. Nesbitt could also join us, but alas, there is so much to be done today. With that said, we could certainly use another skillful hand."

My heart skipped in delight. "I would be honored to be a part of your staff."

"Well, tell me about yourself."

That was easy. I told her everything about my life growing up in Atlanta. I told her about my position as a children's nurse to a maid for a variety of wealthy families in Atlanta. I told her about my twenty-three-year tenure with the Inmans, my time before that with the Hillyers, and also that time I worked as a nurse for a brilliant little blind girl, Elizabeth Pattillo, whom last I heard had become an accomplished pianist and instructor in music at the Maryland School for the Blind.

"You have an impressive résumé, Mrs. McDuffie."

I smiled at the First Lady. "Thank you, ma'am. And please call me Duffie."

With that, I found myself offered a job as a third-floor maid.

This meant I would make beds and look after some of the guest rooms, press clothes for guests, and be in charge of Miss Marguerite LeHand's room. Apparently, the president's personal secretary would also be residing within the White House.

The head housekeeper, Mrs. Henrietta Nesbitt, immediately put me to work that afternoon. Because of the nickname Kathy had given her, I had expected someone a bit more . . . fluffy. Someone stout and rotund. Instead, the older woman was tall and slender, with pale brown, graying hair and large glasses that framed her narrow face. She was the woman in charge of the serving staff, and from what I had gathered in our short meeting, she did not take her position lightly.

"Mrs. McDuffie, we are pleased to have you with us. You will be reporting directly to Mrs. Rogers, but first a few ground rules."

During our brief meeting, I learned that there were six maids in total: the head maid, Mrs. Maggie Rogers, two chambermaids on the second floor, two on the third floor, and a bathroom maid. We all were to report for work at 8:00 a.m., and any changes in routine were assigned by Mrs. Nesbitt herself or Mrs. Rogers. When needed, the housemen would help us with the cleaning until noon.

"Please report to Mrs. Rogers this morning for your first assignment."

With that, I was given my uniform and escorted back to the bedroom that would be the official living quarters for Mac and me for the next four years. It was a decent bedroom with a connecting chamber, but I didn't have time to admire our new space. I quickly donned my black moire dress and dainty white apron. Luckily, there was no cap to accompany the uniform. They never seemed to work well on me—especially on my naturally coarse hair.

I took a quick survey of myself in the nearby mirror, tucked a stray hair into place, and went in search of Mrs. Maggie Rogers, the head maid.

I found her on the ground floor with the other housemaids. To my surprise, Mrs. Rogers, though very fair, was a colored woman. I filed in beside the other maids and was quite relieved to see Kathy standing at the opposite end. It helped my nerves some to see a familiar face.

"Mrs. McDuffie, I presume?" Mrs. Rogers asked.

I nodded. "Yes, ma'am. At your service."

"Excellent." She inclined her head, then turned back to the other maids. Clasping her hands together, she said briskly, "Ladies, we have quite a busy week ahead of us."

Mrs. Rogers, whom I later learned had been at the White House since the Taft administration, gave us our assignments. To my pleasant surprise, Kathy and I were both assigned to work on the third floor, and I soon learned that we worked well as a team. Although the younger woman was a talker, she was also a hard worker.

"How did your husband come to be the president's valet?" Kathy asked as we worked together in one of the larger guest rooms.

"Incidentally, like you, he got the opportunity from a previous client he was shaving at his barbershop."

"Barbershop? So he wasn't a valet before?"

"Once," I clarified. "A long time ago, for a German consul. He must have been discussing this particular client because next thing he knows, the patron was asking how he would like to change jobs. He knew a man by the name of Roosevelt in Warm Springs, where he was doing construction work, who was looking for a valet."

"I've heard that's where the president gets his treatments for his polio," Kathy whispered, as if talking about the subject was taboo.

Perhaps it was. In public Mr. Roosevelt gave off this appearance that his disability wasn't the hindrance that I knew it was. And because I knew how much Mac had to help his boss and how much Mr. Roosevelt relied on him, it was clear his physical disability was much more limiting than he let on.

"Well, apparently, they seem to have liked each other immediately, because my husband went to Warm Springs for an interview on May 1 and returned seven days later with a new job. And here we are now."

"Yes, here we are."

From there, Kathy filled me in on all that she knew about the staff that were now working at the White House. I learned from her that most of the serving staff had been handpicked by Mrs. Roosevelt herself. Some in the group were as much an institution as the White House itself: like Mrs. Rogers and Mr. John Mays, the first colored doorman to work in the White House, and Mr. Ike Hoover, the head usher, who apparently had been appointed to the position by President Theodore Roosevelt. Each of them had been working here for about twenty-five to thirty years, and from what Kathy suggested, they were firmly entrenched in the rigid customs of the old White House practices.

Luckily, Mrs. Roosevelt was a lot more flexible in her vision of how she wanted her new residence to be run. She brought over her personal maid, Miss Mary Foster, who had also joined the family from their New York residence. She was a petite and reserved woman with a gentle demeanor that for the most part she kept to herself. Then there was Mrs. Nesbitt, a neighbor of the Roosevelts from New York, who apparently had quite an extensive experience in running grand households. She had a commanding presence, and from what I could tell, she was a woman of exceptional organizational skills. There was nothing soft or "fluffy" about her, and I had to wonder if the purpose of the nickname was to be contrary.

Except for Mrs. Nesbitt and the chief ushers, everyone on the serving staff were colored. That meant there were a total of twenty-five maids, doormen, hallmen, porters, cooks, butlers, waiters, janitors, and the president's very own valet who were varying shades of black and brown.

By lunchtime, we had managed to get all of the bedrooms clean and tidy. Although I was used to working solo, with Kathy's help we achieved a rhythm that helped us speed through our morning tasks. Soon lunchtime had arrived, and I was immensely grateful for that.

"Lord, I'm starving," I muttered as we made our way to the employee dining room.

Kathy laughed. "Let's hope Fluffy wasn't in the kitchen today."

I frowned, confused, but before I could ask why, a loud shriek followed by several loud bangs erupted from the back of the kitchen.

"Oh, goodness," Kathy groaned. "I wonder if it's the roaches or rats they're battling today."

"*What?*" I couldn't hide the horror from my face or voice. "There are roaches here?"

"And rats," Kathy said, with a slight shiver of disgust. "And I heard they are as big as my foot and as old as this house."

"Oh, my . . ." I looked around, fearful that one would spring out at any minute. I wasn't usually a squeamish woman, but nothing made my skin crawl more than roaches. I was lucky that Miss Emily Inman had felt the same way, and as a result she made sure Swan House was cleared of such critters.

"Don't worry," Kathy said as she led us to a long table where a few of the doormen and maids were already seated. "If Miss Ida made some of her cornbread today, you won't mind seeing a roach here or there."

"Somehow I doubt that," I muttered as I sat down and quickly but carefully surveyed my seating area.

Mac, what have you gotten us into . . .

Chapter 3

A re those a new pair of rubber stockings?"

Mac looked gleeful. This was probably the first morning that we got to actually start our day together. If Mac wasn't running out early to tend to Mr. Roosevelt, I was being asked to help out in another area of the White House.

"They sure are," he said, rolling out the stockings and admiring them. "And these feel even better than the last ones."

Each year, around his birthday, Mr. Roosevelt gifted him with a pair of rubber stockings. Since Mac's birthday was only a few days away, it was nice to see that the tradition between them wouldn't stop just because Mr. Roosevelt was now president.

"Well, be sure to thank him," I said as I pulled on my uniform.

"Of course."

Mac sat on the edge of the bed and began carefully rolling one of the stockings over his injured leg. For a moment, I wondered how much Mr. Roosevelt knew about Mac's injury and how much it still pained him. Although the incident, which had involved scalding hot water, had caused severe nerve and muscle damage to his leg, Mac had persevered. He had continued his work as a barber, standing on his feet and working for hours at a time.

But as the varicose veins in his legs grew unbearable and more painful, Mac made the decision to pursue a less strenuous position. That was why Mac had jumped at the opportunity for the valet position with a resident in Warm Springs. He had been excited that it would mean he wouldn't have to stand on his injured leg for so long. Yet when he learned more—having to tend to a man who suffered from polio and partial paralysis of his legs, not to mention the amount of traveling that would be involved—Mac had initially hesitated before accepting the position.

Now that he'd gotten the chance to work with Mr. Roosevelt, one could never tell that he suffered from his own health challenges. That's how hard he worked for the man.

"How would you feel if we had dinner here tonight, Lizzie?" Mac asked. "I don't think I'm feeling up to dealing with the mess in the employee dining hall today."

I readily agreed, liking the idea. "Yes, let's. I'll make arrangements for our meals to be brought up here tonight."

It had only been a week since we had moved into the White House, and our spacious living quarters were now complete with a sitting area and bath. By converting the adjoining bedroom into a living room, we had managed to make our neat little space on the third floor of the White House's East Wing into a quaint mini-apartment.

We both finished dressing and we left the room together.

As a White House maid, and the wife of the president's valet, I quickly learned that the president wanted to be awakened at eight in the morning. The president also liked to have his breakfast in bed. He liked scrambled eggs, bacon, and toast, and he usually made his own coffee in a Pyrex coffee pot. He also liked fish so much he often had it for breakfast too.

The White House organization was still new to me and Mac, and we never quite got used to the chain of command, but we managed to find our groove with our daily routine.

But today that routine would be broken.

In my short time here, I had quickly learned that the job of maid could overflow into practically every corner of the White House, so I typically held no expectations of what I'd be asked to do on any given day. And because Kathy had been pulled into helping with the upcoming restoration of the White House kitchen, I found myself alone on the third floor, tending to the freshening up of the bedrooms myself. I was straightening Miss LeHand's bedchamber when Mac startled me with his sudden appearance.

"Lizzie," he said as he poked his head around the door frame. "I need your help."

"What is it, Mac?" I asked him, concerned by the visible tension on his face.

"It's the president," he said, hanging on to the door facing. "I need help getting him out of bed."

Though I was always willing to help my husband with anything, this just seemed beyond the scope of my job description. "Mac, are you sure?"

"You know I can usually handle him on my own, but this morning I'm . . . struggling. I'm afraid if I keep trying, I'm gonna drop him."

He appeared distraught by this, and I immediately dropped the pillow I was fluffing and went to him. I hated to see my husband in such distress, but I was also mindful that helping the president in such a private setting as his bedroom may not be welcomed by the man.

"But Mac, won't he be upset or embarrassed if I showed up to help? Can't you ask one of the butlers or hallmen?"

"No, he doesn't want anyone in his bedroom but me. I told him about my trouble this morning and he agreed to let you in the room with me."

"All right," I said, as we left Miss LeHand's room. "But I hope this serves as a lesson for you."

He knew what I meant. That extra nip of rum or gin may have helped ease the pain of his injured leg, but the consequences were that it left him feeling weak and unsteady on his feet, impaired to the point that he couldn't perform his duties. Because of his injury, he wasn't too steady on his feet at the best of times. I didn't understand why he believed adding spirits into the mix would make things any better.

But I didn't harp on the matter further, well aware that he was disappointed in himself. I followed him to the president's bedroom, passing a hallman and two Secret Service men.

For a moment, I expected them to stop me at the door. But they simply nodded as Mac pushed open the door and held it for me. Truth be told, I wasn't very keen on helping Mac with this task. I was used to working with ill or disabled children, not grown men as thin and tall as Mr. Roosevelt. Not to mention that the president and I had never formally met and now I would be entering his private quarters and helping him with such a delicate task.

But it was plain to see from his slow gait that Mac was in pain this morning. I was certain it pained him even more to not be able to help his boss like he wanted.

When I entered the president's bedroom, it was well lit, with the heavy curtains drawn back. The room was larger than the entirety of our apartment on the third floor. It was clear to see that the bedroom could also use some tidying up. The president's finished breakfast lay on a tray on a nearby ornate table in the middle of the room, and there were newspapers sprawled everywhere on the bed and floor. I wondered which maid was in charge of the president's quarters, because if Mrs. Rogers caught sight of this mess she would not be too pleased.

Mr. Roosevelt sat on the edge of the bed, his back turned to me. His chair was positioned in front of him, but his gaze was focused toward the window as if he was drawn to the early morning light. His dark brown hair was peppered with gray strands and combed neatly back.

I couldn't help the thudding in my chest as I drew near. Anyone who worked in the White House couldn't help but have that "Mr. President" feeling rub off on them, even if they knew him before he was president. Though I had never formally met the man, I had Mac's letters and stories to give me some insight into who he was. I clung to the fact that Mac loved and trusted this man, so there was nothing for me to be intimidated about.

"Good morning, Mr. President," I said lightly as I came to stand before him. "I'm Mac's wife, Duffie."

When Franklin Delano Roosevelt turned to me, I was taken by how intense and expressive his deep-set blue eyes were. A small smile stretched across his thin lips, drawing attention to his strong, prominent nose and high cheekbones.

"Ah, Mac's better half. I wondered when we would finally get to meet. How are you doing this morning?"

From his welcoming smile, I felt as if we already knew each other, and that helped ease some of my nervousness.

"I can't complain," I said, returning his smile.

"Bet you weren't prepared for such heavy lifting this early in the morning, now, were you?"

"Nonsense," I said as I stood before him. "You appear as light as a feather."

It was no exaggeration. Despite his obvious height, the president was lean and slender in build. Dressed in a white shirt with a solid blue tie, dark gray pants, and blue and gray socks, he didn't look as if he weighed much. I had flipped mattresses that probably weighed more than he did.

"She's right, Boss," Mac said. "Between the two of us, we'll get you into your chair in no time."

Mr. Roosevelt looked at Mac as if he was right out of his mind. "Now Mac, you know I'm not a small man. I don't want to take you and your little wife down."

"With all due respect, Mr. President, I'm stronger than I look," I said.

He looked me up and down, then asserted, "You appear to be a fine figure of a woman, but I don't need you sustaining an injury on my account. Mac, why don't you have Charles come in and help us out today."

Mac scrunched up his face, letting us know what he thought of that idea. "Now Boss, you know that's not necessary. The leg is bothering me just a little today. I asked Lizzie to help me get you in your chair just for today. I don't need it going around that I can't do my job."

From the sympathetic glance Mr. Roosevelt threw Mac, I realized he understood his dilemma. I was always amazed by how much Mac did for his boss, despite his own leg injury. Though I had come to form some opinions about Mr. Roosevelt and his total dependency on my husband, I did have to give him credit for considering and respecting Mac's feelings on this matter. I imagined no one would understand Mac's need to prove himself capable more than Mr. Roosevelt would. It appeared the president was constantly proving himself in the face of his critics.

Mr. Roosevelt sighed and eventually said, "Just don't drop me, is all I ask. I need to be in shape for my afternoon meetings."

"We wouldn't dream of it," I said.

Mac and I flanked his sides and draped an arm around our shoulders. With a coordinated effort, we managed to lift him from the bed, but his weight was much heavier than I had anticipated. I gritted my teeth as I tried to maintain my hold, but I could sense that Mac was losing his strength.

Mr. Roosevelt sensed the same thing.

"Wait, wait. Put me back down."

We quickly eased him down on the bed. I tried to hide my exertion, but the pinched look on Mac's face was telling. We rested a minute, before Mac spoke up.

"Boss, I think—"

"No, no. Let's try another way," Mr. Roosevelt interjected, rubbing a palm down his leg before gesturing across the room. "Fetch my leg braces, will you, Mac."

He nodded and went to the adjoining room. With Mac out of the bedroom, I hardly knew what to do with myself. In an effort to hide my concern over the situation, I began cleaning up around his room.

"What do you find interest in, Duffie?"

I stopped in my tracks, completely taken aback by the question. Then it dawned on me that the president wanted to fill the awkward silence with conversation. So I answered him honestly.

"Literature," I said, resuming my task of gathering the empty dishes from his breakfast and stacking them on the carrying tray. "I especially like telling stories as much as I love reading them."

"Is that so? What are you reading now?"

I nearly scoffed at the question but quickly caught myself. "Oh, Mr. President. I haven't had a chance to take a breath, much less read anything that's not been the newspaper since moving to Washington."

For a moment, I regretted my blunt honesty. But there was something about his affable eyes that made him seem so laid back and . . . real. And to my relief, he nodded in agreement.

"This is true even for me," he said. "One of these days, we'll need to take a break and visit the White House library. I hear it's impressive."

"I'd like that very much, Mr. President."

Silence once again fell between us, and when I caught him glance at his timepiece, I knew he was getting restless.

What on earth was taking Mac so long?

"Duffie, do you mind pouring me a glass of water?"

"Of course, Mr. President." I found the pitcher of water a good distance away from where he sat and poured him a glass. "Thank you for being so patient with Mac, sir. It's that leg of his, you understand."

"I understand," he said, taking the glass I handed him. "And I thank you for your delicate handling of my condition. Your discretion, of course, is appreciated."

I smiled gently at him. "Of course. My mother used to say to be careful how you treat folks, 'cause they may be the ones to give you your last cup of water."

Mr. Roosevelt glanced down at the glass I had just handed him. "Your mother sounds like a very wise woman. I've told Mac he should bring her by for a visit sometime."

I smiled. "She would like that."

That brief mention of Mama filled me with a sense of homesickness. I realized I hadn't spoken to her since that first day of our arrival in Washington. Life had gotten so chaotic since moving to the White House, I could see now how easy it had been for Mac to get swept away by the job. I couldn't let that happen between Mama and me.

Mac finally returned with the president's leg braces and went to work placing them around Mr. Roosevelt's legs. Not to draw any more attention to the task, I continued tidying around the president's chambers and organizing his newspapers into one pile. To my surprise, I found a copy of the Allied Negro Papers among the bunch.

I lifted up the copy to find that it was indeed the latest issue. The ANP was a publication that predominantly wrote about a wide range of political and social topics that affected the Negro community—both nationally and internationally. It prided itself on being the first to distribute the news to hundreds of Black cities and towns. Mac and I had been reading the publication on and off for years, and some of the stories were not easy to read. For a moment, I wondered how much of the stories and topics the president delved into.

And what he thought of them.

"All right, Lizzie. We're ready."

I placed the paper down and made my way back to the two men, and it dawned on me what the president's new strategy was. He was going to attempt to stand on his own to get to his chair. Without further instruction, I went to his chair and brought it as close to him as I could. As Mac helped him to his feet, I held his chair in place. Together, they managed to shuffle his legs forward until there was enough room for me to move the chair behind him.

Mac gently helped him down as Mr. Roosevelt braced himself against the arms. Good thing the worn-looking chair was a sturdy one.

Once the president was neatly settled in the chair, we all breathed a small sigh of relief.

"Well, that was a fun little dance we just shared, wasn't it?" Mr. Roosevelt chuckled.

"See, now I can tell Mama I've danced with the president," I joked. "Seeing as Mac hasn't taken me out dancing in a while."

Mr. Roosevelt laughed but Mac looked affronted as he knelt down to straighten his boss's legs.

"Is that true, Mac?"

"Don't pay my wife any mind, sir. She's fully aware that I have two left feet, and though I'm not above embarrassing myself, she, on the other hand . . ."

"She, on the other hand," I continued, "has just found herself a new dance partner. Ain't that right, Mr. President?"

I patted him on his shoulder and, to my surprise, he threw me a crooked smile and a wink.

"That's right, doll. Now Mac, fetch me my dancing shoes."

When Mac appeared with a pair of navy blue leather dress shoes, Mr. Roosevelt frowned.

"Mac, where are my favorite brown loafers?"

"I sent them out for a cleaning, Boss," he answered smoothly as he knelt down and began carefully placing the president's feet into the shoes. "But these brogues will make you look real sharp for your meetings today."

I bit back a smile, wondering if those loafers had actually gone out to be cleaned or if Mac had decided that brown loafers would not have been very flattering with his boss's current attire. He had once confided in me that he tended to let his boss believe he was making the decisions when it came to his clothes, but in fact Mac had the final say. Like the morning after Chicago mayor Anton Cermak had been shot by Giuseppe Zangara in Miami. When Mac had held up a rack of ties for Mr. Roosevelt to select, he happened to reach for the same red tie he had worn at the time of the shooting. Because Mr. Roosevelt had been Zangara's original target, Mac snatched it away from him, stating firmly, *"No, sir, Mr. Roosevelt. This is one tie I won't let you wear again."*

Mac kept that particular tie away from him, and that had been that.

As Mac wheeled the president out of the bedchamber, I hung behind to finish tidying his room. As I went about the mindless task of cleaning and organizing, my mind kept drifting back to the president and my initial impression of him. Despite all the stories Mac had told me about his boss, I could draw only one conclusion . . .

Franklin Delano Roosevelt was a lot more complex than I realized.

"Lizzie, Mrs. Nesbitt would like a word with you."

Without a word, I followed Mrs. Rogers into the head housekeeper's office. I couldn't quite keep my hands from trembling, so I kept them clasped before me. I didn't understand why I was so nervous. I knew I hadn't done anything wrong. Despite today's interruption by Mac, I had managed to complete all my tasks on time and without incident. Yet the expressionless look on Mrs. Rogers's face as she directed me into Mrs. Nesbitt's small office left me a bit uneasy.

As we entered, Mrs. Nesbitt glanced up from whatever she was writing and put down her pen.

"Lizzie, you were in the president's chambers this morning. Why?"

Goodness, the woman was direct.

I quickly glanced over at Mrs. Rogers, whose face remained unreadable. I wasn't certain how much I should reveal—or how much Mrs. Nesbitt already knew. All I could be certain about was that I had done nothing wrong.

"Yes, ma'am. I was asked to assist the president this morning."

To my surprised relief, she didn't ask me to elaborate.

"Well, it looks like you made quite an impression," Mrs. Nesbitt said. "The president would like you to be his personal maid. This means that in addition to your other tasks, you will clean his chambers, office, and be on call for whatever aid he may need."

I hadn't expected this turn of events, but part of me was giddy that I would be working more closely with Mac than I could have ever imagined.

Another part of me, however—the perfectionist side of me—was terrified that I would do something to get myself removed from my position.

But I mustered up all the self-confidence that I possessed and jumped right into my new role.

I didn't mind the new assignment, especially when I learned that those tasks had ultimately fallen on Mac. I was astounded but not surprised at just how much work the president demanded of him. But I took to each task with enthusiasm and even a bit of grace. Apparently my hard work paid off, and because Mr. Roosevelt was very selective in whom he allowed into his chambers, Mac and I became the only two servants allowed inside the president's bedroom.

Yet as much as I enjoyed tending to the president, it was working alongside Mac that I enjoyed the most. It gave us a chance to be together for a short time each morning before I was to return to my other duties.

As time went on, I grew to appreciate my position as a White House maid more and I enjoyed tending to the influx of high-profile guests.

Within my first few months at the White House, I became an autograph hound. And with good reason. With people like Amelia Earhart and Will Rogers on hand, it made for a fine hobby. Not that I had much time for hobbies, but I couldn't resist this small indulgence. Second to my love of literature was the theater and reading up on the latest celebrity sensation. And after learning about Bessie Coleman only after her fatal plane crash, I found myself taking an interest in Amelia Earhart. She was a lovely young person, and I wondered what obstacles she'd had to overcome to become a female pilot. I couldn't imagine it was anything like those faced by Bessie Coleman, who, despite beating the odds and becoming the first Negro American female to obtain an international pilot's license, never got the recognition or accolades enjoyed by Miss Earhart. Not even after her tragic death, which was the real shame.

But as the number of celebrity visits grew, so did the level of stardom.

Once at Hyde Park, we got a visit from Shirley Temple. She was about the cutest little thing ever to set foot on the property. She was a beautiful child, and not the least bit spoiled. When she came to Hyde Park, people from the neighborhood worked with us for free just to get a look at the youngster. Mrs. Roosevelt was probably embarrassed because it gave the impression that her place was swarming with servants.

Unlike Mac, I didn't get to just watch these famous people in movies. I got the opportunity to meet them right here in the White House.

Once I left my autograph book in Will Rogers's room with a note, and he wrote in it: *Dear Lizzie, I have had a grand time at the White House. The only trouble is that I'm too nervous to eat.*

I was tickled. The popular actor was confiding in me!

Marie Dressler was also there with her maid, Mamie Cox of

Savannah. Miss Dressler called a group of us in and introduced us to Mamie. She said that Mamie had been with her many years, but for a time the actress had run into a streak of bad luck and she had to let Mamie go. Mamie, however, would still come by her cheap hotel room early every morning and fix her breakfast, then go on to another job.

"I couldn't pay her a thing. Sometimes she even bought the breakfast," the actress said. "Mamie is the best friend I have in the world."

I was intrigued by their friendship but could understand the other woman's loyalty. It reminded me of the same devotion I had toward the Inmans. Even now, having left their employ, I still sent them an occasional correspondence and was delighted when I received a response in return. I could tell from my brief interactions with Mamie that she was a sweet soul, however I knew it was more than friendship or kindness that kept her by Miss Dressler's side.

Like the Inmans had been to me, those two were a family.

Robert Taylor was another at the height of his career as a matinee idol who visited the White House. We got a good look at him when he was being shown around, and one thing we were interested in seeing was whether he looked as much like Franklin Jr. as some of the maids thought he did. I was in the sewing room when he came down the hall. Lillian Rogers, Mrs. Rogers's disabled daughter, was there too. Lillian, who was also a victim of polio and a big movie fan like me, did not let her disability hamper her desire to meet the handsome actor. As Robert Taylor came into sight, Lillian was on her feet, practically running to the door. Without her crutches!

When the movie star saw her, he came over and shook our hands, and I vaguely remember stammering something about his resemblance to Franklin Jr.

"That's quite a compliment," he said, flashing that Taylor smile of his.

Poor Lillian was teased for months about the way Robert Taylor made her forget her crutches.

But that brief encounter helped me recall how, in my heyday, I took private lessons in speech and how I would prop a book up over the sink, memorizing and reciting lines while I washed dishes. I never really had any great ambition to be an actress, but meeting the striking Mr. Taylor—and all the other celebrity sensations—rekindled my unwavering passion for the performing arts. I enjoyed being in plays, making talks, and giving readings, but I didn't quite care to be in the limelight. Heck, I would be happy to play a maid so long as I got to entertain.

But the reality was that there weren't a lot of opportunities for an amateur such as me, so I resigned myself to just meeting as many distinguished guests and collecting as many autographs as I could.

And it brought me great joy to make such acquaintances.

Another personal joy of mine while at the White House was putting in a good word for some of the Negro artists any chance I got. One such artist was Marian Anderson. I had met her years before through the Fine Arts Club, which had brought her to Atlanta, and I had watched her career flourish. She had just returned from a European tour and was singing in Washington, an event sponsored by Howard University. It was then that I spoke to the president about her.

"Perhaps we could have Marian Anderson perform after dinner as a surprise for Mrs. Roosevelt," I suggested.

Because I found Mr. Roosevelt approachable and not "artsy" in his dramatic and musical tastes, I didn't think twice to make the suggestion. He knew how to work and how to relax. He checked his plans and set the time for the first evening after Mrs. Roosevelt return from the West Coast.

Unfortunately, we found out later that night that Marian Anderson had a train to catch at nine that evening.

"We'll move up the dinner hour," the president decided.

This would have been a sound answer, but just as it was time for the concert to begin, here came some officials of some organization to initiate Mr. Roosevelt into an honorary membership.

Mrs. Roosevelt invited the domestic staff to assemble for the concert while we all waited for the president to join us. Finally, when he was rolled in, Marian Anderson, accompanied by Kosti Vehanen, had time to sing only a few numbers before she had to make a dash for her train.

After that night, there were a number of colored artists who got to perform at the White House. And it all started because of a small word from me to the president about Miss Anderson. I couldn't help but feel giddy and proud at that thought. Mac and I were able to help the Morehouse College Quartet of Atlanta, who had once appeared at Warm Springs, come to the White House. They were the first colored group to perform there during the Roosevelt administration. The Howard University Glee Club sang on several occasions. Musical actress Etta Moten Barnett sang at one of Mrs. Roosevelt's dinner parties. Opera singers Dorothy Maynor, Caterina Jarboro, and Todd Duncan were also on White House programs, along with Josephine Harreld, a talented pianist and the daughter of a close personal friend of ours from Atlanta.

For me, this still wasn't enough, but I was glad to see how it opened the door for many more notable Negro artists and entertainers.

The White House, however, was a crossroads for celebrities of every color and from all over. For big receptions, I was lucky enough to help in the cloakroom for some of these popular artists. It was often my good fortune and pleasure to wait on these talented individuals, and I got a bit of a thrill from just being in the same room.

My autograph book was also bursting at the seams!

Yet, somewhere deep inside me, I couldn't help but wonder about life as an entertainer. The closest I had ever gotten to living my dream as a stage performer was putting on plays with the Inman children during the holidays, and I had almost forgotten what it felt like to be in a room with true artists who had a passion for their craft.

Ordinarily, I enjoyed the charged energy and creative zest that vibrated through the room whenever there was a performance scheduled. I reveled in getting more than just a peek behind the scenes with our invited artists, their excitement for their upcoming act somehow fueling my own theatrical spirit.

But not all energy was good energy.

Like that of the young flutist who had somehow arrived without a full dress coat and was visibly shaken to find all the others on the program dressed formally. Watching the poor fellow frantically try to borrow one from another performer exiting the stage was too painful to witness.

As the other performer brushed right past him, my heart went out to the desperate young man.

"Come with me," I said, grabbing at his elbow and pulling him to the back.

"No, wait. I can't. I'm the next one up!"

"I know. But it's clear you're not ready."

The young artist sputtered more excuses, but despite his protests, he allowed me to drag him down the hall to a makeshift dressing room that was usually reserved for the waitstaff when serving a large formal dinner. In that room were twenty-five full dress suits.

"Pick one," I said, shutting the door behind us.

The young man stood in the middle of the room, dumbfounded. I sighed and rushed over to the rack of neatly hung suits. I pulled down several, and one by one we tried on each jacket until we found one that fit.

After his performance, that musician never could thank me enough.

It was in that moment that I realized just how much I loved my job.

Chapter 4

M ac, have you read this?"

My husband waved a dismissive hand. "Lizzie, we don't have time to read any more letters right now. The president is waiting."

I turned to him and read a few lines from the letter. "She says here, 'Dear Mister and Missus McDuffie. You don't know me, but I am desperate for your help. I lost my son during the Great War and, like many mothers, wasn't able to properly lay him to rest.'"

I skipped ahead in the letter as I continued to read: "'The War Department is having a pilgrimage to France and has invited all Gold Star Mothers the opportunity to travel and visit their fallen sons' gravesites. But under segregated conditions. You can imagine those conditions for the Negro mothers are distasteful. We are forced to travel on cargo ships while the white mothers are put on luxury liners. I refuse to dishonor my precious boy's memory by traveling under Jim Crow laws. He fought hard and died brutally for this country. We mothers have all sacrificed and suffered the same great loss. We deserve to be treated the same.'"

My eyes began to tear up as I read those last words. I couldn't imagine the woman's loss, but I could feel her pain in every word. "'I know your time is precious but I would appreciate it if you could arrange a meeting with the president to change these conditions. I know, if given the chance, I can convince him to see the injustice of this all.'"

I glanced up at Mac to find him in front of the mirror, frantically undoing and redoing the knot of his tie.

"Mac, this poor woman is asking for our help and I think we should try to help her."

Although Mac and I received letters from all walks of life, this one stood out to me the most. The woman's pain and desperation leaped from the pages, and I felt moved to do something for her.

"Lizzie, honey, everyone wants an audience with the boss. Unfortunately, he can't oblige them all and we certainly can't do anything about that." Mac shrugged on his jacket. "Now I have to go get the president up. Are you coming?"

He didn't bother waiting for my response before he hurtled out of the room.

I sighed. As much as I hated to acknowledge it, Mac was right, of course. As I tucked the letter away, my heart remained heavy. I couldn't imagine having my deceased child buried thousands of miles away from me with no way to visit his final resting place.

Unfortunately, we couldn't help everyone.

And that thought bothered me the most.

As I made my way to the president's chamber, I couldn't help but think about the other mounting letters that were quickly taking over our living quarters. And I couldn't shake the feeling that we should at least try to help some of these desperate souls.

At first, I was shocked at the amount of mail we received so soon after arriving in Washington. My amazement soon turned into flattery at seeing such a massive amount of correspondence. There was still something dignifying about seeing our names on letters addressed to *The White House*.

Although some of the letters came from those sharing their personal, heartfelt stories—like the mother of a crippled child asking if we could speak to Mr. Roosevelt about getting her daughter into Warm Springs—many of the letters were from those hoping to get their ideas or products in front of the Roosevelts. Someone suggested that I try to get Mrs. Roosevelt to use a certain brand of cosmetics because *"with a little push like that my products would have a great future."*

People mailed copies of newspapers and magazine articles with remarks circled about the president. One man had a fantastic flood control plan he wanted handed to Mr. Roosevelt. Famous composer William C. Handy sent his autograph on a copy of "St. Louis Blues" to Mrs. Roosevelt. In a letter to me and Mac, he wrote: *I have been trying to muster up courage to send an autographed copy of the song to Mrs. Roosevelt. She has done so much for our people.*

Some asked for autographs, which we were usually able to get. One Negro editor wanted autographed pictures of the president and First Lady for his office wall. A Negro orphanage sent a picture that had been taken during Mrs. Roosevelt's visit, asking me to get the First Lady to autograph it. Sailors sent pictures of the president taken on their ships and asked for autographs.

But some requests went beyond just autographs.

There were some, like Walter White of the prestigious NAACP organization, who felt he could bypass a few government channels by writing to me and Mac. The leader of the National Association for the Advancement of Colored People had written about three war veterans who had been imprisoned for allegedly taking part in the Houston riot of 1917, an affray between Negro soldiers and Houston civilians. For Roy, Stewart, and Richard—the three men still in Leavenworth for their part in the Houston riots—this meant execution, court-martial, or life in prison.

Though I appreciated Walter for not trying to leverage our very frail connection as Atlanta collegians to gain special favors from me or Mac, it was hard to ignore his heartfelt plea for the lives of these soldiers. And as much as I regarded Walter and the NAACP in high esteem, I wasn't certain how I could interest Mr. Roosevelt in such a case. In a general conversation on riots, the president had said that in such mass arrests, often the innocent were convicted with the guilty.

And these unfortunate war veterans weren't the only ones being wrongly accused.

Hundreds of letters had been written to the president about the nine Alabama boys who had been wrongly convicted of raping two white women in 1931. The protesters outside the White House were just as vocal. The growing outrage over the Scottsboro case had been the first time I'd seen Mr. Roosevelt take a keen interest in the criminal matters of Negroes. Even Mrs. Roosevelt had been overheard discussing the case with him.

Though I tried to refrain from inserting myself into politics or the president's affairs, all that changed one particular afternoon.

And it was all thanks to Mr. Roosevelt's press secretary, Stephen Early.

On this one particular day, I was hurrying about, trying to complete my duties after helping Mac with the president that morning. Mac had already been up for hours, pressing the president's best suit, making sure his shirt collars were just so, and even giving his hair a quick trim. Mr. Roosevelt always shaved himself. With all this, I stayed longer in the president's chambers than I intended, and that led to my being slightly behind on my tasks.

I had just completed cleaning several meeting rooms in preparation for some important visitors the president was expecting that day. I was passing the press secretary's office when I overheard Mr. Early.

"No, I can't reschedule that meeting to accommodate Mr. Randolph," Mr. Early snapped. "I don't care how important he is or what labor union he's associated with. He is not as important as three Democratic senators. The president has had that meeting scheduled for weeks now. He simply cannot be bothered with some Negro union leader." There was a brief silence, and I soon realized that Mr. Early was speaking on the telephone. "And what does Mr. White want now?"

There was more silence, before he continued with a loud sigh. "When will the NAACP realize the president has bigger issues to tackle than the Negroes? . . . I'm certain whatever those men have to say to the president isn't as important as what is already on his crowded schedule. What? No, no, just tell them we will make every effort to set up a meeting next month, but right now, the president is simply too busy." Another brief silence before Mr. Early burst out: "I don't care! Next month, we'll tell them the same damn thing."

There was a firm click, as if the phone had been brought firmly down on the receiver.

From the little I could gather from the one-sided conversation, I knew he was referring to Walter White of the NAACP, but I didn't know a Mr. Randolph. If I had to guess, I was certain he was an important *colored* man. If this was the treatment these men were receiving from the White House, it was no wonder Mac and I were being flooded with letters from all kinds of colored people—including people like Walter White.

And I couldn't help but feel outraged on their behalf.

In my short time living and working in the White House, my interactions with Mr. Early had been limited. Though my initial impression of the former reporter was that he took his job very seriously, many spoke of him as being a fair and unbiased correspondent, with an open-door policy to reporters and the press. And the Roosevelts seemed to like him immensely.

But what I just overheard was the opposite of what I believed the man to be. Yet Mama would always say: "Give a good deed the credit of good intentions. Give a wicked deed the benefit of the doubt."

Without thinking, I walked into Mr. Early's office and began dusting. I wasn't assigned to clean the press secretary's workspace, but something compelled me to find out more about the man.

"Good morning, Mr. Early," I greeted him politely. "I trust your day has been off to a good start."

He glanced up at me, distracted yet seemingly surprised by my presence. "Um, must you dust in here now? I'm quite busy and I don't need the distraction."

"My apologies, Mr. Early. I didn't mean to be a distraction. I'll come back later." But still I hesitated. "If I may, sir?"

The man barely contained an exasperated sigh. "What is it?"

"I have an acquaintance who is a reporter for the ANP, and he asked me if I could inquire how he can obtain a press pass to attend briefings here at the White House."

I was proud of myself for only partly lying. Mr. Albert Jackson at the Allied Negro Papers may have been an acquaintance, but he had never asked about a press pass. It was as if the colored reporters knew they might as well ask for a seat in the Oval Office.

To validate my suspicions, Mr. Early frowned. "The ANP? Is that the Allied Negro Papers?"

"Yes, it's one of the most popular publications within the colored community. I believe the president is familiar with that paper."

Mr. Early sat back in his seat, his expression guarded. "Unfortunately, there aren't any more available press passes. All of the available passes have been accounted for this year."

"And how does one go about applying or requesting one for next year?"

"It's a long and involved process. Honestly, there may not be any new passes available next year. For security reasons, we cannot issue any more, you understand."

"Yes, of course," I muttered. With a short nod, I left the man's office.

Apparently, my mother was wrong.

Not everyone deserved the benefit of the doubt. Mr. Early and his clearly prejudiced views certainly did not. It didn't take a scholar to see exactly what kind of man he was—or what kind of beliefs he held. Which was a shame, because I wanted to like the man as much as the Roosevelts did.

With a determination I didn't realize I had, I stalked over to Miss LeHand's office. Mr. Roosevelt's personal secretary was the true keeper of the president's schedule. She held the real power of who got in front of the president and when.

"Excuse me, Miss LeHand. May I have a word?"

"Sure thing, Duffie. What is it?"

I forced a smile on my face, but I could tell the woman knew I was upset about something. Miss LeHand was not only a close personal friend of the Roosevelts, but she was also a very kind person. I had always found her nice and courteous toward myself and the rest of the staff.

"How does one go about scheduling a meeting with the president?"

She tilted her head to one side and stared at me curiously. "I don't imagine you're asking for yourself. You probably have more access to FD than I do," she teased.

I smiled. "No, I'm inquiring for someone else. Someone important. He's been trying to gain an audience with the president for several weeks now but has encountered several roadblocks."

"May I ask who's the gentleman seeking this audience?"

I sighed, a bit reluctant to disclose who, but there was no way around it. "Mr. Walter White. He's—"

"The head of the NAACP," she finished. "I'm familiar with the name. And yes, Mr. White has been quite insistent in his request."

"I can imagine. He's written me and Mr. McDuffie in hopes of our assistance in getting a meeting set up. Mr. White's work with the NAACP is very important, and I know that if he is seeking an audience with the president, it has to be for a very important matter."

Based on the letters coming to us, there were more injustices and terrors being plagued upon the Negro community in every corner of this country than I had ever dared imagine. The stories were so overwhelming that Mac had stopped reading them altogether.

Miss LeHand's expression softened as she nodded in what I hoped was understanding. "That's exactly what I tried to convey to Mr. Early. Unfortunately, the president's schedule *is* full. His appointment book is stacked with meetings for the next several months, and try as I might, there is no rearranging his schedule to accommodate anything—or anyone—else. Not until late October, anyway."

I stared at her, stunned. It was only August. Then suddenly the rumors of former resident Theodore Roosevelt having dinner with Booker T. Washington here at the White House came rushing across my mind.

"How about his evenings?" I blurted. "I know the president enjoys a great meal with good company. Perhaps he could meet with Mr. White informally."

Miss LeHand appeared to ponder the idea, though her expression didn't seem to be quite sold on the thought. "That's not particularly a bad idea, Duffie, but I don't want this to set a precedent that the president's evening meals aren't even sacred anymore."

"I don't want that either," I assured her. I knew how hard the president worked and how much he valued his moments for relaxation. "Perhaps the dinner can also include his public policy advisers, the group calling themselves the president's Black cabinet. I've heard Mrs. Roosevelt is close friends with Mrs. Bethune, who spearheaded the council. Perhaps it can be organized into a formal affair with some Negro leaders like Mr. White invited."

This time Miss LeHand's eyes lit up. "Now that sounds like a more solid approach. No one can accuse FD of not making himself available to all Americans, including the Negro." She pulled out an appointment book and flipped through a few pages. "It looks like early next month would be a good time to have this dinner. Which should work out perfectly if we happen to plan something formally."

I smiled, excited by Miss LeHand's efforts to make this happen. "Should I have Mr. White get in touch with you directly?"

"Yes," she said, glancing up from the notes she was jotting down. "But don't mention this possible dinner to anyone yet. It's still very much just an idea that I want to relay to FD first."

"Of course."

For the next few days, I made no mention of my conversation with Miss LeHand—not even to Mac. I didn't want to be the one to spoil something before it had even gotten a chance to take root.

And I was thrilled to learn that my efforts had paid off.

As I entered the president's room one morning to clean, I was surprised by the greeting I received.

"There's the woman I've been waiting to see!"

I hesitated in my steps before I fully entered the chamber. The president was already dressed for the day, in his chair with a paper lying across his lap and a big grin on his face.

"Good morning, Mr. President. I'm glad I could be a bright start to your day," I teased. "Just don't let Mac find out I've taken his place."

Mr. Roosevelt laughed, then scoffed. "I don't think he'll mind as much as you think. I know he's upset with me because I sent him to get my gray sweater mended again. Can you blame me? It's my lucky sweater, and Lillian does a great job on the seams."

I withheld my groan and smiled instead. We were all familiar with that gray sweater by now. For some reason the president was in love with that thing, despite the great selection of sweaters he had to choose from. I remember the story Mac told me once, when Mr. Roosevelt was still just governor, and they were packing his things for a fishing trip.

"Oh, by the way, where is my old lucky gray sweater? It will be just the thing to take along, so let's pack it."

Despite Mac's vehement protests, Mr. Roosevelt had insisted on bringing it. And he was determined.

"Shabby? Nonsense! There's lots of wear left in that thing. Just have it mended up again."

The sweater went along.

"So I hear you've been keeping busy, doll . . ." the president said blithely. "Plotting ways for me to meet with certain Negro leaders, eh?"

For a moment I was struck silent, trying to figure out if he was intrigued or displeased by my interference.

"When the most vulnerable members of our society are in trouble, Mr. President, then the rest of us have an obligation to safeguard them the best we can. Right?"

He stared at me for a moment before his smile widened. "That's right, Duffie. When Missy brought up the idea of a formal dinner with my Negro advisers and a few community leaders, I thought it was brilliant."

Relief and joy spread through me, and for a moment, I didn't know what else to say.

"I almost wish I had thought of it sooner," the president continued. "You know, my cousin Theodore had invited a Negro adviser to the White House for dinner during his presidency, but that didn't go over very well back then. Times, however, have changed, and I don't think anyone would bat an eye now. We have just as many Negroes working in the White House as we do whites."

I nodded, though I didn't want to sully the moment by pointing out that many of us Negroes were in domestic positions. Very few had leadership roles, and none were part of his administrative staff. That small but very visible fact was neither here nor there. The fact that the president was on board for a formal dinner meant Mr. White would get his opportunity to speak to him about matters that truly affected the everyday Negro.

"It's a good thing what you're doing with your Negro advisers, Mr. President. You might be the only president who has established a Federal Council of Negro Affairs. But I think you need someone who is more familiar with the everyday working-class Negro. Someone who has access to those that don't have the time or means to present their issues to you."

"You're right, doll. Everyone I have on my council are more focused on public policy and community issues. I have to admit I don't know what's plaguing the everyday Negro family or laborer."

"I do," I blurted out. "I receive letters every day, from everywhere. Some are nonsense, but the majority of them just want to feel like they are protected and cared about by their government."

"That's easier said than done. I can't solve every individual problem. Even my powers are limited to protecting the many over the few."

"Well, maybe I could help."

He gave me a curious look. "How so?"

"As your self-appointed secretary on colored people's affairs."

I had intended the comment to be a joke, but the way Mr. Roosevelt regarded me said my delivery had fallen short.

The president sat back in his seat and continued to look at me curiously. "And what does this position entail?"

I made a show of thinking about it before replying. To be quite frank, I don't know what possessed me to make such an offer, much less appoint myself to any kind of government position. But I figured that since I now had the ear of the most powerful man in the country, I might as well commit to the role.

"For one, it's voluntary," I offered. "And just like it states in the title, I would present to you all the affairs of colored people. Good and bad. I know the title is long, so you can just refer to me as your SASOCPA."

"My *what*?"

"Your SAY SOCK PAW," I pronounced for him.

The president threw his head back and laughed. "You got to love it." But he quickly sobered and, with a thoughtful look, held out his hand to me. "All right, Madam Secretary. You are duly appointed."

Chapter 5

The end of summer was fast approaching, and although life in the White House was very routine, it was seldom ever dull.

Like the morning the Roosevelts' only daughter came to me with a very sudden and unexpected request.

"Duffie, can you get your things together to leave for Chicago tomorrow? You are to pick up Sistie and Buzzie and take them to Hyde Park."

"Sure thing, Miss Anna, I'll get packing now."

But I never got the chance.

That afternoon, there were a number of tasks to complete before day's end. Like fix a room for someone coming in that night, then pack for someone else going out. When I wasn't cleaning the president's chamber or substituting as Mrs. Roosevelt's maid because Mrs. Mary had fallen ill, I was asked to look after the other Roosevelt children who had come to visit.

I thought I knew what exhaustion was, especially after the previous week when I had helped get the house ready for three hundred guests expected for an evening concert, all while helping in the dressing rooms of the artists in attendance. Though I had to admit assisting the artists was one of my favorite assignments, I was exhausted by the end of it.

Yet by the time Ethiopian noble Ras Desta Damtew, son-in-law of Emperor Haile Selassie, came to visit, I soon forgot my fatigue. His visit created the most excitement among the colored staff.

And it also created a crisis.

I was tidying up the president's room when Mac came bursting through the doors like a madman, carrying a complete change of clothes over his arm.

"What's the rush, Mac?" I asked.

"No time to explain, dear, but hell will be raised if I don't get these formal clothes pressed, get the boss dressed, and in the Blue Room in thirty minutes."

With that, Mac flew out of the room and was down the hall in a blur.

It wasn't until later that I learned that President Roosevelt was to dine with Ethiopian prince Ras Damtew upon his arrival the day before. However, because it had been the prince's day to fast, the visit had been put off for later. So instead, the Italian airman Italo Balbo and a few other Italian airmen had been invited to the White House as dinner guests. But since the Ethiopian prince had arrived in the city first, he had the priority. The president was truly in a conundrum because even though preparations had been made for the Italians, protocol dictated that the president receive the Ethiopian prince first.

It didn't help none that there was currently a strained relationship between Italy and Ethiopia. This made matters even more tense, as having Ras Damtew and Mr. Balbo at the White House at the same time made preparing for their visits extremely difficult.

As luck would have it, both meetings were able to happen without causing an international incident.

On the second floor there was a screened alcove where many of us on staff could see but not be seen. We stood packed in there as we watched the prince make his formal, grand entrance. He wore a bright blue coat trimmed with gold braid, and on his head was a shako made from the mane of an African lion. He presented two lion rugs and a picture of Haile Selassie to Mr. Roosevelt.

Hardly had his footsteps cooled before Mr. Balbo was on the scene.

Needless to say, that had been a tense and highly stressful day.

So when I got the assignment to chaperone Miss Anna's children to Hyde Park, I found it a nice break from all the White House chaos. Miss Anna's daughter Eleanor—who was oddly nicknamed Sistie—and her son Curtis—who was affectionately called Buzzie—were two of the cutest of the Roosevelt grandchildren. By the time I first met her, Sistie was a pretty little thing with long hair down her back, and Buzzie was a round little boy about three who hero-worshiped his big sister. The children were polite and courteous, reminding me of Sam and Mimi Inman, and I took to them immediately.

However, it appeared even during this short trip I could not escape the demands of the White House.

"Mrs. McDuffie, is that you?"

I turned toward the unfamiliar voice, only to find a somewhat familiar face staring down at me. I stood on the train platform waiting to board the late train to New York. Buzzie and Sistie sat on a bench next to me. A Secret Service man wasn't too far behind.

I knew the man had to have been someone I met once in Atlanta. I may not have been able to place his name, but I never forgot a face.

"You probably don't remember me, but we met at the YMCA in Atlanta a few years back."

I remembered him now.

"Oh, yes! Mr. Yergan. How have you been?"

"Well, thank you. I hear congratulations are in order for your new position at the White House."

"Yes, thank you. I decided to follow Mac to Washington during the president's term. How was your missionary trip to Africa?"

That's what I really remembered about him. Mr. Max Yergan was the passionate individual who had spoken about the plight plaguing our brothers and sisters in Africa and his upcoming trip there. I gathered his trip had been a success because he'd recently won the NAACP's Spingarn Medal for his achievements.

"It was enlightening. Truth be told, there is still a lot of work to be done over there."

"Oh, my. Are things just as bad there as they are here for the Negro?"

He pursed his lips and nodded. "I fear, in some instances, it's worse."

He filled me in briefly on the treatment and conditions of the African people and the racial tensions and economic disparity that existed between them and the European "invaders." It was sad to hear that even on their own soil, the African Negroes couldn't have true freedom.

"What's happening over there is an atrocity," Mr. Yergan continued. "I spent quite a few years there and witnessed how the Negro's rights and liberty are being stolen from them. It's something that every American, including the American government, should be aware of."

I didn't disagree with him, but from his intense gaze I suspected he was thinking I could be that gateway to the highest man in office. I instantly felt tension crawl up my spine as I prepared for his request to either be invited to the White House or be connected with the president's advisers.

Neither of which I had the confidence I could make happen.

"I couldn't be more sympathetic to their situation, Mr. Yergan. But do you honestly believe Americans would care for the struggles of Negroes in another nation when they barely care for the struggles of Negroes here?"

"We have to make them care, Mrs. McDuffie. All we need to do is share the truth and open their eyes to our reality. The Negro is a target for prejudice and hate, and apparently it's a global disease."

Though his words moved me, I couldn't think how he believed there was anything I could do to change that. Access to the president was already very limited. President Roosevelt was bombarded with daily meetings, events, and travels. Even now he was off somewhere in the South with Mac and several of his Secret Service men to attend a series of important meetings. Then Mr. Roosevelt would join his family at Hyde Park.

And there, he wouldn't let work interfere with the time he spent with his family.

"It's not my place to tell you how to conduct yourself within your position, Mrs. McDuffie. But there are over 170 million Negroes that can use a voice. *You* could be that voice."

Suddenly there came a shrill whistle that filled the station—a signal that indicated the late train was now arriving.

"Well, sounds like my cue. It was a pleasure seeing you again, Mrs. McDuffie. You have a blessed day."

Mr. Yergan tipped his hat and continued down the train platform, surprising me by not asking for anything—not a meeting or a connection or even a White House tour.

Only that I become the spokeswoman for millions of Negroes.

I sighed, thinking about my conversation with the president on this very similar topic. I had felt so good about myself broaching the subject with the chief in the first place. And having the conversation about the three Houston war veterans. But since that morning, we hadn't had a discussion about the three men—or any other topic concerning Negro Americans.

The guilt that washed over me was nearly debilitating.

As the children and I made our way to Hyde Park, the encounter with Mr. Yergan stayed with me. But as we neared the residence, the man's lingering words quickly curled into a small corner in the back of my mind.

The Roosevelts' Hyde Park estate was just as impressive as I remembered from Mac's letters and pictures. This time I got to see the massive estate for myself, and I was surprised at how expansive the grounds were. I knew it wasn't a fair comparison, but it made Swan House look like a guest lodge.

At the entrance, we were greeted by the president's mother, Mrs. Sara Delano Roosevelt.

"*Nana!*"

Buzzie was the first to reach his great-grandmother.

As I made my way up the grand steps, I couldn't help but notice how pristine and glossy the floors were. They had obviously been freshly waxed for the children's arrival. Unfortunately, however, those shiny floors were about to be my downfall—literally.

I took one step, and before I could catch myself, I went flying and falling on those freshly waxed floors.

Mrs. Delano's brows furrowed deeply. "Duffie, are you all right?"

Despite the hard landing, I laughed to hide my embarrassment, which was fanning hotly across my neck and cheeks.

"Yes, ma'am. I'm as right as rain."

The older woman nodded and returned her attention to her

great-grandchildren. She was very kind and gentle with them. But her mannerisms reminded me of the fine old southern women I'd had more than my share of encounters with in Georgia. This was probably why I felt so at home with her. She was an aristocrat of the old school and made no efforts to mask it, despite her more open-minded son and progressively modern daughter-in-law.

One morning, however, she called me out on the front porch and made me sit down to discuss the theory of pensions with her.

"Don't you think I take good care of my help around this place?" she asked me. "Shouldn't they be able to save money for their old age, and not expect pensions?"

That was a hard one to answer.

"Sometimes it's not always that easy," was all I could think to say, my hands folded tightly on my lap. The blue and white summer uniform we were given felt tight and clammy over my tense body.

"What do you mean?"

I sighed, and for the life of me, I still don't know why I decided to indulge her in this conversation.

"Not everyone makes enough to set money aside, Mrs. Delano," I said more plainly. "Sometimes their wages are barely enough for them to get by."

"But I believe our staff has it quite good compared to others. They have their salaries, their accommodations, and meals, of course. Why couldn't they manage their finances enough to save some aside?"

"Because oftentimes their wages are offset by those benefits you just mentioned." I could tell by her furrowed brows that she knew this to be true. "What are they to do after? When they are no longer able to work and receive these accommodations and meals?"

"I have to be honest with you, Duffie, I don't share your perspective. I believe employment is the means to provide for one's future, and I'm not inclined to shoulder the responsibility of someone else's retirement."

"But Mrs. Delano, many of your staff have devoted their lives to running your household. Isn't it only fair that they be provided with some financial support for their later years?"

She paused and looked thoughtful for a moment. "I see . . . I just don't understand how that would be financially viable for me or anyone else in my position."

I guess Mrs. Delano found it difficult to understand some of the social programs her son and daughter-in-law were putting into place. I sensed that their liberal actions bothered her a little.

And that wasn't something I could help her come to terms with.

Thankfully, as we awaited the arrival of Mr. Roosevelt, there were no more talks of pensions or staff satisfaction. Not that I didn't appreciate the open discussion, but I didn't quite have it in me to comfort the older woman in her backward beliefs. And perhaps I was too much of a southern woman of the old school myself because I eventually grew fond of the president's mother and didn't want her antiquated ideals to further sully my opinion of her.

During our visit to Hyde Park, I overheard that the First Lady was off visiting Camp TERA, the all-women's interracial camp in New York that she and Secretary Frances Perkins had managed to get government funding to open. From what I managed to gather about the camp, it was an innovative way to get women impacted by the recession to learn a new skill set and trade. It seemed the First Lady was doing all that she could to keep the camp open, and I couldn't blame her for choosing to be there rather than here with her overbearing mother-in-law.

Luckily, I was able to hold my own with Mrs. Delano.

It was another two weeks before the president and Mac finally arrived to Hyde Park.

They arrived at the mansion with a few Secret Service men late in the evening. I stayed close to see if Mac would need my assistance in helping Mr. Roosevelt into bed. I wasn't the only one who hovered nearby.

Mrs. Delano also stood just outside the president's bedchamber. "Oh, Duffie, you and Mac are so loyal and faithful. Thank you for being so gentle and careful with my son."

There was an overwhelming emotion in the other woman's eyes that tugged at me. Despite her usual conservative, sometimes rigid, demeanor, it was clear that she was still a mother who held a massive amount of love for her son.

"It's an honor to be at his service, Mrs. Delano."

And it really was a privilege to serve Mr. Roosevelt.

At Hyde Park, there was no talk of politics and such. Here was where the president got to be himself—a father, son, and husband.

I got to see the Franklin D. Roosevelt that many others didn't get to see. For one, he was a man who loved to laugh. He laughed when one Sunday the picnic table fell down, taking with it all the fancy salads and tiny sandwiches. He laughed at me whenever I slipped on the freshly waxed floors, which for some reason seemed to be often.

Once a jar fell off a mantel and landed on Mac's head. During his retelling of the incident, Mr. Roosevelt had a good laugh: *"My Mac says it fell on his head, but I know that Lizzie really hit him with it!"*

And just like that I was "Lizzie" to the president.

Maybe it was the country air or having a lot of his family around, but at Hyde Park the president was a different man. Not only was he quite jovial, but he took great pleasure in being with his children and grandchildren. He turned to his grandchildren for relaxation, and that summer there were plenty of them around. Every evening, it was Mr. Roosevelt's custom to receive them in his study just before dinner, and sometimes in the morning right after breakfast. Sistie and Buzzie called him Paw-Paw, and he talked and played games with them like any grandfather would. And Mr. Roosevelt never lost patience with them.

Despite their minor squabbles, he and Mrs. Roosevelt had brought up their children well.

Of all the Roosevelt children, I was more familiar with their daughter, Miss Anna. Perhaps it was because I had spent so much time caring for her sweet girl, Sistie, and her shy boy, Buzzie. The Roosevelt boys I never knew very well, but from what I saw of John and Franklin Jr., I had become a little partial to them. John was the youngest and the most reserved. I could see that Franklin Jr. seemed to be the most affectionate. He also resembled his father in appearance and personality the most.

When the boys would come to visit, Mr. Roosevelt didn't just let them hang around and do nothing. This particular summer, he put them to work.

Some days they worked as regular farmhands, other days they helped cut roads through some new land Mr. Roosevelt had bought. From the way they came shuffling into the mansion with their faces flushed and shirts sticky with sweat, I knew it was hard work.

As much as Mr. Roosevelt loved his family, he was a strict disciplinarian when it came to his children. And who could blame him? Those children were constantly subjected to temptation—more so than others. I grew another level of respect for him and Mrs. Roosevelt in their abilities to rear and ground their children and grandchildren.

And I grew to love the Roosevelt children as much as I had the Inmans'.

It was one quiet afternoon, while I was cleaning the patio, that I realized how much Mac and I were appreciated by the Roosevelts.

Mr. Roosevelt typically enjoyed an early lunch outside, so I proceeded to wipe down the tables and chairs and sweep away the dirt that had crept into the corners. I was lost in thought, thinking about Mac and grateful that he had been able to relax some since arriving at Hyde Park. I thought about Mama and the letter I'd been meaning to mail off to her. I even thought about my goddaughter Hazel and how I missed watching her grow into a lovely young woman.

Suddenly, my train of thought was interrupted by a piercing sound. I looked around and found a little yellow bird sitting on the freshly polished deck railing of the open patio. The little birdy was a tiny thing with a large voice. He sang as if he had not a care in the world—nor that I had just wiped down the wooden handrail.

I stopped in my tasks and studied the small yet outspoken critter. "You are one pretty loud fella."

The little yellow bird responded with another series of chirps and song. I smiled. By the way his beak turned up and his throat swelled, it was clear he was giving it everything he had.

"Hope is the thing with feathers," I recited. "That perches in the soul . . . and sings the tune without the words . . . and never stops at all."

I held out my hand to the bird, and to my surprise, he didn't fly away.

"And sweetest in the gale is heard . . . and sore must be the storm—"

"Lizzie, who are you talking to?"

Mr. Roosevelt's curious voice startled the bird, and it flew away. I turned to the president, who was being wheeled onto the patio by Mac. They both regarded me strangely, and I couldn't help but laugh to mask my embarrassment.

"I had just made a new friend, Mr. President. Unfortunately, you scared him off."

Mr. Roosevelt chuckled. "Or perhaps he simply grew tired of the conversation?"

"Perhaps," I said, making room for Mac to sit him facing the great landscape. "But I do make for fine company."

Mr. Roosevelt inclined his head. "That you do. And entertaining too. We do love your orations."

"Thank you, Mr. President."

Suddenly, one of the kitchen staff brought out a cart with covered dishes and a pitcher of lemonade.

Mac began to uncover the president's lunch and I went to aide him. He glanced up at me and gave me a look of silent appreciation. He'd been unusually quiet that day, and I knew it had to be from a lingering headache. The kind caused by too much drink the night before. But he'd had a bad night with his leg and I couldn't reproach him for trying to ease his pain. His increased drinking, however, worried me.

As we prepared to serve the president his meal, the little yellow bird came swooping back to the patio and landed again on the handrail.

"There's my friend," I said with a short laugh. "I believe he would like to join you for lunch, Mr. President."

Mr. Roosevelt grabbed a piece of lettuce from his salad bowl and tossed it to the little bird. The bird swept down, grabbed the small leaf, and soared off.

"I didn't know birds ate lettuce," I mused out loud.

"Leafy greens are actually good for birds," Mr. Roosevelt said. "I think our little canary friend will quite enjoy it."

"Listen to him, Lizzie," Mac said with a nod. "The chief knows his birds."

"I've always been a fan of the species," Mr. Roosevelt said, dunking a corner of his grilled cheese sandwich into his tomato soup. "Did you know they used to take one of those beautiful little birds down into coal mines, in a cage? When the bird cocked up his toes and fell down to the bottom of the cage, they knew it was time to get out of the coal mine. Seems like a terrible waste of an extraordinary creature, if you ask me."

I was mortified. "Why would they do such a terrible thing?"

"They were used to detect the presence of carbon monoxide," Mr. Roosevelt explained. "Once they succumbed to the poisonous gas, it gave the miners a chance to react in time."

I shook my head in disgust. "Couldn't they come up with other methods? I find it incredibly cruel to take something so innocent, so full of life, and end its life so . . . callously."

"I agree," Mr. Roosevelt said, wiping his hands on his napkin and taking a sip of his lemonade. "And when the most vulnerable members of our society are in trouble, then the rest of us have an obligation to safeguard them the best we can."

In that instant, I recognized my own words spoken to him not too long before and was deeply impressed. "Your memory is frighteningly astute, Mr. President."

"Thank you," he said simply with a small grin.

"But maybe those who are truly defenseless can find some protection under our laws," I added, including Negro lives in my assertion. It was clear, however, that the president was still thinking of those innocent birds.

"Unfortunately, I can't say if that practice will ever come to an end, but rest assured there are about fifteen different species of canaries in Africa and I can't imagine they have that same practice over there."

"I would hope not!" I hated the thought that any other people, particularly Africans, would participate in such a barbaric act. "Maybe I could ask an old acquaintance of mine if he's seen such a practice. He's just completed a mission trip there."

"Is that so?" Mr. Roosevelt looked genuinely intrigued. "Which part of Africa?"

"I'm not certain, but I do know that wherever he was, the Negroes there are suffering."

His brows pulled together. "How do you mean?"

I told him about Max Yergan and his mission to Africa. To my surprise, the president asked to meet with him, to gain some first hand information on Africa.

I was caught off guard by the request but didn't hesitate.

On August 5, I arranged a meeting between the two men right there at Hyde Park. Both Mr. Roosevelt and Mr. Yergan thanked me. The president, who had been very welcoming and courteous to Mr. Yergan, said he had gained a good deal of insight into African problems after their discussion.

I never felt so proud and yet so humbled by such a small accomplishment.

And I would never forget that summer at Hyde Park.

It had been a long and gloriously entertaining one with the Roosevelts. But above all, I would never forget, near its end, the person who had almost slipped right past me.

I had been picking up the after-dinner tea tray when Mrs. Delano asked me if I knew the rest of the line of a song that began "Can a mother's tender care . . ."

I was able to quote it. For added flair, I intoned in my finest aristocratic accent: "Can a mother's tender care cease toward the child she bear?"

To our amazement, Mr. Roosevelt dissolved into robust laughter. My cheeks flamed with embarrassment. Though my short rendition may not have been worthy of praise, I didn't think it warranted his mocking.

"Franklin, what has gotten into you?"

He wiped at the corners of his eyes before he explained, "Forgive me, Mother. I wasn't laughing at your recitation, Lizzie."

"Then what do you find so funny?" Mrs. Delano demanded.

The president chuckled again. "I remember hearing that song when I was a child. For the longest, I had thought the line was referring to a she-bear. Imagine a she-bear saying that line in *that* accent."

At his explanation, we all couldn't help but laugh at the thought.

Suddenly one of the president's sons, James, came rushing toward the house, calling out for me. I met him at the foyer, where I found him looking a bit too flustered.

"Lizzie, I need your help."

"Yes, of course," I said, rushing forward. "What do you need?"

He informed me of his friend Miss Phillips, who was waiting outside. He explained that her plane had just landed in some water. Luckily she was unharmed but all splashed up.

"We need to get her dry and comfortable. Can you do that?"

I nodded and went to grab several towels and a blanket to help the poor woman. When I stepped outside, the young woman was soaked.

"I'm a frightful mess, just frightful," she said with a laugh as she draped the blanket around her shoulders.

I helped her dry off and combed her hair a bit before she started for Val-Kill, Mrs. Roosevelt's cottage. It was when she was about halfway there that I realized that "Miss Phillips" was in fact Katharine Hepburn!

My mouth hung open for the rest of that evening.

And oh, how I regretted having left my autograph book back in Washington.

Chapter 6

March 24, 1934
White House

S o, Mr. McDuffie, how did a bright but small-town barber from Atlanta end up becoming the president's most trusted valet?"

I barely suppressed my annoyance at the young reporter's exaggerated approach to asking a simple question.

Initially, I was excited when the Allied Negro Papers had invited Mac to do an exclusive interview, capturing this special moment in history. They had sent Mr. Albert Jackson to conduct the interview, and as the wife of the now "famed" valet, I was allowed to sit in during said interview.

But my excitement quickly turned to exasperation, especially when it was becoming plain to see that Mr. Jackson had already come into this interview with his own formed opinions about Mac and the president.

"Well, it was all thanks to a client of mine," Mac began. "I had forgotten I had spoken to him about working as a valet before. For a German consul."

"And this was the barbershop you worked in that served only white patrons, correct?"

Mac nodded, not at all bothered by Mr. Jackson's pointed question, as I was. There was something about how he stated it that made the question feel . . . disparaging and critical.

"Correct. My client informed me that he knew about a job opportunity that I may be interested in. He asked me how I would like to work for Franklin Roosevelt."

Mac sat back in his seat, and I could tell he was warming up to the story he had told countless times to family and friends who had asked about how he'd happened upon his new and unique position.

"I told him 'fine,' and that following Thursday I got a telegram from Mr. Roosevelt to come to Warm Springs and that I would be met at the station. After ten minutes of conversation, Mr. Roosevelt and I had closed the deal. I went back to the barbershop and got a leave of absence for a year. Because I didn't know just how I would like the job, you know. But after ten days of working with Mr. Roosevelt, I knew I would like him, so I sent in my resignation to the barbershop."

"Fascinating," Mr. Jackson whispered as he jotted down more notes. "And as his valet, what are your duties?"

Mac shrugged. "Nothing crazy. I shine his shoes, clean and press his clothes, keep his hair neat and trim. President Roosevelt does his own shaving with a very good Durham duplex razor. I wake him up every morning for breakfast and prepare him for his day. Other than serving his meals, I have nothing to do with the actual preparation."

Mac fell silent as Mr. Jackson jotted down more notes. I glanced over at Mac, but he kept his gaze trained on the reporter. I knew he was trying to be careful about how much he shared, but part of me was a little stung that he didn't mention the assistance he received from me in preparing the president for his day. I liked to view us as a team. I was "Duffie" to his "Mac." But it was clear he didn't see it that way.

"So tell us . . ." Mr. Jackson continued, "now that FDR has made the move from governor to president, what is his daily routine like?"

"Well, after breakfast, the president reads the morning papers, including the leading Negro weeklies."

"I hope the ANP is included in that," Mr. Jackson joked.

Mac laughed. "I won't confirm or deny that, but the president does a lot of reading before he gets up. He is very well informed and open-minded. He's certainly one that the humblest need not fear to approach. In fact, I can frankly say that the president does not think in terms of races but in terms of Americans. He believes the Negro is an American. I heard every speech he made during his campaign and never did he single out colored people. It was always *Americans*."

Mr. Jackson nodded. "That's good to hear, because I think I can speak for the majority of Negro Americans when I say that we are counting on him to include us more in his New Deal programs."

"I don't doubt he will," Mac said confidently.

"And are you making it a point to get in the president's ear about the issues in our community?"

Mac shook his head. "I learned early not to talk unless there is an expedient opportunity for the conversation, which I don't usually get, as the president is a very busy man. I especially refrain from discussing politics or his personal affairs with him."

Some of that was a blatant lie, but only I knew that. Mac's stance on politics differed a bit from what others might have believed. It wasn't that he didn't believe in the work of the NAACP or other organizations actively working to improve the lives of the Negro.

He simply believed that we as a people shouldn't lean too much on government for assistance when we should be doing for ourselves.

And though I could understand why Mac wanted the reporter to believe their relationship was strictly a professional one, I didn't see the harm in sharing that they held a special camaraderie of sorts. He and the president may not have discussed politics, but they did hold deep, personal conversations. They also shared a lot more in common than people would have thought.

"Can you tell us, Mr. McDuffie, what you most enjoy about your job and working for the president?"

"The traveling," Mac said without hesitation. "I don't have a formal education, but the experience I have gotten as valet from working with the president has been an education that one cannot get in schools. What other people talk about, I have seen. I have nearly circled the United States twice. I have been to Canada by water three times, to Montreal, Paris, the Bahamian Islands, and lots of other places."

"My husband is very well-read too," I added, knowing Mac would be too bashful to mention the many forms of literature he'd been exposed to. "He's read all of the Harvard classics, Balzac, Emerson, Tennyson, Byron, Shakespeare, and of course the Bible."

Mr. Jackson looked intrigued. "That's very impressive, Mr. McDuffie. You must be very well-read."

Mac simply shrugged.

"I have sources that say you are also afraid of flying," Mr. Jackson continued. "That you didn't accompany the president to Chicago when he went to accept his nomination because of that fear. Is this true?"

Mac shifted in his seat uncomfortably, and I figured that short laugh he let out was to mask his embarrassment. I disliked the reporter even more at that moment.

"I'll be the first to admit that I'm not ready to fly," Mac offered. "But if the president had insisted that I fly with him that day, I would have gone. I'll go with the president anywhere by land or water. Flying, however . . . Let's just say that I've always managed to get out of that in a diplomatic way."

"Well, speaking of sources, it's been said that not only does the president use a man by the name of Sean O'Grady as his double at certain events, but that you too have a double, Mr. McDuffie." He pulled up a few sheets to check his notes. "A Rufus Strother?"

I tried to contain my surprise that anyone outside of Mr. Roosevelt's closest confidants would mention the doubles that they had begun using for the president and Mac during select public appearances. Mac glanced at me, also surprised. It was clear from his pursed lips that he was at a loss as to what to say to the reporter.

I held Mac's gaze for a moment before I addressed the young reporter. "Off the record, Mr. Jackson?"

For a moment the reporter was silent. It was clear from his stunned expression that he was taken aback by my awareness of the phrase.

"Sure," he eventually agreed, laying his pen down. "Off the record."

"That's not something that we should be mentioning in this interview," I said. "With what has happened in Miami, and the continuous threats the president has received, getting a double is more for the president's safety than anything else."

"So the double isn't to trick the public into thinking the president is in good health and isn't dependent on his chair or leg braces?"

"No," Mac and I lied in unison.

Though it wasn't a complete lie. The president did receive threats, and it was only wise that the Secret Service had put in place a double who could keep him safe. It was nerve-racking to learn that Mac also needed a double, but I was grateful for the added precaution to his life as well.

Mr. Jackson simply nodded and picked up his pen. "Before we wrap up, Mr. McDuffie, what are some of the challenges you've faced working as the president's valet?"

Mac laughed. "There isn't much, but he sure can work five men to death while still lying in bed."

We all laughed.

"But he's still a good man," Mac said.

"Is that the impression you want to leave the Negro American about President Roosevelt?"

"Yes, because it's true. He's the greatest humanitarian I know. Anyone who is slightly acquainted with the president loves him. He is not only the leader of this great country, he is also president of the Warm Springs Corporation and he allows people to come there and take baths for free. As an individual, I think the president is the finest man in the world."

"And as a boss?"

"You know," Mac said, steepling his fingers, "I may call him 'Boss,' but I don't think of him in terms of a boss. He never gives orders but makes requests. Honestly, I think of him not as a boss but as a friend. One thing I can truthfully say: I work for one great man."

I glanced over at Mac, surprised that he had finally admitted that much. In that moment, I was proud of my husband for sharing his true feelings without regard to what others may think or feel about a Negro man expressing his admiration for his white employer.

After that interview, many who had read about Mac's history with the president began pouring letters to us.

I had never seen anything like it.

"Goodness, Mac, do you see this?"

I tried organizing the haul of mail we had just received by date and then by weight, my rationale being that the thinner the envelope, the quicker the read. There was a pile for me, a pile for Mac, and one with letters addressed to us both. But the more I organized, the more letters seemed to materialize. I was beyond overwhelmed. This was nothing at all like the vast amounts of mail that had inundated us when we'd first arrived at the White House.

"How are we possibly going to get through all of this?" Mac mused as he sifted through one stack of envelopes. He was clearly just as baffled by the influx of mail as I was. "These people do know we have duties to tend to, right?"

"I don't know how," I answered, still grappling with the sheer amount of correspondence we had just received. "But these people took the time to write us, so we need to at least make time to find out why."

With that, I made it a point to read a few letters before bed each night. Occasionally, Mac and I would read a few letters together.

We discovered that most of Mac's letters were fan mail—some sensible notes complimenting him on his service as valet, others not-so-sensible notes from colored high-school girls. Most of what I received was tragic, begging letters about situations or circumstances I could do very little about.

Then there were the crackpot letters.

Like the woman who wrote about the pictures she made from fish scales and chicken bones, or the milliner who wanted to know what shade of brown was Mrs. Roosevelt's new suit so she could send her a matching hat.

All sorts of people wrote us, on all sorts of topics.

Unfortunately, many of them overestimated our power within these grand walls. We were just one maid and one valet. Aside from the occasional autograph from the president and First Lady, there wasn't much we could do.

But it didn't stop me from reading the letters.

"LIZZIE, HONEY, YOU need to quit while you're ahead."

I ignored Mac as I sifted through more of the letters we had received just that week alone. I had grown tired of listening to his "warnings" that I was overstepping by inserting myself into matters that "didn't concern me." People were writing us on important matters and I couldn't just let them go ignored.

It had taken months for the president to form an unofficial "cabinet" of Negro leaders and advisers. It had taken just as long for him to have a formal sit-down with all of them in one room.

Last night's dinner with the president's group of Negro advisers and community leaders had been a success from what I could see. I had been tasked to serve at the dinner and I had been delighted, and inspired, to see a room filled with prominent Black men—and even one Black woman—having a moment with the most powerful man in the country. I had learned that Mr. Randolph was in fact A. Philip Randolph, a very prominent civil rights activist and union leader from New York City who didn't mind challenging the president to include Negroes in his New Deal programs. Mrs. Mary McLeod Bethune was a very personable and pleasant woman. I was inspired to hear her speak among a crowd of men and hold her own. I could see why she and Mrs. Roosevelt were such good friends.

The evening had gone off without a hitch.

Well, almost . . .

There had been that one awkward encounter with Edgar G. Brown, which still left me cringing. Though I had heard a lot about Mac's former brother-in-law from his first marriage, last night was the first time we'd met in person.

It was a meeting I could have done without.

"Lizzie, are you listening to me?"

I sighed and finally glanced up at Mac. "Yes, honey, I'm listening. You just haven't said anything that will change my mind. How can you feel comfortable ignoring all these people?" I held up the letters in my hand. "Especially when we can at least *try* to do something to help them."

"And you're willing to risk our position here? The boss may be entertaining this SAS—whatever—you're calling yourself, but what happens when the wrong subject gets discussed at the wrong time and things between you and the president go from friendly to sour?"

"Why are you being so pessimistic about this, Mac?"

In that moment, Mac reminded me of my own father.

Pop-pop, who had been born a slave, had once confessed to me that as a boy his reaction to "freedom" had been fierce disappointment. All because his mistress had promised him that when he got older, he could be her coachman. He had dreamed of the day when he would sit behind her team of fine horses and ride through the fields. He loved horses and dogs, and his nine-year-old heart was broken when he had to say goodbye after the Emancipation Proclamation had ended slavery.

Though he was a little ashamed to recall this, for William Hall, it had been a dismal day when he and his parents stacked their little pile of worldly goods on a rickety wagon and drove out through the gates of Butts County Plantation.

Mac was that nine-year-old boy, not recognizing the opportunity for a better and brighter future. But I wouldn't let my husband be blinded by the status quo.

Perhaps it was the scene that still stayed with me during that fearful march of my people after the Atlanta riot. Or maybe it was remembering how I had worked in service clubs for the Negro soldiers during the Great War, how I had recited for them and mended their socks. I needed to remember the woman that I was in Atlanta—the woman who worked for interracial groups after the war, who even today was still a member of the Young Women's Christian Association—the YWCA—and the Urban League in Atlanta.

As much as I loved literature and film and recitations, I couldn't forget that at my core I was a woman who loved to be of service to others. My job at the White House had now become more than just a job.

It was starting to feel like a small crusade.

And if Mac could only see things the way I did, then he would join me in my efforts. But I couldn't fault him. He'd lived a more sheltered life than I. The Great War had ended just as Mac was slated for the next draft, so he never got to see firsthand the ugliness of battle or the sacrifices our people were willing to make for a country that treated us as second-class citizens.

"Lizzie, I'm only trying to get you to see the reality of the situation. You don't understand how easily, or quickly, things can go from good to bad. Just like that." He snapped his fingers to emphasize his point.

"Are you speaking about me or you?"

I fixed him with a level stare and he knew what I was referring to. It wasn't a secret between us that the First Lady had called him into her office the other day for a private meeting. Neither Mr. Roosevelt nor Mrs. Nesbitt had been present, and Mac hadn't disclosed to me what the meeting had been about, but from the tension that had been with him since that meeting, I had an inkling that it had something to do with his self-medication method, which others would view as an overindulgence with alcohol.

"I understand your concern, Mac, I really do. But I can't just sit back and do nothing but make beds and sweep carpets while we're here." I stood up and went to him. I took his hand and gave it a gentle squeeze. "You remember how that Frenchman made you feel when he told you about that lynching in your hometown?"

He nodded stiffly, his lips pinched together. "How can I forget? It was my first time in Paris with the boss. And I had been really enjoying my time there."

My grip tightened again in sympathy. "Right. But it took one taxi driver to remind you where you come from."

Mac scoffed. "'Til this day I can't remember his name, but I'll never forget how he made me feel. They took a regular ole taxi driver to act as our chauffeur during our trip and here he goes judging me."

The bitter anger from that moment was still sharp in his voice. We had never gotten a chance to actually speak face-to-face about the incident. He had first recounted it to me in one of his many letters while he'd been traveling with Mr. Roosevelt overseas. I had tried to bring it up once during one of his late phone calls, but the call had been rushed and it was quite obvious he'd been too embarrassed by the situation to discuss it further.

His shoulders sagged. "Here I go boasting about Georgia to these people, telling him and anyone who'd listen all these wonderful things about my town, flat out denying that we have a lynching problem, and here he goes pulling out that damn paper about the lynching that had just happened in Elbert County. Right in my hometown!" He shook his head ruefully. "Yeah, I felt all kinds of funny then . . ."

It felt odd not knowing how to comfort my husband. Touch or humor were my usual responses, but those didn't seem like enough. It had been almost two years since that incident, yet the stiff set of his shoulders told me it still bothered him.

Heck, it still bothered me.

"I can imagine you must have felt a little less proud to call yourself an American, much less a Negro, right?"

His downcast eyes told me he had.

"Well, that's how I feel when I read these letters and do nothing more than set them aside. I know you must think I have my head in the clouds, but believe me, I'm not that naive. I know we can't fix everyone's problems, but we can try to help some."

"Not if it puts our jobs here at risk," Mac insisted. "There's just some things we shouldn't be getting involved in, and some people who are just too militant to be diplomatic. Like your friend Walter White."

I frowned, confused by that unexpected comment. "What do you mean?"

"I guess you haven't heard about the heated conversation Mr. White had with the boss after dinner last night. Apparently, the man brought up some anti-lynching bill that he wants the president to push through Congress. Clearly, Mr. White doesn't understand the chain of command, and the boss had to remind him of that."

I was surprised by what I was hearing, though not about Mr. White's lack of understanding. It was true that very few people realized that the word of the president was *not* law. All he could do was suggest things, and the suggestions would have to pass through a dozen officials, any one of whom could stop the whole thing. There were several legislative bills in front of the House at the moment that would have had an effect on people in the South and people of color. These were sensitive times for the president.

"They are both educated and well-spoken men," I offered. "I'm sure despite their disagreements, they still remained respectful."

Mac scoffed. "Only because Mrs. Roosevelt was there did

things remain civil. If the man was so smart, he should have known that bringing up an anti-lynching bill at dinner wasn't the time or place."

Though I somewhat agreed with Mac, I couldn't imagine that lines were crossed. Even if Mr. White hadn't gotten out of the meeting what he had hoped to gain, he appeared appreciative of the opportunity. He had even found time during the dinner to pull me aside and thank me for arranging the affair. He may be passionate about his beliefs, but I wouldn't go so far as to call him militant.

Edgar Brown, on the other hand, was another story . . . But I kept those derisive thoughts to myself.

"Well, I'm not discussing legislative bills with the president," I defended. "I'm simply bringing him issues that are far less controversial. Like this gentleman currently living in France, Leroy Commons. He's a war veteran who speaks several languages and is trying to get a job as a guide in a memorial cemetery. He's asking us to see if the president could help with getting him that job. It's an innocent enough request. It may not seem like much, but it could possibly change this war hero's life."

Mac shook his head. It was apparent he still didn't understand, but I hoped that over time he would come to see that this was the right thing to do.

"Let's hope, Lizzie, that in your efforts to help a few, you don't cause a riff that could cost you your job."

I watched as Mac made his way to the washroom, taking his words to heart. A part of me did agree with him, but the other more defiant part of me didn't care. There were human lives at stake, and I felt compelled to do more than just sweep rugs and dust counters all day.

I sat down at my desk, ready to pen down some of the issues I wanted to address with the president, when I saw an unopened letter peeking through today's newspaper. I picked up the envelope and tore it open. The letter inside was from a name I didn't recognize.

Dear Mrs. McDuffie, you don't know me but I need your help.

Tears blurred my eyes at the woman's words. Her letter addressed the detainment of her husband, who was a Great War veteran. He had been convicted with two other veterans for starting a riot.

She was Roy Tyler's wife.

In her letter she shared with me their life and who Mr. Tyler was as a husband and provider. They had four young children together whom he hadn't seen since he'd been wrongly convicted for the Houston riot in 1917. Her fear was that if he was left to rot in prison, she would be forced to raise their four kids alone.

Her plea for my help in getting her husband out of prison tugged at my heart, and I knew I couldn't turn my back on her.

The next day, while I was cleaning the president's bedroom, I was further assured that what I was doing was right when the president said, "Lizzie, I don't think I thanked you properly for arranging that dinner event. There were a lot of excellent points raised that night, and I'm glad I got the chance to hear them all."

I was a little taken aback by the appreciation, especially after hearing about the heated argument between him and Walter White. But I didn't dare bring that up now.

"You're welcome, Mr. President. Not bad for my first year as your SAY SOCK PAW, huh?" I teased, emphasizing each letter in the SASOCPA acronym.

He chuckled. "No, not bad at all. Now, what else do you have on your agenda?"

"Well, since you mention it . . ."

I proceeded to tell him about Mr. Commons and the request for a job in the American memorial cemetery in France. While on the topic of war veterans, we revisited the conversation regarding the three war veterans in Houston who had been wrongly accused of participating in the riot.

"Roy Tyler, Stewart Phillips, and Richard Lewis all have families they will never see again, children they will never get to see grown, all because of an *accusation*. Where's the justice in that?"

Mr. Roosevelt sighed and his expression was unreadable. "Riots are complicated affairs, Lizzie. In the end, those that are involved are never really without guilt."

"I understand, Mr. President. But I find it our duty as a country to make sure that the men who risk their lives for us, for this country, be given the opportunity of a fair and just trial. Most especially Negro men."

To my surprised delight, the president nodded in agreement.

"All right, Lizzie, I'll have Missy gather more information regarding the cases. This may not change anything, but it doesn't hurt to gain some insight on the matter."

I hid my joy at his words as he quickly jotted down some notes. Afterward, he put down his pen and sat back in his chair, a pensive look on his face.

"You know what, Lizzie? I feel like a good swim and a good meal . . . When Mac gets back, could you help him pack my things? I'd like us to leave for Warm Springs tomorrow."

I smiled at that. This was a man who knew how to work hard, then enjoy a dip in the pool after. I could see now why Mac was so fond of him. I sincerely hoped, for the sake of the country, that the presidency didn't change him because he was exactly what the country needed right now.

He was what the Negro needed right now.

Chapter 7

One year later...

The president's love for Warm Springs was infectious.

There was something about the small town that made Mr. Roosevelt feel that a trip there could solve any problem.

And I felt the same way.

During my two-year tenure with the Roosevelts, we had made multiple trips to the small town that had been dubbed the Little White House. There in the pine-scented slopes sat Mr. Roosevelt's main cottage. Flanking the white and black cabin was a small guest cottage and the servants' quarters.

FDR, as the press was regularly calling him, was a man who knew how to relax. He ate and slept well—and there was a lot of good eating here.

At Warm Springs, the small staff consisted of simply myself, Mac, and Mrs. Daisy Bonner, the cook—and she was a very fine cook at that. My waistline always seemed to spread an extra inch after each visit. Of course, there was Charles Fredericks, the president's bodyguard and lead Secret Service man. Miss LeHand often joined us, and though there was also a room for Mrs. Roosevelt, she rarely came down to visit.

Though I didn't have much to do with the preparation of the food, I would help serve, and I would get a kick out of Mr. Roosevelt asking for second helpings—something he never did at the White House. It felt good to know that, like many of us staffers, even the president didn't care too much for the White House food. Though his favorite meal was steak and French fries, there were not many things I ever saw him pass up from Daisy. He was fond of clam chowder, cheese soufflé, scrambled eggs, small peas, pheasant served with a hot bread-crumb sauce, and of course Daisy's famous "Country Captain"—a dish composed of chicken, tomatoes, onions, and raisins, all stewed in a curry, thyme, and garlic sauce, served over a bed of rice.

Daisy's signature meal always left the main house smelling like what I imagined summer in the Caribbean smelled like—sweet spicy earthy goodness. Those who got a whiff of the savory dish couldn't resist it.

Myself included—and my waistline hasn't forgiven me since!

But as much as Mr. Roosevelt enjoyed the food at Warm Springs, he enjoyed the pools and fresh air more. He treated his visits here with joy and adventure, and it was a pleasure for us all to see him come alive. With the world's problems crowding his desk, the president never shied away from seeking fun distractions in the company of his family or friends—or even those of us on his staff.

Even when there was "business" to conduct, he would find a way to joke and have fun. We were very much alike in that way and I always delighted in his pranks. Like that one morning when he notified the press to come to the cottage. The reporters had no idea what was happening, but they all rushed over in full force to hear what the president had to report. I stood just outside the servants' quarters, watching as the flock of reporters in their heavy overcoats followed the president, their cameras at the ready.

Very solemnly, Mr. Roosevelt led them to a quiet spot in the woods on Pine Mountain where they witnessed the dedication ceremonies for his secretary Marvin McIntyre's "Possum Preserve."

The reporters were not very happy about this unexpected journey, seeing as it was an early December morning and so cold that the water in the pipes had frozen over.

The president thought it was a hoot.

With all of the criticism Mr. Roosevelt was getting in the press about his policies and performance, I thought it served them right to frost their tails a bit.

Like Hyde Park, Warm Springs was Mr. Roosevelt's home away from home. With the help of his attorney and friend Basil O'Connor, they managed to turn Warm Springs into a great institution available to all people, especially those who needed it most.

And I had grown to love it here as well.

Despite the constant flow of guests, I found myself more relaxed, and more at home, at Warm Springs. Mr. O'Connor, who was often at Warm Springs and the White House, was one frequent visitor Mac and I enjoyed. Mac respected him above all of the president's friends, and Mr. Roosevelt always looked forward to his visits.

But it was longtime friends like Louis Howe that gave me a better insight into who Mr. Roosevelt was. Mr. Howe was as homely as homemade sin tied up in a carpet rag, and he was the first to admit it. Once I came upon him standing in front of a mirror at the White House after an important ceremony. He cocked his head from one side, then to the other, and grimaced.

"An awful lot of people turned out today to get a look at this face, didn't they, Duffie?"

Despite this self-awareness, he would lounge all day in his room wearing a disreputable dressing gown that did nothing for his looks. He was also a sick man who had asthma, and his room always smelled of some kind of steaming medication that he kept burning. Mr. Roosevelt, whom I had come to learn was a fastidious person, would sometimes flinch at Mr. Howe's appearance. One evening, Mr. Howe rang for Mac and asked him what the president's plans for dinner were.

"Mac, tell him if he is going to eat in the study, I'll come in and eat with him," Mr. Howe said.

The president's study was the Yellow Oval Room in the south side of the White House on the second floor. Typically, Mr. Roosevelt would dine with his secretary Miss LeHand when Mrs. Roosevelt was away and there were no guests to attend to. That night, however, Mr. Roosevelt was open to Mr. Howe's invitation but only under one condition:

"You tell him he can come down, but he will have to be dressed."

Poor Mac carried the reply back to Mr. Howe, couched in gentler terms, of course.

But Mr. Howe still hit the ceiling.

"Is that so? Tell him to go to hell," Mr. Howe growled. *"I will not dress!"*

Mac reported back to Mr. Roosevelt: *"Mr. Howe says he has changed his mind. He will eat in his room."*

The president shouted with laughter. *"Oh, no! That's not what he said! Tell me, now. Tell me what he actually said!"*

Needless to say, Mr. Howe did not eat with the president that evening.

But under Mr. Howe's surface gruffness was a kind heart, and

I soon came to enjoy his company. And I could see why Mr. Roosevelt took to him as well. Mr. Howe was the one true friend who never feared to argue hotly with the president. He was also the one friend with whom Mr. Roosevelt could truly let down his guard some. Sometimes their arguments would go on for days, with neither of them giving an inch. But it appeared all in good fun and it was nice to see the jovial side of the president.

Whether at the White House, Hyde Park, or Warm Springs, Mr. Roosevelt seemed to have the most fun with Mr. Howe around. The president loved to laugh and joke, and with his friend around, he did a lot of that. And that added to part of the fun in working for Franklin D. Roosevelt.

But if anyone asked where I preferred to work the most, I would have to choose Warm Springs. I always loved our trips there. What I personally loved about our visits was that it wasn't too far from Atlanta. During our days off, Mac and I would go and visit with family and friends.

During this last trip to Warm Springs, we finally managed to introduce Mama to the president. The meeting hadn't gone as I had imagined, but Mama, being the woman she was, didn't easily impress. And I think that was what Mr. Roosevelt liked about her the most.

"Lizzie takes very good care of us," he told her upon the first introductions.

"And I want you to take good care of my Lizzie, Mr. Roosevelt," Mama replied. "She's still my baby, you know."

And when the topic of his performance came up, my mother surprised us all with her candid response.

"I think you're doing the best you can, Mr. President. But I would be lying if I didn't say you could be doing more. Especially for our people."

Mr. Roosevelt took it in stride. "That's a criticism I often hear a lot. From all sides and groups."

"Then do better," Mama said casually. "You take the big cookie, you better take all the crumbs that go along with it."

To my surprise, the chief seemed to enjoy and appreciate her candor.

But it was one afternoon, after his lunch of Country Captain, that I learned our trip to Warm Springs this time around wasn't all just for relaxation.

"Lizzie, how would you feel if I told you I was running for a second term?"

It was not a surprise to me that he was already making plans to run again. Most presidents did, and based on the repair the country still needed, four years wasn't enough to make any real progress or change.

"I would be surprised if you didn't," I said honestly. "You're the right man for the job."

I, for one, was definitely in support for a second term. Though I distinctly knew that a reelection would mean Mac and I would be in Washington for another four years.

"Excellent. Because I'm going to need your help."

"What exactly do you need me to do?" I asked, as I began to clear the empty dishes before him.

"You've got such a way about you, Lizzie," Mr. Roosevelt began. "A very good and solid presence. And you do great in front of an audience. I think you would be the best person for this assignment."

"What assignment?"

He smiled. "Lizzie, I would like for you to campaign for me."

My eyes rounded, and for a moment I was speechless. "But Mr. President . . . I've never been a politician."

"It doesn't take much," he said casually. "You can meet the public and you can talk. So just tell them what we are trying to do here."

"But . . ." I stammered. "My oration skills are limited to plays and poems I have memorized. I can't speak to crowds. Not politically. I wouldn't even know where to begin!"

"That's exactly why I want you on my campaign trail, Lizzie. I don't necessarily want a politician. I have enough of them in my camp. I want a person who can connect with people, and on a very real and personal level."

Though I was flattered by the president's confidence in me, I wasn't sure that speaking to a crowd of people about issues that have or could have a major impact in their lives was something I could do well. And the president could see my apprehension.

"Do you believe in me, Lizzie?" He cleared his throat and quickly rushed on. "By that I mean: Do you believe I should be president?"

I offered him a tender smile. "Yes, of course. I can't think of anyone else who would be able to fill your shoes during these times."

Though it may not have appeared so to those outside the president's circle, Mr. Roosevelt was truly a man for the people. Though he knew how to maneuver among the best within this political machine, he also knew very well how to separate the president from the father and friend.

Even with those of us on his staff.

I never felt like an automaton in a black and white uniform. To the president, I was simply Lizzie McDuffie.

"Well then, if you have such faith in me, then believe me when I say you are the right woman for this. I believe in you. Just be yourself and speak from your heart."

When he put it that way, how could I say no?

So I jumped at the opportunity.

"Okay, Mr. President. How exactly do I get started?"

He grinned. "Let me discuss with Louis on the best cities for you to visit on your speaking trail," he began. "I'll be sure to have the Democratic committee send you some literature. I'll also have Missy send you some speaking notes. And get Edgar Brown to help you. He knows politics."

I bit back a groan at the idea of having to work closely with Mac's former brother-in-law. But I couldn't let my feelings toward the man interfere with this very important role. As I gathered up the dishes to take back to the kitchen, I released a determined breath.

"All right, Mr. President. This is not what I had in mind when I appointed myself as your SASOCPA, but I'm always up for a challenge."

He laughed. "My dear Lizzie . . . Welcome to politics."

PART 2:

The Road We Trod
(1936)

Chapter 8

My dear Mrs. McDuffie:

You probably have heard the good news already but fearing that it may not have come to you yet I want to tell you that the War Department wrote us yesterday that Roy Tyler is to be released. A large part of the credit for this should go to you for your persistent efforts, and I send you my warm congratulations.

—Ever sincerely, Walter White

The president had a memory the size of an elephant.

I don't believe he ever forgot a face or a name, and to my delight, he hadn't forgotten about Roy, Stewart, or Richard—the three war veterans who had been sent to Leavenworth for the Houston riots. The president, as promised, had looked into the case further and, based on what he learned, had decided to grant them a full pardon. All three men would finally be set free.

Roy Tyler was the last to be released.

Though the president and Walter White still didn't necessarily agree on certain matters that impacted the Negro community—namely the anti-lynching bill—the president still did what he could to make a difference. And the pardons of the three war veterans earned the president the NAACP leader's slight approval.

I found the other great characteristics of Franklin D. Roosevelt were his curiosity, his open-mindedness, and his commitment to seeing something through to the end. Like in the case of the Scottsboro Boys back in '33. Though the boys still languished in prison, their death sentences had been commuted down to life. I was convinced it had to do in part with the brief conversation the president had initiated with David Bibb Graves, the incoming governor of Alabama. During a governors' conference at Warm Springs, Mr. Roosevelt had asked the governor to remain behind for a while, and Mac had overheard the president saying:

"Governor Graves, I know I haven't a thing to do with this matter officially because it is purely a state affair. I don't know how you feel about the Scottsboro case, but won't you do all you can to clear it up?"

Governor Graves promised that he would and he ultimately ordered the National Guard to protect the young boys from lynch mobs that had gathered.

It wasn't much, but these were small victories.

While some of Mr. Roosevelt's efforts made an impact, there were some of the other matters he couldn't do anything about, like that of Mr. Leroy Commons. The president had asked Miss LeHand to write some letters in support of Mr. Commons getting the job at the memorial cemetery, but sadly, the job didn't pan out. I couldn't help but feel a profound sense of defeat when that unfortunate news reached me. I had hoped that if anyone could make a difference in the man's situation it was the president of the

United States. Here was a man who had the power to influence the fate of a nation. Surely, he could change the life of one individual.

Except he couldn't.

That moment served as a stark reminder to me that even the most powerful people in the world had their limitations. It also made me realize that Negro laborers needed a union or organization that would mobilize and protect them the same ways in which the American Federation of Labor protected their white workers.

Yet, here we were, in the middle of another election year, and this one was perhaps the most important of the president's career. It certainly was an important one for the country. Campaign flyers and posters were littered all around Washington. It was the main topic that filled the papers and radio. I was even featured in a good share of newspapers and journals for my campaigning efforts.

WIFE OF F.D.'S VALET CAMPAIGNS, wrote the *Afro American* paper this past October in one of their columns. I couldn't remember giving that interview, but the reporter on that column had been thorough. Though they referenced little of my campaign message, they did feature the lovely little anecdote about the Ethiopian prince Ras Desta Damtew and Mac's frantic attempt to avoid a massive diplomatic faux pas. It was a story I had shared countless times—one I was almost sick of recounting.

But no one could resist a funny story, so I gave the audience what they wanted.

In that same paper, I was surprised to see that I was referred to as "Mrs. Lizzie McDuffie." A nickname once reserved for family and friends was now casually used by people whose names I didn't know. I can't say when it happened, but eventually those close to Mr. Roosevelt began to call me Lizzie as well. Except for the children, of course. They continued to call me Duffie. And I didn't mind the informality. It made me feel a bit closer to the Roosevelts. They made me feel as if I was more than simply their maid or servant.

And that made my decision to stay on for another term a bit easier.

Before arriving at the White House, I had never considered a second term with Mr. Roosevelt. Our time here was supposed to be just four years, then Mac and I were going to resume our life in Atlanta. This was supposed to have been just a job that allowed me and Mac to be together while planning for our future. But the reality was that we couldn't leave now. Despite his wins and losses, Mr. Roosevelt was the right person to lead the country again and there was still important work to be done. Knowing that we couldn't walk away yet, that we still had important work to do for our community, filled me with an unwavering sense of determination to see this job through.

That thought left behind a complex mix of emotions in me until a bittersweet acceptance settled in my heart. There was no question that we needed to keep Mr. Roosevelt in the White House, and acknowledging that fact was what drove me forward in accomplishing that goal.

Campaigning for Mr. Roosevelt was the most demanding yet amazing development in my "crusade." For my upcoming tours, Mac helped me collect data, and he was surprisingly more supportive in this venture than he was with me bringing the problems of the people to the president. I think he may have been proud to have learned that the president had personally asked me to campaign for him.

Everybody else, from Henry Morgenthau's secretary to Walter White, also contributed to the preparation of my speeches. I was looking forward to Mr. Howe's contribution, since he had been so influential in all the president's other campaigns. Unfortunately, he passed away just before I was to start my "tour." He was sorely missed by all of us at the White House, particularly the president. Louis Howe had been the last to realize what an important part he had played in building the chief's career. He would say that no one ever "influenced" Mr. Roosevelt.

He was *almost* right.

Mr. Howe had the capability to influence the president more than any other person, and upon his passing, Mr. Roosevelt gave him a state funeral in the East Room of the White House. It was a somber moment, and I wondered if Mr. Howe left here knowing just how much the president really cared for him.

And it appeared the passing of Mr. Howe only fueled the president's ambition to win this next election. With a solidly formed campaign staff at his side, Mr. Roosevelt was bound to secure his reelection.

Now I just needed to fulfill my part.

Before I was to leave for my first series of campaign speeches for him, the president would tease, *"Now don't fall down, Lizzie."* I knew he meant that literally and figuratively because of my misfortune with freshly waxed floors.

Of course, I fell just before my first speech in Springfield, Illinois.

That memory tugged a small, quick smile from the corner of my lips, though at the time I had been absolutely mortified.

As I stood in the other room of the large assembly hall, I couldn't believe I was about to give my first ever political speech—in front of hundreds of people! The crowd's murmurs and the excitement in the air made my heart race. Despite my love of recitations and public performances, I was overwhelmed by the task before me.

But I was determined to see it through.

Mr. Roosevelt had believed in me enough to send me on this mission. I wouldn't let him down. More important, I wouldn't make a fool of myself.

Or so that had been the goal.

Just before my cue to step forward on stage, I took a deep breath. The lights glaring toward the stage were blinding, so I could barely see anything leading up to the platform. I was also so wrapped up in my nervous energy that I completely missed how pristine and glossy the stage floors were.

Yet with as much confidence in my stride as I could muster, I calmly took to the stage, ready to face the crowd. Before I could fully reach the podium, my foot slipped on the slick surface and I went flying. With arms flailing wildly, I barely had time to brace my fall before my bottom landed hard on the ground.

The loud gasps from the audience were quite audible and perfectly in unison. I could also make out a few nervous chuckles. In a flurry of clumsy movements, I was helped to my feet.

"Oh, my! Mrs. McDuffie, are you all right?"

I was too busy trying to regain my composure—and get past my embarrassment—to focus on who had asked the question. I was slightly bruised but mostly intact. Strangely enough, my main concern was with my hair and whether the curls were still pinned in their rightful place. I would rather not look as disheveled as I felt inside.

As I assured the organizers and host that I was quite fine to continue my talk, I turned to face the crowd with a wide smile.

"You know, before I left DC, President Roosevelt told me to break a leg tonight," I said to the sea of stunned faces. "I'll be happy to report to him that I did not."

The crowd erupted in laughter and applause, and I couldn't

help but laugh along with them. Suddenly, I felt a strange calm come over me. The ice was broken, and I was finally truly at ease.

With newfound confidence, I began my rehearsed speech, and despite the rocky start, I managed to slip my way into the hearts of those citizens of Springfield. Their warm reception further fueled the anticipation for my next speech.

When I faced that next overflowing crowd in St. Louis, I could tell they were restless. From the folks walking out, I could also tell I was boring them. So I stopped right in the middle of reading the rehearsed—or what I considered the "nice talk"—part of my speech. I knew that the crowd wanted to hear the little stuff that went on with the president and within the walls of the White House. They wanted to know what it was like to live in that great house and what sort of person the president was behind closed doors.

I told them as much as I dared.

"President Roosevelt is a stickler about leftovers," I told the audience. That comment was met with some chuckles, so I pressed on. "We all know better than to throw anything out, because he'd always have a suggestion as to what we can do with some leftover chicken."

As I paused for their reaction, a sea of mostly black and brown faces gazed eagerly up at me, all gathered to hear a bit of gossip about the nation's leader.

"Once at Warm Springs, we had pheasant," I continued, smiling as I recalled the memory. "It's the president's favorite. He told my husband, Mac, 'Let's serve this for breakfast tomorrow.'"

Murmurs of approval and agreement rippled through the crowd. I myself didn't care to be wasteful, and it was clear the good people of St. Louis appreciated a leader who was just as thoughtful.

"The president didn't know this, but that same day we had

already made sandwiches with the leftovers for a tea party we had not expected. And I'll tell you that was the first time in my life I had ever made *pheasant* sandwiches!"

The audience erupted in laughter.

"Y'all should've seen how Mac was wringing his hands, sure that President Roosevelt would ask for the bird in the morning. And of course, he did."

The crowd leaned in, rapt with attention. I found myself picking up their excited energy. My senses sharpened and my focus narrowed on the crowd and their response to my every word. I couldn't remember ever feeling so enlivened to speak in front of an audience before.

"So what happened next?" someone shouted from the front.

I smiled and zeroed in on the portly old man with a balding head who stared up at me with great intrigue.

"Well, sir, I explained to the president that we had used it for the tea party. And I said to him, 'I also noticed you enjoyed those sandwiches too.' His eyes twinkled back at me and the subject was dropped, 'cause we both knew how he had polished off that tray of pheasant sandwiches."

The audience, which had hung on my every word, suddenly erupted into laughter and cheers. My willingness to share these stories with the crowd served to show the everyday citizen that Franklin D. Roosevelt was a leader like none other. In the few years I had known him, I found Mr. Roosevelt always courteous. He was generous, but no one could accuse him of being extravagant. He played with his grandchildren. He kidded all of us.

And I got the opportunity to show others these many sides of him.

Over time, it became easier to speak to people about President Roosevelt and the reasons why he should be elected to a second term. Some were easier to convince, especially when it was the popular opinion that Republican governor Alfred Landon didn't stand a chance against him. And my duty now was to try and change the opinions of those who had doubts about the president and his New Deal policies.

At the campaign events at which I was asked to speak, I would hand out printed handbills and pamphlets for President Roosevelt. I don't believe any other White House servant championed the president's cause more than I did. And quite honestly, I also gained a lot from the opportunity.

Not only did I get to visit some exciting and diverse cities, I got to meet a ton of fascinating people. I especially wouldn't forget my run-in with a particular young and resilient woman during my tour in Lansing, Michigan.

Of the many people I'd gotten to meet during my campaign stops, she was the one person who came across my mind the most. I don't know how long the woman had waited around to speak to me after my speech, but I was glad on that particular day that I wasn't in any rush to return to my hotel room.

"Hello, Mrs. McDuffie."

I turned to the soft, timid voice and smiled at the petite light-skinned Negro woman. She appeared nervous and uncertain, and for a moment I wondered if I was the cause.

"Hello." I offered her a friendly smile and held out my hand, hoping to ease her anxiety. "Please call me Lizzie."

She took my hand. "It's a pleasure to meet you in person, Mrs. Lizzie. I really enjoyed your talk."

I couldn't help but wonder where the woman was from. Her accent was distinct, yet I couldn't place it.

"Thank you, Miss . . ."

"Sorry. My name's Louise Little."

"Are you by any chance from Louisiana, Louise? Maybe French Creole? I picked up an accent and was curious about it."

Louise offered me her first smile. "I'm actually from Grenada, but I do speak French."

"Oh, how nice. I've always wanted to learn how to speak French," I confided.

"*Ce n'est pas difficile à apprendre.*"

"Pardon?"

Louise laughed, and from the rustic sound, it wouldn't have surprised me if that wasn't an action she indulged in often.

"I said, 'It's not hard to learn.' I actually found English harder to pick up."

"I'm not surprised, especially when there's two kinds: white English and Negro English."

Louise nodded in agreement. "My husband and I used to discuss that all the time. I think it's important for our children to learn to speak the white man's way. He, on the other hand, didn't think we should be so quick to assimilate."

I pursed my lips, wondering if her husband was like some of the Negroes I had encountered before. The ones who believed that speaking with a "proper" vernacular was "putting on airs"—or, worse, kissing up to the white man.

"Well, tell your husband it's not assimilation. It's called survival."

I tried to keep the sharpness from my tone, but from the dejected look on her face, I didn't quite succeed.

Suddenly a young boy who couldn't have been more than eleven or twelve years old came rushing to her side.

"Mama, it's time to go now."

"Malcolm, don't be rude," Louise admonished. "You see I'm talking."

The young boy turned to me, looking sheepish. "Sorry, ma'am."

"Now go wait with your brothers and sister. I'll be there in a minute."

The young boy pouted. "But you said we could go to the candy store after. It's gonna close if we don't hurry."

She sighed, and that small sound spoke volumes. "Don't make me repeat myself."

The young boy looked like he wanted to argue, but from the look in Louise's eyes, he wisely decided against it. He darted back to where the other children sat on a nearby bench, his copper-red hair a blur. His unique coloring was different from that of his other siblings, but they all shared similar features. But it was his polite brazenness that stood out the most, and I found it adorable in a Negro boy his age.

"Sorry about that, Mrs. Lizzie. My kids usually have better manners than that."

"You have nothing to apologize for. I've been a child nurse, a nanny, and a maid for over thirty-five years now. I can tell he's being raised right. But kids will be kids. Don't be too hard on him."

"Oh, I adore my children, but sometimes they can be a handful. Especially Malcolm. He's my hotheaded one, and of my seven—"

"*Seven?*"

I could imagine my eyes were as wide as saucers in that moment. Though I knew plenty of women who had a large number of kids, I had never met one who appeared so young.

Louise nodded. "That's right. I've been blessed and highly favored to bring seven lives into this world. But it's been hard, especially after my husband was murdered."

I gasped, and my hand instantly flew to my mouth. I was now mortified after what I had said about her husband.

"Oh, my. I'm so sorry, Louise. How—"

"He was lynched," she interrupted bluntly.

I didn't know what else to say, so I said nothing and simply offered her what comfort I could. During my time in Michigan, I had learned about the countless Negro men lynched in various parts of the state, and I could only imagine what this petite woman and her children were enduring.

"Thank you, Mrs. McDuffie, but I was hoping you could help us get justice for my husband, Earl Little. He was killed here in Michigan. According to the police it was an accident, but I don't believe that for a minute."

"Why not?"

"They claim he got run over by a trolley. Said he was drunk and fell on the tracks. But my husband never drank a day in his life."

"Oh, Louise, I can only imagine your suffering. But in this case, it would be hard to prove otherwise."

Her eyes flooded with tears but none fell. For the first time since she approached me, her voice was thick with anguish and rage. "Everyone around here knows it was the Klan. They lynched my husband in plain sight and have the audacity to still call it an accident."

I knew there was nothing I could say to ease the woman's pain, so I simply pulled her into a hug. Unfortunately, her story wasn't uncommon, and I knew from experience that the president wouldn't intervene. There just wasn't enough there to prove that his death wasn't simply an accident.

"I will share your husband's story with the president," I promised. "But tell me how else can I help you and those sweet children."

To my surprise, she opened up to me about how she and her kids were struggling to survive in Lansing. I learned that although she had received a portion of her husband's life insurance, she had to rent out a room in her home just to make ends meet. For a moment, I thought of a place like Camp TERA and how the First Lady's program could perhaps be of help to her.

But then what would happen to her seven children?

It was moments like this that I wished the president's New Deal programs had more to offer women, especially unmarried and widowed mothers rearing children alone, like Louise.

And as I continued my tour, I met many women like Louise.

My journey took me from state to state, from Ohio to Illinois to Indiana and then Pennsylvania, where I spoke to more interracial groups than in any other state. I also met many families who just wanted to share their stories of struggle and how they were placing their faith in the president to turn things around for them. I listened, I took notes, and I assured them that the president was certainly keeping the American people at the top of his mind.

It felt good to use some of what I had learned in school about giving speeches and giving recitations to help in the campaign of a worthy president. But what felt even better was that I was able to make a difference.

At least on some occasions.

On other occasions, I was challenged at every opportunity. My support for the president was also not seen favorably by some staunch Negro Republicans. There were some colored-only establishments that refused to serve or house me during my campaign, and I often found myself hosted in the homes of other Negro Democratic supporters.

And I was ever so grateful to them.

I didn't let these small prejudices stop me from my mission, however. While President Roosevelt proved he had what it took to ease the nation's poverty, unemployment, and debt crises, his opponents worked to undermine what he had managed to accomplish thus far. Several other politicians also wanted to know why the president did not appoint more Negroes to important positions. Or even give them major speaking engagements.

Secretly, I wondered the same thing too.

At my first opportunity upon returning to the White House, I shared everything I had learned with the president and presented that very question to him.

"Lizzie, the leaders in your race are constantly speaking against segregation, so why should I segregate a race or minority?" the president countered. "I'm running for the presidency of the United States and all its people."

When Franklin Delano Roosevelt spoke of "the forgotten man," he referred to them all—the Negro, Jewish, and Chinese laborer. He refused to lower his standards and principles in the hope of gaining extra votes. Even if it meant losing the upcoming election.

I wasn't sure if I completely agreed with his sentiments. Not many viewed the world in the same ways he did, and without proper representation in the places where it mattered, there was no guarantee that these forgotten men would truly have their voices heard.

So I tried to be that voice for them.

During our discussion about the peoples' feelings and attitudes toward him, I spoke to Mr. Roosevelt about Earl Little and those who lived in constant fear of being lynched because it went so widely unpunished. I spoke to him about the many families I had met along the way who still struggled to make ends meet despite his labor and work programs.

However, I couldn't fault the president for holding true to his beliefs. He was a politician. but he was democratic without posing. In my humble opinion, he was a true friend to the Negro without being patronizing, and that was the message I worked hard to get across to the public.

And on the day of the election, it all seemed to pay off.

On November 3, 1936, Franklin Delano Roosevelt once again won the presidency in a landslide victory. The president managed to carry every state except Maine and Vermont. His victory was impressive, but not all that surprising. Not to me, anyway. Many Americans saw what I did:

That President Franklin D. Roosevelt was the one who would lead this country toward prosperity.

Chapter 9

Some mornings were absolutely serene.

I would roll onto my side and watch as the morning sun peeked through the thin opening of our drapes, leaving slanted rays of golden light streaming down the sheer curtains beneath. I would watch as motes of lint floated in pure symmetrical brilliance in the air that smelled of old spices.

Other mornings like today, however, were unbelievably brutal.

It was as if I could feel every inch of my fifty-five years of age. Especially after celebrating the president's second win, where we were all up well into the night receiving, entertaining, and cleaning after guests.

But no matter what the morning started like, waking up in the White House didn't change the fact that I was still a maid to the Roosevelts and had duties to attend to.

For the next four years, this was where I would wake up each morning, where I would have my meals, and where I would spend my evenings.

I wasn't sure how I felt about that.

And quite frankly, there was no time to dwell on it. I dragged myself from my cozy, warm bed and made my way to the large windows. I pulled the curtains wide apart so that the light flooded the room, stunning Mac out of his sleep.

"Lizzie . . ." he groaned, rubbing the sleep from his eyes as he struggled to pull himself out of bed. "What time is it?"

I glanced at the clock hanging nearby. "Fifteen minutes past seven."

With a short exclamation, Mac stumbled to his feet. I bit my tongue, keeping my disapproving words to myself, as I watched him fumble around the room. I was certain he was nursing a massive headache this morning, after the amount of drink he had indulged in last night. Granted the election results were definitely cause enough to celebrate, but if Mac couldn't practice some restraint then there wasn't much I could say at this point.

"You might want to hurry before you end up getting to the president late this morning."

Mac grunted in agreement before heading to the washroom. I shook my head as the door shut behind him. It had been a while since I had seen Mac drink so heavily, and I was taken aback at how strongly of spirits he smelled when he'd finally come to our room last night. It had also been very disappointing. I could understand that there were times he needed a stiff drink to help ease the pain in his leg, but I couldn't understand why he couldn't have it in moderation.

But I wouldn't widen the tension between us this morning with an argument. Mac would have to spend the next few hours dealing with the consequences of his decisions.

As I busied myself tidying up our chamber, I couldn't help but think about what our lives would be like these next four years at the White House. Mac's drinking was steadily increasing, and deep down I wondered if he could still handle the demands of being the president's valet.

While I felt our presence here was very much needed if we were to continue getting the president's attention on issues that impacted the Negro community, it certainly came at a cost, and the price was Mac's health and our marriage. I was beginning to wonder if our sacrifices were worth it . . .

A sudden knock on the door jolted me out of my thoughts. It was still early yet, and I wondered for a moment who it could be. I rushed to the door just as the knock came again.

"Coming!" I called out.

I pulled the door open to find one of the messengers holding out several pieces of mail, and I knew immediately they were letters from people around the country wanting—oftentimes *needing*—the president's attention.

"Mrs. McDuffie, these just came in for you."

I flashed a brief smile and took the envelopes from the young man. "Thank you, Adam."

I shut the door and sat down at my small desk to go through each letter. They were mostly appreciation letters from Negro women in Washington and across America. I spent time over every letter, committing the words that crawled across the pages to memory. The words of encouragement and praise from these people I had never met or spoken to reminded me why I had spent months campaigning for the man I felt would give us a chance of being heard and seen. I couldn't regret my decision now.

There was still work to be done. And I was willing to continue doing it. Even if that meant setting aside my own goals and ambitions.

Later that evening, President Roosevelt summoned me to his study. Mac was seated right in front of him just as I came into the room. I imagined the president would have been surrounded by his staffers, either still celebrating his recent win or planning for the next term to come.

"Lizzie, please join us."

"Thank you, Mr. President." I took the seat beside Mac, guessing hard on what this meeting would be about. I noticed a bottle of champagne sitting on the desk with three empty glasses. I stared pointedly at the bottle. "What are we celebrating?"

"You, my dear Lizzie." The president's smile was contagious. "I've had a lot of staff work with me over the years, but you and Mac here have been remarkable."

I returned his smile. I knew his words came from a place of gratitude. The Roosevelts had always treated us less like servants and more like trusted friends.

"I couldn't come to trust or appreciate a more devoted pair than you two," Mr. Roosevelt continued. "Despite Mac tossing out one of my favorite ties."

"In my defense," Mac began with a small chuckle, "that tie was nothing but bad luck."

Mr. Roosevelt raised a brow. "Was it? How can we be sure it wasn't the shoes I was wearing that brought on that maniac Zangara to take aim at me? Or better yet, how do we know it wasn't the suit I had on?"

Mac shook his head. "Every time you've worn that tie, we always ended up getting entangled in some unfortunate situation."

"Hmm, perhaps you're right," the president agreed with a short nod. "But we can debate about that later. I brought you both here to celebrate and commend you for the work you've done during the campaign. You have done a lot during the course of your time here, serving me and your people well."

The president uncorked the champagne bottle and poured some gold sparkling liquid into each glass. I couldn't help but think about the celebrating that Mac had done the night before, and I hoped tonight didn't result in the same outcome tomorrow morning.

"It was my pleasure, sir," I said, trying to tamp down my rising tension. "You have done good by us and the country. It was an honor to share all that you've done, and are still doing, for the American people."

"Thank you, Lizzie. We are now about to enter a new era," the president said. "This one will be more challenging than the last. It's my greatest pleasure to have you both by my side as we continue on this journey, moving this nation forward."

"You have our full support, Boss," Mac said. "That will never change."

Mr. Roosevelt picked up his glass and raised it high. Mac and I followed suit.

"Here's to the continuous effort we've all put forth in serving and moving this country forward. And to you, Lizzie dear. Thank you for taking to the streets to campaign for our cause."

We all brought our glasses to our lips and took a sip of the sweet champagne. I wasn't much of a drinker, so the bubbly bite that followed took me by surprise, and I succumbed to a fit of coughing. Both men put their glasses down and stared at me with concern.

"I'm fine," I managed to croak, placing my own glass down. "My palate is just not used to so much excitement."

The president laughed. "Well, we're going to have to change that now, won't we?"

I joined in the men's laughter with a forced one of my own. I couldn't help but keep my focus on Mac as he finished his first glass and poured himself a second. Not wanting to sour the celebratory mood, I kept my potentially volatile comments to myself.

But I later regretted my silence when Mac didn't return to our chamber until late that evening. He didn't reek of alcohol like he had the night before, but I could tell by his stumbling that he had overindulged. Again.

"Mac, you can't keep on like this."

He sat on the edge of the bed and kicked off his shoes. "Lizzie, what are you going on about now?"

I shook my head in disgust. "Mac, please don't play me for a fool. I don't say anything about your drinking because I know you're in pain, but you need to slow down. Sooner or later, people will start to notice."

"Bah!" Mac said dismissively. "You worry too much."

He pushed off the bed and disappeared into the washroom. I reined in my anger and decided to drop the matter. For now.

Though Mac's increased drinking was the main source of my constant worries these days, it wasn't the only issue that occupied my mind. We had just secured another victory for the president, yet I couldn't help but feel a sense of uncertainty for our future, both as servants and activists, in the White House. It was hard to find much joy in the job anymore when my every thought was centered around how I could foster more change in our community.

There was one joy, however, that I could still find pleasure in.

The White House library.

Lately, I found myself wandering in there at every opportunity. I had been in there so much that it now felt like my own personal safe haven. Mrs. Roosevelt was also a frequent patron, sometimes startling me when I found myself lost in a story from off the shelf, yet always encouraging me to read as much as I could.

And I would take full advantage.

On one particular afternoon, after spending an hour cleaning every nook of the large library, I perused through the tall shelves filled with over two thousand books. I eventually settled on a book about Greek mythology and sank into my favorite armchair in the middle of the room. I could feel the chair envelop me in its warm embrace as I reclined, the tome of a book heavy on my lap.

I felt right at home.

I hadn't fully settled into the large chair before I heard the soft scrape of the door opening behind me. I swung around, half expecting to find the First Lady walking in. Although she would encourage me to spend as much time in here as I wanted, I didn't feel quite comfortable lounging about in her presence.

Instead, I was surprised to find the president's bodyguard and Secret Service man Charles Fredericks standing at the door. He looked just as surprised to see me there.

"Oh, excuse me," he rushed out. "I didn't expect anyone to be in here."

"No excuses necessary," I said, getting to my feet. "I was just taking a break myself."

He nodded briskly but continued to stand at the door. Though I'd had many encounters with the large strapping man, I knew him to be a person of few words—not very uncommon for a Secret Service man, but it certainly made for awkward moments such as now.

After a brief, uncomfortable silence, Mr. Fredericks made his way past me to the bookshelves. I don't know how I missed the tome he was carrying, but as he passed me, I caught a glimpse of the title.

Gone with the Wind.

The cover of the book didn't necessarily catch my interest as much as the large bold text of the title did. I had heard whispers of the book being either very good or a disgrace—depending on who was asked. Being that the author was from my hometown of Atlanta and the book was set in the same place, my curiosity got the better of me.

"What did you think of it?" I asked the man, staring pointedly at the book. "The novel?"

Mr. Fredericks glanced down at the book, then back up at me. If I wasn't mistaken, I could have sworn there was a bit of color forming across the man's cheeks.

Was he blushing?

"I've heard mixed reviews about it," I said, hoping to ease some of his obvious discomfort. "But it looks like a book I'd fancy."

He shrugged his broad shoulders and glanced down at the book again. "I enjoyed it. I think it did a good job balancing action, adventure, humor, and a bit of romance. If you're into that sort of thing."

His brief description piqued my interest.

"I am. What is it about?"

I was surprised by how the man's eyes lit up as he started with his assessment of the story.

"Well, it's about a southern belle named Scarlett O'Hara, desperate to save her home during the Civil War . . ."

Mr. Fredericks went on to give me a detailed description of the story, careful not to say too much. His obvious excitement over the story further piqued my interest, and I was hooked.

Besides, it might be a nice change from the political papers and ancient classics I had been consuming as of late. And if what Mr. Fredericks claimed about the novel were true, I could use a bit of romance in my life right now.

"I think you sold me, Mr. Fredericks. If you're done with it, I would love to give it a read."

"Of course." He handed me the book, a wide smile stretching across his lips. "You're a woman from the South, right?"

"Born and raised," I confirmed proudly, stuffing the encyclopedia into a nearby shelf and taking the book from him.

"Then I think you'll thoroughly enjoy this book."

Mr. Fredericks was right.

I did enjoy the book.

So much so that I found myself reading the massive tome for a second time . . .

Scarlett O'Hara was not beautiful, but men seldom realized it when caught by her charm as the Tarleton twins were.

The opening line of the book always arrested me, and for the next few days, I read and reread the book cover to cover. There were days I would ache to go back to my quarters just so I could recline and continue where I had left off in the story. It had been a while since a book had captivated me so. I had even felt compelled to write to Miss Margaret Mitchell, on White House letterhead, about her wonderful job on the book.

I secretly hoped it grabbed her attention enough to write back a response.

In the meantime, I found myself once again engulfed in the story, and it didn't take too long before I began memorizing some of the lines in the book. One of my favorite lines in the story, which not only gave me a chuckle but also rang very true, was:

Death and taxes and childbirth! There's never any convenient time for any of them!

And I found on one afternoon, during my days off, that there was no convenient time for reading either.

It was on a particular day off, as I found myself once again lost in the sweeping saga of the popular novel, that Kathy not only managed to interrupt my quiet time in the library but also managed to ruin my enjoyment of the story.

"Lizzie?" Kathy called out as soon as she entered the White House library. "I've been looking all over for you. Why aren't you down in the kitchen enjoying some birthday cake with us?"

I glanced up at the younger woman, closing the book and resting it down on my lap. "Oh, I didn't know. Whose birthday is it?"

Kathy thought about it for a second. "I think it's Mrs. Rogers's daughter. Lillian."

"Oh, I'm sorry I missed it."

"There still might be a few slices left over," Kathy said, walking over to where I sat and looking down at the book on my lap. "What are you reading so deeply that has you locked away in here all the time?" She leaned over to read the title on the dust jacket. "*Gone with the Wind*," she muttered, then shook her head. "Oh no, Lizzie. Don't tell me you're actually reading that garbage."

"Garbage?" I frowned over at her, confused. I had heard just as many criticisms of the book as I had praise, but never anything so harsh. "Have you read the book? It's not garbage."

"That's not a book you should be wasting your time on."

"Why not?"

Kathy tsked. "You mean you haven't seen anything wrong with the book so far?"

I squinted. *Was I missing something?* "None yet . . . Tell me, have you actually read the book?"

"Yes, and I despised it. I couldn't even finish it."

"Really? Why?"

"It offended my sensibilities, and it was hard for me to read and get into any of the characters. I'm sure southern whites found the book very much enjoyable."

"Well, what do you expect? The author is a southern white woman," I reminded her. "Our stories are different from theirs. You have to understand that she did not write this from the experience of a Negro. She's probably a descendant of slave owners, maybe even grew up on a plantation. Who knows? I imagine she told the story she knew."

"Then she shouldn't be writing about things—or people—she knows nothing about. The author of that book made light of the brutality of slavery and watered it down to the point you would think every Negro in that book was an ignorant buffoon, a violent criminal, or a scared little slave happy to stick by their master."

"I think you're being too judgmental, Kathy. The book is meant to be a work of fiction. Let us not be so consumed by the details of history that we fail to see the artistry of the book itself."

"Art is subjective," Kathy said. "But I wouldn't call that book of lies art."

"Lies?"

"Yes! Do you really think those happy-go-lucky Negroes in that book were happy working on that plantation? And don't get me started on the Prissy and Mammy characters . . ." Kathy scoffed and threw her hands up in disgust.

"Hmm, I can see why you'd have an issue with Prissy, but what about Mammy? What was wrong with her character?"

Kathy scoffed again. "What *wasn't* wrong with her? She acted more like a paid servant than a slave. She also cared a little too much for the main character for my liking. Acted as if the woman was her own daughter!"

"Well, she was a house Negro who raised Scarlett from birth. What do you expect? And I actually liked her character in the story."

I left out the part where I could actually relate to her as well. No, I wasn't a slave when I worked for the Inmans and I hadn't worked under those conditions, but I had helped raise the Inman children and grandchildren as if they had been my own. And like Mammy, I had come to care deeply for the family.

"The depiction of those Negro women was a disgrace," Kathy continued. "Never mind how the Negro men were portrayed. Not to mention how the author romanticized the idea of slavery a little too much for my liking, which made it uncomfortable for me as a Negro woman to read. Especially when a lot of slaves are still alive now, including my parents. They were born into slavery, you know."

"So were mine," I said. "We're all descendants of slaves. We can't escape that fact."

"Right. That's why this story is an insult to us all. I'm surprised you're not as offended as I am by this book."

"It's just a book, Kathy. I don't know about you, but I read for the fantasy of it, not to be reminded of my reality. Besides, the author presents flaws from all sides. Scarlett O'Hara was probably the most unlikable character in the beginning—"

"And throughout," Kathy interjected.

"But it's the flaws from the characters that make them interesting and feel real. No one is all good or all bad, and I like that the author makes a point to show that."

Kathy sighed and, with a slight shake of her head, made her way toward the door. "Well, I'm not convinced. The book is still bad, but enjoy your *fantasy*. I'll talk to you later, Lizzie."

I shook my head as I watched Kathy shut the door behind her. I understood her point of view and she had every right to her opinion, but I resented her stealing my enjoyment of the story.

Art is subjective, I reminded myself, repeating Kathy's very words.

For me it was just a story told from a white woman's perspective, and because I understood that, I didn't make the story more than what it was—a sweeping saga about love, loss, sacrifice, and perseverance.

A few weeks after I had finished *Gone with the Wind* and returned the book to the White House library, I found Mr. Fredericks standing just outside the president's office and couldn't wait to discuss the story with him.

"Mr. Fredericks, why didn't you tell me how good that book was?" I admonished with mock outrage.

The Secret Service man graced me with one of his rare wide smiles, and we descended into a lengthy discussion of the book.

"Are you as excited about the film as I am?" he gushed.

It was a delight to see a man of his size and stature express his excitement over something so small with such abandon. But my brow furrowed in confusion as my curiosity got the better of me.

"What movie?"

"Oh, you haven't heard about it? They're making a movie from the book. I hear they're opening for auditions next year."

"Oh, really? So soon?"

Mr. Fredericks shrugged. "I imagine they want to do it while the book is gaining in popularity. I would love to try my hand at a role as a soldier, if I didn't already have this job."

"So would I," I teased. "If I had any acting skills to speak of."

He chuckled, and I shared in his laughter. Perhaps in my younger days, I would have given the thought some serious consideration. In grade school, I had put more time into programs and school plays than anything else. The predictions at graduation were that Elizabeth Hall would be destined for the stage.

But as an adult, I knew better.

At my ripe age of fifty-five, I wasn't so naive as to think I could break into acting now. Besides, of all the things I found myself involved in, there was no room in my life to even consider the silver screen.

Chapter 10

January 21, 1937
White House

The president's second inauguration was impressive, though it wasn't anywhere near as thrilling as the first.

Mrs. Roosevelt, with her usual foresight, saw to it that inauguration invitations were sent to all the servants in Washington, Albany, and Hyde Park. Their efforts to get invitations out had been so thorough that the president had even received one. It was a head-slapping moment, and we all had a good laugh over that one.

It had rained that entire morning of the inauguration, and unlike the first, the crowd had dispersed immediately after the president's speech. But I still wouldn't have missed it for anything.

The next morning after the ceremony, it was business as usual. As I prepared to leave our small living quarters in the East Wing of the White House, the telephone rang. I hesitated for a moment before I decided to pick it up.

"Hello? Mrs. McDuffie?"

"Speaking," I said cautiously, not recognizing the voice on the other end of the line.

"Yes, good morning. This is Albert Jackson, from the—"

"Allied Negro Papers," I finished for him. "I remember you, Mr. Jackson. How can I help you?"

"Well, here at ANP our aim is to address the lack of representation of the Negro perspective in the mainstream media by exposing our experiences to the world," he said.

I couldn't contain my eye roll. "I'm familiar with the publication, Mr. Jackson."

"Yes, of course," he rushed out. "I'm not going to take more than a minute or two of your time, Mrs. McDuffie. You've been on the campaign trail for President Roosevelt and have been a big advocate of his. I would love to interview you. Would you have some time to offer a few words about your experience at the White House?"

I was torn between curiosity and suspicion. Before now, Mr. Albert Jackson hadn't given a hoot about my experience. His last interview had centered on Mac solely. That part I didn't mind so much, but the fact he suddenly cared to hear from me gave me pause. The man was now earning a reputation for being one of the president's loudest critics in the press. I didn't want him to use my words to hurt the president.

"I'm sorry, Mr. Jackson, but I can't—"

"Mrs. McDuffie, you're the closest link the average Negro has to the president. Don't you think they want to know what the man they elected has planned for their future?"

"Yes, which is why they should be sure to listen to him when he's on the radio and pick up the paper when he's discussing those very matters."

"I'm afraid that's not enough, Mrs. McDuffie," Mr. Jackson said. "The president is not addressing matters that are relevant to *us*. This week alone, there have been fifty reported lynchings in this *great* country of ours. Why hasn't the president spoken up about this?"

I didn't have an answer for that. Even now, the topic of the anti-lynching bill was a sensitive subject to bring up with the president. Despite even the First Lady's efforts, the president refused to budge on his stance regarding the bill. He still believed he had too much to lose if he supported a bill that he knew would turn his own party against him.

"Mr. Jackson, I'm just one woman," I said. "Though I have the interest of my people at heart, there's only so much I can do. Just like the president. There are things he would like to support, but he needs the support and approval of Congress to push them through."

I knew I was saying too much, particularly regarding what the president would or wouldn't do, but I needed the reporter to understand that the man he was condemning as a "panderer of the Negro vote" was genuinely interested in helping better the lives of the American Negro. Even when I wasn't sure if a lot of colored people would support him, I still believed in him enough to go and express my support. I believed his support of the Negro cause was genuine. I just needed to convince others of that.

"With all due respect, Mrs. McDuffie, you need to open your eyes. Your president spent an entire first term in office and did nothing to uplift or better the lives of the Negro. Yet he has you trotting around the country securing him the Negro vote."

It took everything in me not to slam the telephone handle down on the receiver. The only reason I didn't was that it was important for me to let Mr. Jackson understand that he was wrong to expect change overnight.

Or to expect change from one man.

"Mr. Jackson, you are entitled to your opinion, but it's clearly coming from someone who doesn't understand politics. If you think the president wields all this power to change things, you are sadly mistaken. In the democracy that we live in, there are steps and channels that everything must go through."

"Even so," Mr. Jackson interjected, "the president doesn't need Congress's permission to come out and condemn acts of violence. He doesn't need to draft a legislative bill just to voice his support for civil rights and equal justice."

"'I see millions of families trying to live on incomes so meager that the pall of family disaster hangs over them,'" I quoted from the very president Mr. Jackson was criticizing. "'I see one third of a nation ill-housed, ill-clad, ill-nourished. But it is not in despair that I paint you that picture. The test of our progress is not whether we add more to those who have much. It is whether we provide enough for those who have too little.' Were you not paying attention to the president's inaugural address yesterday, Mr. Jackson?"

The reporter was silent for a moment before he said, "Fancy words with no real action behind them."

"Exactly, Mr. Jackson. 'Well done is better than well said,'" I recited, quoting Benjamin Franklin. "Action is what is needed now. Not more words on a page. White people lobby. They believe in it. What the Negro needs to do is become more lobby minded—more willing to pay for what he both wants and needs."

"Haven't we paid enough with our lives and dignity?"

I sighed and shook my head, realizing the man would continue to remain combative with me if I let him. "Listen, Mr. Jackson. I'm simply a maid here at the White House. I have no political office, therefore no real power. I can't make or change the laws, so I don't quite understand what it is you expect me to do."

"We expect you to do more."

"I fully support the cause, Mr. Jackson, but I'm no civil rights activist."

"You wouldn't be saying that if it was your son who was lynched in Tennessee just last week. Or your husband who was laid off because a white man applied for his job. Maybe it's because you've been living behind those white high walls for so long, like some modern-day house Negro, that you forget what life is like for a Black woman on the streets of America."

I gripped the phone tightly but refrained from engaging with him further. "If you'll excuse me now, Mr. Jackson, I have to get to work."

"Don't forget who you are, Mrs. McDuffie," Mr. Jackson said just as I brought the telephone down.

Though I tried not to let them, the man's words truly punctured my spirit. Was that what some in our community thought of me? Of Mac? That we were just some "house Negroes" living safely away in the White House?

I was afraid to acknowledge that there might be some truth in his words.

Later that morning, I made my way to the Yellow Oval Room, the room the president had turned into his main study. An air of urgency hung heavy in the air as rushing staffers almost collided with each other along the corridors. I wasn't exactly sure if the urgency was a result of the post inaugural excitement or from the protesters outside the White House, challenging the president's second term. Despite his second landslide victory, he was still plagued with very vocal critics.

Mr. Jackson was just one of many.

By the time I arrived at the doors to the president's study, my palms were sweaty. I didn't know what I planned to say, but I couldn't shake what Mr. Jackson had told me. The urge to say and do something weighed heavy on my heart.

The entrance was flanked by two Secret Service men. I waited for one of them to hold the door open for me and I quickly stepped inside.

The president's office was a large space, decorated by old yet sturdy mahogany furniture. The room itself was spacious and well appointed, with tall windows that let in the natural light, giving the room an air of openness. Entering it always filled me with a moment of mixed awe and reverence. The president's office was a place of power, authority, and gravitas, and as a maid, I had the privilege of maintaining this space where the nation's most important decisions were made and where history was shaped.

How could I not feel the pride and pressure of my role every time I walked into the room?

Behind the grand desk sat Mr. Roosevelt, engrossed in a few documents scattered over its surface. The room seemed to exude an air of seriousness and purpose, and I couldn't help but feel the weight of the responsibilities that rested on his shoulders in that moment.

Stephen Early was also in the room, and I bit back a groan. I was hoping for an opportunity to speak to the chief in private, perhaps hint at some of the issues Mr. Jackson had brought up to me that morning, without the cantankerous press secretary hovering nearby.

Both men glanced over at me, but it was Mr. Early's expression that was most telling. The man was obviously annoyed by my presence.

"Good morning, Mr. President. Mr. Early."

"Good morning, Lizzie," Mr. Roosevelt said, a small smile removing the seriousness of his earlier expression. "Just the woman I wanted to see today."

I returned his smile as I inched closer to his desk. It was a nice feeling to know that the president had no qualms about letting others know how much he valued my services. I was especially pleased to have that knowledge made known in front of Mr. Early.

"Yes, Mr. President?"

"I wanted you to change these flowers," he said, gesturing toward the daisies on his desk. "I asked Mac to bring the same ones you had brought in last week, but he brought these instead. I much prefer the others. What were they called again?"

"African violets," I said, trying to mask the hollowness in my tone. Of all the reasons I could think of for the president to want to see me, flowers had not been on the list.

"Right!" the president exclaimed, as if the name had suddenly dawned on him. "Those smelled very refreshing and were a nice touch in here."

Stephen Early remained silent.

"Mac isn't familiar with these things," was all I could think to say.

"Of course not." After a brief pause, the president then asked, "Have you seen the protests, Lizzie?"

Mr. Roosevelt gestured toward the television set and I squinted at it. The volume had been turned down low but it was clear that there were loud chants coming from the crowd.

"I have, sir. I believe the roads have been blocked all morning."

"Mr. President," Mr. Early said, "I've made arrangements with the leaders of the group to see how issues can be ironed out."

There was something condescending in the way he said that, but it was clear the president didn't even notice.

"Better yet, have Missy arrange a meeting," President Roosevelt said as he turned toward the press secretary. "I'm certain we can get this resolved by giving them some time on my schedule."

"There's no need for that, Mr. President," Mr. Early said, as I watched the exchange between the two men. "There are more important issues lined up on your schedule. I assure you, I can speak to the leaders of this group and will fill you in with a comprehensive report."

My heart stung a little by Mr. Early's words that there were more important issues for the president to tackle. There were tens of thousands of protesters marching across Washington for a better life, desperate to be heard. Yet people like Stephen Early thought it was not important enough for the president to address these groups or civil rights issues, which was hurting the president's chances of gaining their support. Organizations like the NAACP were still largely divided about supporting Franklin Roosevelt, many still believing that he wasn't working in favor of colored people.

And it was up to the president to change that.

The fastest way to do that was to openly support the anti-lynching bill, but I knew as well as anyone else that he would never do that. Winning the favor and support of the southern Democrats was more important. And that knowledge was a bitter pill to swallow.

"All right, Stephen," President Roosevelt said. "Be certain to have Missy in these meetings taking notes."

Mr. Early nodded, then picked up some papers from the president's desk. He locked eyes with me as he strode across the room and out the door.

When the door was shut behind the surly man, I was surprised by the president's next words.

"I might not be able to walk, Lizzie, but I see quite well."

The corners of his eyes wrinkled behind his eyeglasses and I returned his smile. The voice in my head kept urging me to tell him what I felt about the protests and how I wanted him to address the movement himself. But something held me back. I didn't want to overstep and have my words cause any friction between myself and the press secretary.

As if reading my mind, he flashed a reassuring smile. "Don't worry. Stephen may be a lot of things, but he's a very efficient man. Reliable too. I'm sure he'll do as I've asked. And if it's anyone I can trust to be fair in her reporting, it's Missy."

I pursed my lips. "I'm glad to hear you have a lot of confidence in Mr. Early's abilities, sir, but that doesn't change the fact that he isn't as . . ." I struggled to find the right words. "Supportive of the Negro cause as you are. In fact, no other American president in recent times has had in mind the interest of the Negro as much as you, sir. But there are about 11 million Negroes in this country, and we all share one common problem—unreasonable hate."

"I understand, Lizzie. Really I do. For years, your people have been hewers of wood and drawers of water, but now they are going to get those rights which are theirs. In due time, it will come."

I shook my head and moved closer to his desk. Mr. Jackson's words still echoed in my head, forcing my initial hesitation about keeping my thoughts to myself right out the large high windows.

"With all due respect, Mr. President, we've been told to wait and be patient for change for decades now. Many are tired of waiting." *I was tired of waiting.* "These are fundamental issues that do not need the lifetime of a presidency to restore. We just need your voice. Your support on large issues like the anti-lynching bill could change the tide for my people. Perhaps then we would be looked at as an integral part of this nation, not just second-class citizens."

Mr. Roosevelt pulled his eyeglasses from his face and pinched the bridge of his nose. "You have to understand by now, Lizzie, that politics is a game. It's all about strategy and staying ahead of your opponent, letting them have the smaller wins so you can ultimately score the bigger victory. I'm not ignorant of the Negroes' plight, but that is a battle that is going to require a lot more patience *and* time to win. And it may be a victory that does not come during my presidency, but we have to believe that it will eventually come and soon."

"And what if it doesn't? What if you are our only chance? Slavery may have ended, but our pain and suffering have not. We are treated like the dregs of society while others get to enjoy the freedoms and liberties of this country. It's not fair."

"It's not," he agreed, leaning back in his seat. "But there are 122 million people in the United States, all of whom have their own unique and collective problems, and yet I make it a point to listen to the individual plight of the Negro through my maid and valet."

I frowned, not appreciating the insinuation of his words. Perhaps some of the president's critics were right. Perhaps Mr. Roosevelt was so blinded by his own liberality that he couldn't see where he could in fact be doing more.

"Have you ever stopped to wonder, sir, why my people need a back door into the White House just to get to you? We cannot be satisfied with where we are right now. Not when there is still a lot of work left to be done."

He sighed and sat back again in his seat. "I understand your position, Lizzie. I do. But there are a lot more of your people who are finally getting a fair shake for a change, and that's partly thanks to you and your efforts. Progress, no matter how slow it comes, is still progress. Front or back, the door has finally been opened for the Negro, and I will make it my mission to open many more."

The look in his eyes was sincere and determined. Despite the continuous criticism from people like Mr. Jackson and those who didn't get to have these kinds of candid talks with the president, I believed he wanted us to build a pathway to economic and financial freedom, to ensure our continuity of progress and success. I believed that he did want us to succeed and thrive. Not only as a people, but as a nation.

I believed him.

For my peace of mind, I *needed* to believe him.

It was always an eventful day at the White House.

The air inside was, as usual, burdened by the chaotic burst of urgency, which seemed to be the usual energy as of late. Staffers hurried through corridors and rooms, looking occupied and flustered. I met Mrs. Nesbitt in the kitchen area. She wore a bright smile when she saw me striding toward her. I had recently learned from Kathy why some of the servants called her Fluffy, and after having Mrs. Nesbitt's cooking, I could understand why.

"*For someone who cooks so badly,*" Kathy had said, "*she should be skin and bones. If you ask me, she's fluffier than she ought to be!*"

"Good morning, Lizzie," Mrs. Nesbitt called out, with a smile stretching both ends of her lips. Though she had a reputation for being a stern, business-minded housekeeper, she smiled more often at me than she did the rest of the maids. We had a good working relationship, and I didn't mind her as much as the other maids did.

"Good morning," I said as I approached her.

Not too far from her was the head maid, Mrs. Rogers, yelling instructions to another maid. They were fumbling with a large cloth-covered bundle.

Mrs. Rogers let out a low grunt. "Lift the—no, no, not that way. Turn it . . ."

"Shall I help them?" I asked Mrs. Nesbitt as I inched closer to join them in their task.

"No, they can take care of that." Mrs. Nesbitt flashed a smile again. "You're coming with me to see Mrs. Roosevelt."

I glanced over my shoulder to catch Mrs. Rogers's disapproving frown. I could only imagine what was going through the other woman's mind, but I didn't have time to ponder it as Mrs. Nesbitt whisked me away.

We found the First Lady sitting at her desk, reading a journal. She was often regarded as a bookworm, which gave us a lot in common. I enjoyed discussing popular literature with her. She chose her words the same way she took her steps—purposefully, with a lot of intent.

When we entered the room, Mrs. Roosevelt glanced up from what she was reading, then rose to her feet.

"Good morning, Henrietta. Lizzie."

"Good morning," Mrs. Nesbitt and I both chorused.

In the few years I'd been in Mrs. Roosevelt's employ, I'd come to realize that she was every inch a First Lady. Not only was she intelligent and outspoken in her public life, but in her home she was a gracious hostess as well as a kindly mother and grandmother. She was untiring in her efforts to make the White House more of a home and less of an institution. We all marveled that she found time to do so much.

As the head of her house, she told us that if there was ever anything that we could not settle through Mrs. Nesbitt, we were to feel free to come to her directly. She meant it too, and every now and then she would be called in to pour a little water on the embers. Even the problem of housekeeping at the White House could get turbulent at times.

"I trust you're getting the preparations done for our upcoming event," Mrs. Roosevelt said. "You have the list, correct?"

Mrs. Nesbitt nodded.

It was no secret that Mrs. Roosevelt was always eager to give young artists a break by putting them on programs at the White

House. On her trips, she would hand out invitations to any and all to "Come see me in Washington." With a heart as big as all outdoors, the First Lady extended the invitation genuinely, and they did come. They also wrote letters that kept her secretary, Miss Malvina Thompson—Tommy, as Mrs. Roosevelt called her—very busy.

Now we were to get ready to receive yet another large group and had only days to get everything in order.

"Excellent," Mrs. Roosevelt said. "I want you to make provisions for two hundred guests."

"Two hundred?"

"Yes," Mrs. Roosevelt confirmed. "Please work with Lizzie to get the things we might be missing from the list."

"Yes, ma'am," Mrs. Nesbitt said.

We left the First Lady to her affairs as I prepared myself mentally for the arduous task of planning for yet another large event.

"Who do you think will be at this event?" Mrs. Nesbitt asked as we strode out the doors of the White House and down the short flight of stairs and into the waiting car.

"I'm not sure," I said with a smile, "but I'll definitely be sure to have my autograph book handy."

We both laughed.

"Well, let's hope there are not too many foreigners."

Though her words came off a bit callous, I understood where the other woman was coming from. It required extra work to tend to the needs of foreign guests. One needed to be mindful of the culture and customs or risk the danger of offending said guest. And though tipping at the White House was generally a problem for some, the overseas guests especially struggled with this concept. Frequently, I was asked quite innocently, *"Am I supposed to tip you in this country?"*

"No hardworking American would ever turn down a token of appreciation for their services," was my usual answer.

Most of us, from the ushers on down, weren't averse to receiving a tip, although we didn't stand around and wait for one. Usually, some money would be left for the maid, although sometimes there was none.

"At any rate," Mrs. Nesbitt continued, "I hear it's going to be a big affair. I should probably tell Miss Ida to prepare for extra guests since the president always adds extra guests."

Inside the presidential service car, I inched closer to the window so I could feel the rush of cold wind whip across my cheek as the vehicle sped through the busy Washington streets.

"Autumn is my favorite season," Mrs. Nesbitt said as she huddled deep into her coat.

"I myself enjoy the sights and smells of winter," I said, keeping my eyes on the rows of shops and scattered lines of commuters going about their daily business.

These outings during my shift were rare, but I enjoyed them. Though I didn't need for much at the White House, moments such as these made me realize how isolating it could be living at 1600 Pennsylvania Avenue.

"But if I had to choose, I would say summer is my preferred season."

Mrs. Nesbitt smiled and nodded. "I can see that. You're so lively and full of zest. Summer definitely suits you."

I smiled in return.

"My least favorite is winter, of course," she continued. "I only look forward to it because of Christmas, though I'm happy to be spending my winters here in Washington. Winter in New York is bitter and long."

"The sky of brightest gray seems dark to one whose sky was ever white," I recited. "To one who never knew a spark, through all his life, of love or light, the grayest cloud seems over-bright."

Mrs. Nesbitt was silent for a moment, as if she was processing the meaning of the words. "That was lovely, Lizzie. Who's it from?"

"Paul Laurence Dunbar. One of my favorite poets. That one is a favorite of mine that speaks about perspective. You being a woman of the North, and me from the South, our view of the sky—or, rather, the weather—will certainly differ."

I left out the part about how our perceptions especially differed because she was a *white* woman from the North. I didn't want to sully our lovely drive with talk of race.

Suddenly the car jerked to a stop, startling and jolting us in our seats.

"Joseph!" Mrs. Nesbitt exclaimed to the driver. "What was that about?"

"Traffic jam, ma'am," Joseph said. "Roads appear to be blocked."

I peered out of my window, only to find a long line of cars, stretching in both lanes.

"Oh, goodness . . ." I breathed. The roads were hardly ever congested. Not around this time of day. This was strange.

"What is all this about?" Mrs. Nesbitt murmured.

Joseph whistled over to another Negro driver and shouted out the window, "Hey, brother. What's the holdup?"

"There's a big protest up ahead," the other driver shouted back. "I heard they're marching up to the White House. It's about to be a long day."

"Oh, lord. We don't have time for this today." Mrs. Nesbitt fumbled through her purse and pulled out her watch. She fidgeted with it before returning it back to her bag.

I caught Joseph's eye from the rearview mirror but said nothing. I didn't know what the protest was about, but I was all ready to defend those who were out there simply wanting to get their grievances heard.

This just further highlighted how the other woman's perspective of things differed ever so greatly from mine.

By the time we had gotten closer to the heart of the protest, we could see that the crowd marching by the side of the road was massive enough to intimidate anyone.

Loud and passionate Negro people of all ages, shades, and genders chanted and held placards raised high up above their heads.

WE DEMAND DECENT HOUSING

WE MARCH FOR EQUAL RIGHTS

WE MARCH FOR INTEGRATED SCHOOLS

They all marched along the street, some old, others young, some carrying children on their shoulders, all protesting and expressing the same message.

SLAVERY IS STILL ALIVE

STOP LYNCHING US!

There were men in three-piece suits and women in floral printed dresses, their foreheads furrowed in deep frowns. Peppered among the crowd were a few white supporters—both men and women. They were all coordinated as they demanded more from their government, from their country.

Everything about their words resonated with me and reverberated through my mind and soul. I read the picket signs, and I
knew that not even the walls of the White House could shield me
from this country's racial discrimination. I couldn't stop the car
to join the march, but I could join their protest from inside the
White House.

The crowd swarmed past our car as other cars honked their
way through the congestion. Our driver, however, crawled
through the crowd like a snail. It was unlikely that we would
be recognized as White House employees, but I was still glad
the driver took measures to avoid drawing attention to us.
That didn't prevent some of the protesters from jumping on
the car's hood and hitting it.

Mrs. Nesbitt jumped in her seat when an unexpected bang vibrated through the car.

"It's fine, ma'am," Joseph assured her. "We'll be out of this
crowd soon."

"Sorry," Mrs. Nesbitt said as she forced out a smile. "I just have
a thing against . . . crowds. They make me nervous."

I peered out the window, Mrs. Nesbitt's words sending a wave
of anger and sadness rushing through me. I knew what she really
meant with those words: that too many Negroes gathered around,
shouting, is what truly frightened her.

I tried to excuse her reaction, but this time I found it hard to
do. Whether she understood or agreed with their method, how
could she—or anyone, for that matter—not be in support of our
desire for basic human rights?

I hoped that was the message the president received when the
protesters reached the White House.

A man kicked the door of our car with his legs and screamed,
"Come! Join us!"

Soon others joined the man, gesturing to Joseph and me to come out of the vehicle and join them. I wound up the window, and luckily Joseph maneuvered his way out of there before it got ugly.

It took about twenty minutes before the roads started to clear up. Grumbling drivers rushed back into their cars, trying to make the most of the space before the traffic stopped again.

Our trip was a failure.

Shops were closed, and I imagined the majority of them shut their doors, not wanting to risk damage, theft, or violence from the crowd.

Mrs. Nesbitt sat there in silence, staring out the window. I knew she was still shaken by the mass of people. Despite my annoyance over her overreaction, I reached out and patted her hand. She shot me a glance and smiled for a millisecond before turning back to look out the window.

I couldn't shake off the scene of the protesters either.

Today's protest weighed down on my mind as we drove back to the White House. It especially bothered me to think what the protesters thought of me and Joseph as we simply drove away.

By the time we got to the White House and to the First Lady's office, Mrs. Nesbitt still looked shaken by the day's events. Her eyes told the story before any of us could tell it.

"Henrietta?" the First Lady asked as she rose from her seat and moved from behind her desk. "What's the matter? You look like you've seen a ghost."

"We couldn't complete the trip to the market," I began.

"There was a mob outside, ma'am," Mrs. Nesbitt cut in at the same time. "They tried to attack us."

Mrs. Roosevelt's eyes rounded in shock. "What?"

"Yes," Mrs. Nesbitt confirmed. "It was awful. The crowd was massive. They've shut all the shops along several avenues and blocked the roads."

Mrs. Roosevelt turned her gaze over to me and I shifted from foot to foot. I suspected she wanted me to either confirm or correct what Mrs. Nesbitt had just said, but I didn't know what to say.

So I simply gave my perspective of the matter.

"It looks like it was a civil rights protest, ma'am," I said. "The crowd was large, but relatively peaceful."

The First Lady went to the window, as if to see if she could find any evidence of the protest from where we were. "Are they heading here?"

I nodded. "I believe so."

"I haven't heard of any protests happening today," the First Lady said. "But I'm sure the Secret Service has everything under control if they do happen to bring the protest here." Mrs. Roosevelt turned to Mrs. Nesbitt, who appeared a bit calmer now. "Henrietta, let's go find Ida and Maggie and figure out what we can improvise or remove from the list. Lizzie, you may return to your duties."

"Yes, ma'am," I replied, as I followed them out of her office.

I shook my head as I watched Mrs. Nesbitt hurry behind the First Lady, trying to match her strides. As I returned to my task, my mind drifted back to Mrs. Nesbitt and Paul Laurence Dunbar's words . . .

The sky of brightest gray seems dark . . . to one who never knew a spark . . .

Chapter 11

It was late in February, a month after the president's inauguration, when I read the news in the Allied Negro Papers about the Ethiopian prince Ras Desta Damtew.

I remembered his visit back in '33 and how impressed I had been by the man. It was my first time meeting a nobleman—a colored one at that!—and though he had appeared larger than life, his passionate spirit to defend the rights of his people had endeared me to him.

It now saddened me to read how such a fearless warrior, the last of the "fighting Rases," had been shot by the Italian army.

All I could think after reading the news was that war was an ugly thing.

As I lay in bed watching the sun peek through the thin opening of my curtains, I forced my bleak thoughts to last night's more pleasant moment. It was one of those rare occasions when I had come to our chamber much later than usual, only to find Mac sound asleep. I wasn't surprised. He had looked tired all throughout the day. It seemed as time went on that working for Mr. Roosevelt wasn't quite the break from barbering Mac had hoped it would be.

But it wasn't long before I was dressed in my nightclothes and slipping between the warm sheets to lie beside my husband. I cuddled up close to his side and placed my hand on his chest. Each rise and fall from his breathing was a soothing reminder that no matter our disagreements, we would always have each other.

And I fell asleep with that comforting thought.

When I woke, however, Mac was nowhere in our bedroom.

I sighed and pushed back the covers, determined to start my morning on a high note. It was my day off, but I had no idea how I would spend it.

As I busied myself tidying up our living quarters, I stumbled upon an old NAACP flyer. I couldn't recall where we had picked it up—or if it was something sent to us in the mail—but I was intrigued. Not only were they advertising their upcoming meetings and speaker events, but there was one happening today. And Walter White would be the keynote speaker.

To think that of all days for them to have a meeting, it would fall on a day that I was not on duty and could potentially attend. It was practically serendipitous. I couldn't dare pass up this chance.

After locating the address, I quickly got dressed, picked up my handbag, and made my way out of the White House gates. The bitter wind whipped across my face as I stepped out into the streets.

I managed to hail a cab, and as I climbed in, I was greeted by the smell of tobacco and strong coffee. The driver drove toward my requested destination, and I couldn't help but notice how the scenery began to change. We moved farther away from the large marble buildings and towering monuments toward neighborhoods that buzzed with life and energy. Negro men draped in sharp suits and trendy hats strode across the sidewalks looking every bit as indispensable as time. The women were dressed just as conservatively, but their strides were light and unhurried.

Every one of them embodied an air of class, dignity, and strength. And they reminded me of being back home in Atlanta.

As the cab pulled up to the five-story brick building, I was taken aback by the white words printed on the black flag, waving lazily in the wind right above the entrance.

A MAN WAS LYNCHED YESTERDAY

Those bold words on the flag were enough to evoke a mixture of anger and disgust from me. Those emotions quickly turned my excitement into anxiety.

But I didn't second-guess my decision for another minute. I climbed out of the cab and headed straight toward the front doors of the building.

"Mrs. Lizzie McDuffie?"

My attention shifted to the young man standing on the sidewalk, a cigarette hanging from the corner of his lips. He was clad in a black suit and a gray hat. He was just about a head taller than I was, with a heavy mustache canopying his upper lip.

"Yes?" I asked cautiously. I wasn't in the habit of speaking to strange men on the street, but he looked harmless enough.

He put out the cigarette and pulled off his hat.

"The name's Woody," he said, a small smile gracing his slender face. He held out his hand. "I'm one of the newer staff members here at the NAACP."

I shook his hand, a bit flattered to be recognized by a complete stranger. "Very nice to meet you, Woody."

"The pleasure's all mine, Mrs. McDuffie. Mr. White didn't say we would be expecting you today."

At the mention of Mr. White's name, I flashed him a quick smile, until his words finally sunk in. For a moment, I wondered if I should have called ahead to reserve a seat. Did I need to be a member to attend today's event? I instantly regretted my impulsive decision to come and felt like an interloper.

"I hadn't told anyone I was coming," I said faintly.

"That's all right. We're honored to have you here today. Did you come alone?" He looked over my head as if to see whoever had accompanied me suddenly materialize behind me.

"Yes," I said. "I came alone."

"Is Mr. McDuffie not coming?"

"No, my husband works directly with the president. He rarely gets time off. Neither do I, for that matter. But I heard the cookies were worth it," I teased.

Woody threw his head back, his eyes creased up with laughter. "Next time I'll be sure to bring some. Just for you." He repositioned his hat on his head and offered me his bent arm to grab hold of. "Shall I escort you to your seat then? I believe Mr. White is about to speak."

"Yes, thank you."

He ushered me inside, his stride and entire demeanor confident and unapologetic. The large room was packed with people, and it smelled of a hundred different perfumes and colognes. Women and men, Black and white, young and old, filled the auditorium, taking up every available space, and everyone sat wherever seating was available—not by color or social status. A few people smiled at me as I passed them, and I wondered if it was out of recognition or civility.

Occasionally, Woody would lean over to whisper the names of people who offered us a nod or smile, his breath heavy with the scent of tobacco. Many I didn't recognize, but I still offered a smile in return.

As I walked beside him, I couldn't help but swell with pride at the number of people who had gathered together for a common goal: equality.

Woody found available seats for us in front, and I was grateful for that small advantage of being closer to the stage.

"That's Mary Ovington," Woody whispered to me, nodding toward an older white woman a few seats away from us. "That man over there is Oswald Villard." He pointed to an older man walking down the aisle. "Both are foundational members of the NAACP."

"Foundational members?" I raised my brow as I turned to him for clarity. Before now, it never occurred to me that white people were not only regular members of the NAACP but also founding members.

"Yes," Woody confirmed. "Not all white people are animals like those running around stomping on every Black person they see." He gave a wry laugh just before he pointed to another white man walking toward a reserved seat in front of the stage. "That there is Joel Spingarn."

"Of the Spingarn Medal award?"

Woody nodded. "He's also the organization's current president. He has used his influence to help grow the organization. He's dedicated much of his life thus far in support of the NAACP and our movement."

"Incredible," I murmured.

The hall erupted into applause as Walter White walked across the stage to the podium on which the microphone sat. He was clad in a drape suit and no hat, just his neatly combed hair and glasses. He tapped the microphone twice to make sure it was sound.

The crowd once again fell silent.

"Why was everyone cheering?" I asked, leaning over to Woody, whose eyes remained fixated on the fair-skinned man standing on the stage.

"Mr. White's been away traveling through the South, investigating the rising number of lynchings there. He just returned yesterday, and I know he has quite a few stories to share with us."

I returned my attention to the petite, light-skinned man as he leaned over the lectern to speak.

"Good afternoon, everyone. And welcome."

The crowd applauded him again and he beamed with a charming smile before raising his hands to calm the excitement sweeping through the audience.

"Yesterday," he began solemnly, "a man was lynched in Texas."

Complete silence fell across the crowd as Mr. White waited for his words to sink in.

"Two more were lynched the day before that in Georgia," he continued. "And, sadly, more will be lynched by week's end."

Murmurs of anger and disapproval flittered through the crowd. I sat rigid in my seat, my hands clasped tightly on my lap and my attention focused intently on Mr. White.

"Before I left for Texas," he said, "I prayed in my heart that the reports about lynching in the South weren't as bad as they were recorded. But I have to tell you something . . ." He paused and looked around the crowd as if searching for the right words. "Unfortunately, it is worse."

I followed his gaze around the room and I saw the anger and frustration on many faces. I was sure their reactions mirrored mine.

"Lynchings have since tripled in the South recently," Mr. White continued. "Last month, five men were reported lynched in South Carolina. This month, ten men were found hanged throughout Mississippi, Alabama, and Florida. And it isn't any better here in Washington either."

He shook his head in disgust. "There's nothing I can tell you now that you haven't heard before. There's nothing I can say to you that we haven't said before. Lynching isn't new. Segregation isn't new. Our struggle isn't new!"

The crowd erupted in applause and shouts of agreement.

"I have said this before, and I'll keep saying it: There's no justification for murder based on someone's color or creed. We're all created equal, and in a country where the law is the supreme entity, it should be a crime against humanity to lynch a man just for existing."

"That's right!" someone from the crowd shouted in response.

Leaning into the podium, Mr. White almost resembled a preacher as he spoke into the microphone.

"There's always going to be a new lynching case somewhere here on American soil. Down South, I've heard and witnessed some of the most heinous crimes. I have seen men strung up on trees. The ones they do not kill publicly, they slaughter in the shadows. There have been reports of men going missing in several cities. Black men, women, and even children! The police aren't doing anything about this. Our politicians aren't doing anything to stop this. I say enough is enough!"

"*Yes!*"

The crowd chorused with another round of applause and cheers, including from Woody.

I joined in on the applause, captivated by the man's passionate words. I couldn't help but feel moved by the crowd's energy and Mr. White's speech.

"We can no longer remain silent," he continued. "We must let our voices be heard. We must speak up and protect each other. Silence means acceptance. Silence means we are complicit. Silence means we have accepted our role as inferior—and *that* we are not!"

"No, we are not!" I couldn't help but shout back.

I felt moved and enlivened by his speech. The last time I was in a gathering with such passion and energy was at my church back home in Atlanta.

Mr. White glanced in my direction and a quick smile graced his lips. "There is an anti-lynching march that's being organized for next month and I encourage you all to attend. We need to show them that we've had enough of this. We cannot keep losing our brothers and sisters so brutally. We need to show them that we will not keep silence against injustice. No more!"

"No more!"

The crowd shouted back as if echoing a deep-rooted rallying cry. Gooseflesh crawled up my arms from the passionate energy that seemed to fill the room. With a brisk nod of satisfaction and quick wave of his hand, Mr. White walked off the stage. The room thundered with the sound of everyone's applause. It bounced through the walls and reverberated beneath my feet.

"What a charismatic man," I said to Woody just before someone else jumped on stage to make a few more announcements.

"That he is."

When the last speaker finally made his way from the stage, Woody leaned over to me and said, "Let me introduce you to Mr. White and some of our other members."

"Oh, it's okay," I rushed out, suddenly feeling shy and uncertain. "I'm sure they have other things to attend to . . ."

Woody scoffed. "Don't be silly. You're quite popular among the members. They would be honored to meet with you."

Though I had spoken with Mr. White over the phone and shared plenty of correspondence, we had never been officially introduced to one another. Just as Woody led me through the aisle, a couple materialized before us, huge smiles lighting up their dark brown faces.

"Mrs. McDuffie," the man said, extending his hand in greeting. "I'm Kendrick Thomason." He gestured to the short yet robust woman beside him. "This is my wife, Josephine."

"Very nice to meet you both," I said to the couple, wondering where I had heard those names before.

"My wife wrote you a few months back about this special walking stick I'm designing for the president."

"My husband is a fine wood carver," Mrs. Thomason chimed in. "He used to own his own furniture shop, you know, before the crash."

It was then that I remembered the couple who had been insistent on gifting the president a cane to use during his second inauguration. They believed that not only would the president appreciate the hand-carved walking stick, but it would also bring awareness to Mr. Thomason's product.

"I'd still love to gift the president one of my creations," Mr. Thomason beamed. "But I need to know how tall he is and would he be walking with it most of the time or just some of the time. I see he's been doing a lot of traveling, so it would be nice if he could carry my cane with him at all times."

"Umm, I—"

"Right now is not the time or place for such conversation, Mr. Thomason," Woody interjected.

It must have been the flustered look on my face, but whatever it was I was grateful for his interference. I had no idea how to answer their questions because, truth be told, I didn't know if Mr. Roosevelt used any of the walking sticks that were gifted to him— and he had a new one sent to him practically once a week.

"I'm sure Mrs. McDuffie will address your queries when she gets some time. Now if you'll excuse us."

"Good day," I managed to say before Woody whisked me away.

As we made our way to Mr. White, who stood surrounded by a small cluster of people, a handful of other NAACP members tried to stop me. Luckily, Woody managed to maneuver around them as well. As we approached, the NAACP secretary inched away from the small crowd and started toward us.

"Mr. White," Woody began. "I wanted to introduce you to Mrs.—"

"I know who Mrs. McDuffie is, Thurgood," Mr. White said, as he took my hand in both of his.

I turned to the man who had introduced himself as Woody and raised a curious brow. I wasn't in the habit of keeping company with strangers, particularly those who weren't who they said they were . . .

"Thurgood?"

Mr. White chuckled. "You really need to stop going by that schoolyard nickname."

The other man shrugged. "I prefer to go by Woody."

Mr. White shook his head. "Thurgood Marshall here is head of our new legal defense team. He's going to do great things for the organization and our community. I just know it. He just needs to get used to putting himself—particularly his real name—out there."

Woody shrugged again.

Not sure how to respond to Mr. White's reproach of the younger man, I simply stretched my lips into a polite smile.

"Well, it's been a pleasure being here with you all. That was a great speech you gave up there earlier, Mr. White. The last time I saw someone so charismatic it was my pastor back in Atlanta."

We all shared a good laugh at that.

"Well, thank you. We're glad to see someone from the Big House out here with us today. I'm especially excited to have you as part of our cause."

"I'm happy to help in any way I can."

His eyes lit up. "Well, I'd love to get a meeting with the president if you could arrange that."

I groaned inwardly. *I can help in any way but not with that.*

"It seems getting even just a message to him is impossible," Mr. White continued. "Never mind having a conversation."

You can thank Stephen Early for that, I thought dryly.

"It's no secret that white supremacists run this country," Woody said. "Yet for whatever reason, the president won't come out and publicly condemn them."

Mr. White shrugged. "That's because he would rather strike us with one hand while he feeds us crumbs with the other."

My lips pursed at the men's unfair assessment of Mr. Roosevelt. Had I not worked so closely with the president, I would have shared the same sentiments. But I knew better than anyone the fine, fragile line he followed when it came to this game of politics.

"Have you tried getting in touch with his secretary, Miss Le-Hand?" I suggested. "Perhaps you would have better luck—"

Mr. White shook his head. "The only women in that White House I will have any luck with are you or Mrs. Roosevelt."

He was right about one thing . . .

The First Lady would be his best bet in getting to the president. It was what she was good at. Whatever the president didn't address publicly, she would unabashedly speak up for or against. Mrs. Roosevelt was hardly coy about her support and loyalty to the NAACP and had publicly shown her support for the organization numerous times.

Mr. White suddenly pulled out a couple of papers from his briefcase and handed them to me.

"What are these?" I asked, taking the letters.

"In addition to the physical brutality our people are dealing with, we are facing challenges in the workplace. What you're holding are complaints by colored workers here in Washington. Not Texas. Not Mississippi. Not Baltimore. Right here in Washington."

I skimmed through some of the letters, surprised at the issues being brought forward, particularly in a city that I had believed to be more progressive than most.

"We have overly qualified workers in many of these places," Mr. White said. "And they are making a third of what they are rightfully owed. They are forced to work under terrible conditions at these low-paying jobs because they have no other options outside of them."

"And these are the jobs they are offered under the president's work programs," Woody muttered.

I glanced up from the papers I was reading, my heart heavy as I processed what they were telling me and what I had just read. It was all so overwhelming, and I didn't know where to begin to address some of this. I certainly didn't know how I would broach this matter with the president.

What I did know was that a face-to-face meeting with the president and the NAACP secretary was very much warranted.

"I really do want to help, Mr. White. But I think this part is a bit above me. I can try to have Miss LeHand set up a meeting with you and the president. Perhaps even coordinate a lunch meeting to help ease the conversation."

"Whatever you can do to help would be appreciated. And if you would do me this last favor . . ." Mr. White gathered a few more documents from his briefcase and handed them to me.

"Could you please get these to the First Lady? Among these letters is one I wrote personally to Mrs. Roosevelt. Please be sure to deliver these to her."

"Yes, of course," I said vaguely, a bit overwhelmed by his overconfidence in my position at the White House.

How in the world was I to get the extremely occupied First Lady involved in this cause? How were we to get the president?

With so much at stake, how could I not try?

Chapter 12

It was early June when Amelia Earhart visited the White House for the last time.

It was just before she left for her flight across the Pacific Ocean. She had visited the White House many times over the years while the Roosevelts held office, becoming fast friends with the First Lady. I remembered her earlier visit back in '33 and how excited I had been to meet a female pilot—and how she and the First Lady had snuck out for a spontaneous flight to Baltimore! Even now, I was in awe of her graciousness and bravado.

And if it hadn't been for her last visit, I perhaps wouldn't have been able to steal a small moment of the First Lady's time.

It was during that time that I used the opportunity to follow up with her regarding Mr. White's request for a meeting with the president. Mrs. Roosevelt's schedule had been packed for months now, yet Mr. White's words kept resounding in my head. I knew she had gotten his letter and the many others he had given me. I had hand delivered them to her myself, but I had no idea if the First Lady had gotten a chance to read any of them, much less his.

Now that Mrs. Roosevelt was back in the White House, I made it a point to get on her schedule at the earliest opportunity. But before that scheduled meeting was to arrive, Mrs. Roosevelt summoned me into her office.

As I entered her office, I was greeted by the strong scent of coffee and a sweet floral fragrance in the air. The First Lady sat on a small two-seater sofa, her long legs crossed as she sifted through a few papers. I immediately recognized the documents Mr. White had handed me.

Mrs. Roosevelt glanced up at me as I made my way to where she sat. A wide smile graced her lips and she gestured for me to have a seat across from her.

"Lizzie, my dear, how are you?"

"Very well, ma'am, thank you. And yourself?"

I fell into the single armchair and clasped my hands tightly together. Normally, I wasn't so nervous around the First Lady, as she was very open and approachable. But it had been a while since I'd been in her presence, and I didn't quite know which topic I should broach to her first—the recent letter I had received from the young mother of seven I had met during my campaigning in Michigan or Mr. White's request.

"I'm still alive so I guess I don't have much to complain about," Mrs. Roosevelt said with a shrug. She laid the papers down and looked at me squarely. "I called you here today because I read through the papers you left for me. It was quite a read, I'll tell you."

I winced and decided to wait before mentioning Louise's letter.

"I can imagine—and I apologize for burdening you with all of this, but Mr. White is eager to arrange another meeting with the president and we felt that your being more sympathetic to our cause could help set that up."

"Of course I am, Lizzie. But after their first meeting, FD accused me of priming the man, which I did, but still . . ." She shrugged. "It was very presumptuous of him. Now he and his administration believe I'm a bit *too* sympathetic toward causes that could jeopardize his gaining support on other issues. I'm afraid the president won't be as inclined toward meeting with Mr. White this time around no matter what I say."

Mrs. Roosevelt's words reeked of frustration, and my shoulders slumped. I knew what she was saying was true. The First Lady had grown popular among the Negro community across the nation because she didn't shy away from her support for equality and basic human rights. She was at the forefront of every fight for women, Negroes, and many other minority groups. In fact, I believed she was still an active member of the NAACP.

Now we were on the brink of losing even her support.

"Lizzie," she said, reaching out to take my hand in hers. The warmth of her grip was a reflection of who she was at her core—sincere and tenderhearted. "Please don't despair. You and your people will always have my support."

Her kind smile managed to force a smile from me in return, and I placed my hand over hers.

"Thank you, Mrs. Roosevelt. Right now we could certainly use your support with this anti-lynching bill."

She pursed her lips and nodded resolutely. "I know. It's perhaps the most important, yet most controversial, dossier on the president's desk right now. And unfortunately it is the one act of legislature that FD refuses to take a stand on." She sighed. "Then again, he wouldn't be president today had he done so earlier."

"Then how can we get more support around it? We just need to convince enough members of Congress to vote the bill into law. Can they not understand that just signing this bill could potentially save thousands of lives?"

"Oh, Lizzie, you don't have to convince me. I'm quite aware of how important this bill is to people of color. But unfortunately, these things are about timing, and right now the anti-lynching bill is simply falling on deaf ears."

My shoulders slumped again. Although she was right, I resented the thought of pushing this matter aside. For me, there would never be a better time than now to bring about change—especially with an issue as important as this one.

"I know that's not what you want to hear, but we have to begin thinking about other important matters. The ones we can bring change to now."

Again, she was right. There were other issues that desperately needed attention, and I couldn't lose focus on that.

"What matters are you thinking of, ma'am?"

She stared pointedly at the papers I had handed her a few months back. "After going through these documents, I've come to realize that we've let a more practical opportunity go undeveloped."

"And that is . . . ?"

"A labor union for colored workers." The First Lady beamed at me as if the answer had been obvious.

Now I was intrigued.

"For the longest, the Negro worker has been cheated and excluded from fair working conditions and livable wages," Mrs. Roosevelt continued. "We can change that by setting up a union for these workers, both men and women, who have been exploited for so long. It would be an opportunity for all disadvantaged, low-wage earners to finally have their voices heard."

"This sounds like a wonderful idea, ma'am. Tell me how I can be of help."

"I want you to take the lead in setting this up," she said. "It'll be up to you to find the best people to help get this going. There are a ton of resources available to you here, so reach out to them. If it helps, feel free to use my name to grab their attention. And their cooperation. I suggest perhaps recruiting members from our own staff to get started. In no time, I believe this could be a very powerful, very effective organization."

For a moment I stared at the First Lady, stunned that she would entrust me to organize something this significant. This was bigger than anything I had done as the president's SASOCPA, and an avalanche of pride and responsibility surged through me.

"I am honored by your confidence and trust in me, ma'am. I would be happy to take the lead on this."

"Excellent! Though my schedule may not always allow, I want to be involved in this as much as possible, Lizzie. Give me direct reports on everything."

As the First Lady rose to her feet, signaling the end of our meeting, my mind raced, wondering how I would get started in organizing something this big.

"In the meantime, I'll work on getting that second meeting with Mr. White on the books."

"Thank you, ma'am," I said, also rising from my seat. I shouldn't have been surprised by her commitment to my earlier request, yet I was. And, of course, I was profoundly grateful she would even put in the effort. "I'm sure Mr. White would be immensely appreciative."

The corners of her eyes creased as the First Lady gave me a wide, cheeky smile. "I said it would be hard, Lizzie. I never said I wouldn't try."

THE FOLLOWING MONTH, on July 2, 1937, it was reported that beloved aviator Amelia Earhart had vanished over the Pacific Ocean. The news shook the nation—and those of us at the White

House—as there was no evidence of plane wreckage and absolutely no sign of her or her navigator. President Roosevelt authorized an immediate search for the pair that week, and the country waited on pins and needles for the outcome.

That very same week, I received more stunning news. A letter from a representative of Mr. David O. Selznick's office came addressed to me at the White House. In the letter, I learned that Mr. Selznick, the film studio executive who was producing the upcoming movie *Gone with the Wind,* wanted me to audition for the role of Mammy.

The invitation left me staggered.

Yet thrilled.

I spent the rest of the day debating the decision to go or not. I already had so much on my plate that I couldn't even keep track of it all anymore. Between my responsibilities at the White House—which was enough work for two!—I was also in the middle of gathering key personnel for the creation of the United Government Employees union, a name the First Lady and I arbitrarily came up with just to give our project some officiality.

Despite all of these inescapable duties, I couldn't help but give the invitation to audition for the role some serious consideration. And I had very little time to ponder the decision. Auditions were now open, and the talent scout wanted me to be in New York City immediately to screen-test for the role.

Imagine me in New York City!

It would be a massive departure from my duties here, but all I could think was that I would be passing up the opportunity of a lifetime. When else would I be given the chance to showcase my theatrical talents—as minimal as they were?

And who knew, perhaps this would be my big break onto the silver screen.

I giggled. The more I thought about it, the more giddy I became over the idea.

I could be a movie star!

I had read, studied, and digested the book in its entirety. I knew the character Mammy well because I saw so much of myself in her. I knew I could embody her spirit and bring her to life on the screen. And the fact that I had been sought after to read for the role was all the encouragement I needed.

By the end of the day, I had made my decision.

"I'm leaving for New York City next week."

I made the announcement to Mac later that night as we lay in bed together.

"What's happening over there?" he murmured sleepily.

"An audition."

"What audition?" Mac propped himself up and stared down at me curiously.

"For a movie role," I said demurely, not wanting to say too much. And not wanting to jinx my chances.

He remained silent for a brief moment before he asked, "Are you not going to tell me what movie?"

I sighed as I too propped myself up and adjusted my pillow. "It's for a new movie. You know that book I've been reading—"

"*Gone with the Wind*?"

I smiled, pleased he remembered. "Yes, that book. They're making a movie of it and I got invited to New York to read for the part of Mammy."

"Who?"

I waved my hand dismissively. "She's a character in the book. A very important character," I added.

"Well, ain't that something," Mac murmured in amazement. "My wife's gonna be a movie star."

I laughed. "Don't say that," I admonished playfully, though I couldn't help but like the sound of that. "I haven't even read for the part yet."

Mac pulled me to him and planted a kiss on my temple. "You're going to do great, honey. I know it."

Surprisingly, his encouragement and support were just the thing I needed to ease some of my nervousness. "Aren't you going to wish me good luck?"

He pulled me into his arms and I snuggled in close. "Good luck, honey," he whispered into my ear. "Or like they say in show business . . . Break a leg."

Unfortunately, I needed more than just luck.

Upon my arrival in the great big city, my nerves about this new venture were strung so tight, I was afraid I wouldn't get out my first line before I retched all over the stage. I was glad now that I hadn't told anyone other than Mac and the First Lady about the audition in case that very thing happened.

The thought of the First Lady only added to my anxiety. She had made it possible for me to take a short leave of absence without word getting out to Mrs. Nesbitt or anyone else about the real reason for my trip. She had also gone out of her way to send a letter of recommendation to Mr. Selznick in hopes it would help with my chances. I couldn't let her—or Mac—down because of a few nerves.

Needing some encouragement, I decided to phone Mac. In the small room of my New York hotel, I placed a call to the White House. Mac had once said that Miss Hackmeister from the White House switchboard—whom we all called Miss Hack—never forgot a voice. Only Mac knew that I was to arrive in New York today, so I decided to test her out.

When I finally got through to the White House, I deepened my voice to the level of Mrs. Nesbitt and spoke slowly into the receiver.

"Hel-lo."

"Why, hello, Lizzie McDuffie," Miss Hack responded. "What are you doing in New York?"

I was so completely taken off guard by the woman's easy recognition of my voice that I couldn't respond right away. I couldn't recall what I said to her, but there wasn't any point in disguising my voice any further. Apparently, I wasn't a very good voice actress.

"Hello, Miss Hack," I said in my normal voice. "I'm just here visiting."

I hoped the woman wouldn't pry any further, as I didn't want to have to lie. But I didn't want to expose my secret either. I was sure it would come out soon enough. For now, however, I'd rather keep this departure to myself.

"Could you please pass me through to Mac?"

Unfortunately, he never came on the line, but I wasn't surprised. It was midday, and I was certain the president was keeping him very busy.

I tried not to let my disappointment overwhelm me and forced my entire concentration back to the reason I was in New York. It had been a long time since I had spoken on any stage, much less performed on one, and I was determined to have memorized every line I was to rehearse.

On the day of the audition, I had a bit more confidence and was prepared to give the reading my whole heart.

"Mrs. McDuffie, are you ready?"

I nodded to Miss Katherine Brown, the talent scout who had arranged for me to be there. I was handed a hair bonnet, and after carefully wrapping it around my head, I was then given a script and practically shoved onto the stage. The three casting directors sat behind the camera, shrouded in shadow from the glaring overhead lights that beamed brightly from above.

To my chagrin, Mr. Selznick was not in attendance.

"Okay, let's take it from the top."

I cleared my throat and started my lines, not needing the script to recall the most emotional and heartbreaking scene in the story.

"Miss Melly, this here's done broke her heart," I began in a low, anguished pitch. "But I didn't fetch you on Miss Scarlett's account. What that child got to stand, the good Lord give her strength to stand. It's Mr. Rhett I's worried about. He done lost his mind these last couple of days."

I put in all the pain and despair that I could imagine was in the character's voice at that time.

"Oh, no, Mammy, no," one of the casting directors read back to me in a flat tone.

I continued with the same anguish in my voice. "I ain't never seen no man, Black or white, set such store on any child. When Dr. Meade say her neck broke, Mr. Rhett grabbed his gun and run out and shoot that poor pony. And for a minute, I think he gonna shoot hisself!"

We continued on like this until the end of the scene, and by the last line I had genuine tears in my eyes. My love for literature and recitations was nothing compared to transforming into another character in front of the camera. I managed to embody Mammy in that moment, and I had never felt more alive—or more in tune with a character's emotion.

I received neither praise nor criticism from the casting directors, but after Miss Katherine's smile and encouraging words, I left New York feeling proud and confident in my efforts.

I was further encouraged when I was called back four more times to complete the screen test.

But as I predicted—my secret audition did eventually get out.

Before I knew it, my trip to New York and the audition for the role of Mammy had made headlines. And that alone catapulted me into stardom. Making the papers wasn't anything new with all the campaigning I had done for the president. But this was different. I received endless letters and telegrams from all over, wishing me luck on the role. Some went as far as to predict that I had already landed it, though I had not received the official call.

"See, I knew you would do great, honey," Mac said as we sat in bed reading one of the news articles.

I stared down at the paper, still at a loss for words. It was flattering yet overwhelming to be the center of so much attention, and to my surprise, I didn't really mind it. For a moment, I was starting to feel very much like a celebrity.

And, truth be told, I kind of liked it.

Chapter 13

July 30, 1937:

My dear Lizzie McDuffie:

I was very glad to learn your address from the story about you in this morning's paper for I have been wanting to get in touch with you since you phoned me several days ago. Of course, I want to see you and hear about your moving picture experience. Would it be possible for you to come to see me this afternoon between four and five o'clock? I expect to go to the country for a little vacation tomorrow and may not return before you leave Atlanta . . .

—Sincerely, Margaret Mitchell Marsh

See! It says right there that she wanted to see me at her apartment before she left town."

I held up the letter from the popular author, but Kathy simply rolled her eyes and didn't bother to give it a glance.

"Still doesn't prove anything," the younger maid said. "I still think she's a bigot."

"Would a woman who had racism in her heart invite a Negro maid to her home to chat about books and movies?"

Kathy shrugged. "Maybe. I never know what's going on in a racist's mind."

I waved her presumptuous words away and tucked the letter back into my keepsake box. That letter from Margaret Mitchell was one of the highlights of my summer. I found her to be kind and courteous, and also one of my biggest supporters in landing the role of Mammy. Though I never got to have that meeting with her, we continued to correspond through the mail. She eventually came to see me while at Warm Springs and told me again that she hoped I would land the role.

And for a while it looked as though I had the part.

When news columnist Walter Winchell announced that I had been selected for the role, the White House was abuzz with excitement. Mr. Roosevelt and many others had begun congratulating me, Mac brought me celebratory flowers, and I sat back waiting for the official call to come.

Unfortunately, we had all been crossing the creek before we came to the bridge.

As it turned out, I didn't get the role after all.

I couldn't be upset about the loss. I was no actress. The role deserved to go to a professional, and the fact that it would be played by a Negro woman was still a win for me. When Miss Hattie Mc-Daniel was named the actress who had landed the role of Mammy, I was especially pleased. I knew she would do a wonderful job because she had done so in many of her other movies.

Several days after the announcement, the letters of disbelief, condolences, and outrage came pouring in. I was comforted by this show of love and support. I may have been a tad disappointed in the news, but I didn't let the disappointment sag my shoulders as much as others might have believed. I not only had the experience of a lifetime, but had gotten to connect with people I had never dreamed of meeting before this opportunity. Perhaps it had been my inexperience that was telling, or my mastery and passion for the character weren't enough. None of it mattered. They had sought a more experienced actress and had found her in Miss McDaniel.

She was, in the end, the right one for the part.

Now that the summer—and my moment in the spotlight—had come to an end, I was back to my full-time role as an actual maid. And as I went about my daily tasks around the White House, I couldn't shake the words from the recent letter I had just received. Unable to dismiss what I had read, I made my way to the president's study. The two Secret Service men standing outside his door didn't even stir when I knocked once, then pushed open the door.

"Good morning, Lizzie," Mr. Roosevelt said, placing the paper he had been reading down. "You look like you have a lot on your mind."

"Well, actually, I do . . ." I pulled out the envelope from my apron pocket. "I received this letter yesterday and I thought you'd like to read it . . ."

I handed him the letter, realizing there was no way I could accurately express to the president the pain of the woman who had written me about her situation. The president stared at me with curious eyes for a moment before reaching to take the letter from me.

"This dear woman wrote me about her current circumstances," I began, "but I thought perhaps it was best if you read it yourself."

As the president began reading, I couldn't help but compare this mother of four's situation to that of Louise Little and her seven children. It had been weeks since I had sent Louise a response to her last letter practically begging for assistance. The poor woman was now pregnant with her eighth child and in desperate need of support. And though I hadn't been able to offer her much other than encouragement, and a promise to bring up her plight to the First Lady, I was hoping the president would have more to offer.

Though both mothers were raising children on their own with very little resources to help ease their burden, things were made harder for a mother who couldn't work and who didn't have family she could lean on. It saddened me to think that so many more women—particularly mothers and widows—were experiencing a life with so much responsibility yet very little support.

I watched the president as he carefully read through the letter. His eyes moved along every line, and I secretly hoped he was digesting the woman's pain and sorrow the same way I had. Sadly, the woman's story wasn't that uncommon, and that presented a much larger problem.

President Roosevelt put the letter down and gestured to the chair in front of him. "Lizzie, please sit." His gaze shifted from the letter over to me. "As you know, every American has problems," he began.

My heart sank to my stomach. I knew where this speech was headed. I stared back at the president, tense, wondering if he was about to dismiss the woman's plight.

"Some issues are larger, and more traumatic, than others—"

"Mr. President," I interrupted before he could continue. "Hundreds of displaced Negro farmers are roaming the country, looking for work, because the Agricultural Adjustment Act drove them off their lands. This woman didn't just lose her husband from natural causes. She lost him from a New Deal program that was supposed to help the American people but instead forced them out of their home and right into poverty."

He sighed and rubbed the bridge of his nose. "And I feel sorry for her, I do. This was not the outcome we were hoping for when we proposed the AAA, but there are too many stories like hers, and unfortunately we can't change things now."

"We may not be able to change her story," I agreed, "but we can certainly try to ease some of the burden. Especially after losing her husband the way she did. Taking a life is bad enough. Taking your own life . . ." I shuddered at the thought.

"It's unthinkable," Mr. Roosevelt finished, sitting back in his seat in defeat. "So, my dear Lizzie . . . what do you suggest we do?"

"I can't do much, Mr. President. But I know that with one phone call, you could potentially change her life."

His look was contemplative for a moment, then he nodded briskly. "All right. I can have Missy look into housing for this woman and her four children. I also have some favors I can call in. Perhaps there's a job I can unearth for her down in Texas."

I smiled at him, relieved that he wasn't going to just dismiss the woman who had been brave enough to reach out and share her very personal story with me, a person she didn't even know. This small act of empathy from the president may not have been on the larger scale of signing the anti-lynching bill, but it was enough to restore my wavering confidence in him and his interest in the Negro plight.

In the few weeks that followed, I was able to interest Mr. Roosevelt in cases of discrimination within the postal service and stories of discrimination against Negro women by the Works Progress Administration. Because I helped serve as an unofficial liaison for Mary McLeod Bethune, the new director of the Division of Negro Affairs of the National Youth Administration, I was able to get these stories firsthand. On occasion, I also worked with Mac's former brother-in-law, Edgar G. Brown, in the Civilian Conservation Corps.

Though Edgar and I never quite saw eye to eye in the past, we began to get along better these days. I realized he was simply passionate about matters that were important to him, and that intensity often made him come off as too abrasive.

Because Edgar's passion was just what I needed to get the union project going, I enlisted him in helping me organize the United Government Employees union, or the UGE as we were calling it these days. It didn't take much convincing.

"Starting a union isn't going to be a small feat, Lizzie," he cautioned me. "We'll need a solid plan, and support from our colleagues."

"I know it's going to be a process, Edgar, but I believe with the long-term benefits, it'll be worth it. Besides, we already have the support of Mrs. Roosevelt," I reminded him.

"Yes, but there will be resistance from others, so be prepared for that."

"I'm prepared, but not worried." That was a lie. I was beyond anxious about what the response would be to this new union, but I didn't let him see that. "Why don't we begin by setting up a meeting to gauge interest? We can address any questions or concerns then, and hopefully enlist some members."

He nodded. "That sounds like a good start, but let's ensure we have a solid foundation before moving forward."

"Absolutely."

He sat back in his seat, a small smile curving his neatly mustached lip. "Now, I just have one question for you . . ."

"Yes?"

"Where do you find the time for all of this?"

I had not a clue.

But I was constantly on the move and didn't have time to think about it all. Of course, my time with Mac and the president was shortened, and finding time to indulge in small pleasures like reading was nonexistent. I knew, however, that these were small sacrifices to make now for bigger rewards to come later.

When the president got wind of our budding organization, he too threw his support behind it.

"The only way to gather support is to lobby through organizations," Mr. Roosevelt advised. "Present your case to the right committee, and change will come."

So that's what we did.

With the president's help and support, we managed to put together a strong committee of leaders and were well on our way to gaining in popularity and membership. In just a few weeks of its formation, a massive turnout of Negro men and women swarmed the union.

Edgar took the helm and became leader of the UGE, and I was fine with that. I became a member and secretary, and later that year, we held our first annual event, where the president even gave a small speech.

In the months that followed, the UGE was standing on its own. Under our new union, lower-paid workers now believed they had a voice and a body representing their interests. We succeeded in getting pay raises for government laundry workers and other progressive measures.

My efforts, however, didn't stop there.

Over the coming months, I continued to receive letters from many people from across the country, people I had met in the past and people I never once met. Many of them expressed their appreciation to the First Lady, myself, and even the president. I continued to present Mr. Roosevelt with core issues that he could act on immediately while supporting his efforts with the New Deal programs.

From inside the White House, I was also entrusted with a multitude of confidential letters that I had not been privy to before. If not for this correspondence, I would not have believed the level of discrimination that plagued many of the New Deal programs. One of the letters had a note attached to it that read:

Missy: Show this to Lizzie and then file. —F.D.R.

The letter referred to the president's appointment of Negroes to supervisory positions in the Civilian Conservation Corps. Whether those appointments actually happened remained to be seen, but it was nice to see the president putting in the effort to achieve equality in the workplace.

And I had never felt more a part of his administration than in that moment. I may not have had the official title, but that small note made me feel every bit his secretary on colored people's affairs than ever before.

Another letter that I was privy to see was addressed to the president from Mrs. Roosevelt. She noted across the top:

F.D.R.: There is no doubt that slowly the colored people have been weeded out in many departments. Could you check? —E.R.

The letter suggested that an interracial committee be appointed to investigate discrimination in civil service appointments. Such behind-the-scenes correspondence provided me with useful information I presented to the UGE committee, so we could potentially use this information to get ahead of these injustices and begin facilitating change within these agencies.

Toward the end of the year, however, I was operating on fumes. But I kept going.

It was never easy finding a balance being a wife, a maid, and a bridge that connected our people to the White House. As much as I despised Mr. Albert Jackson's earlier approach, I had him to thank for spurring my hesitant soul into a series of actions that would later be of great help to a large number of Negroes.

"God emancipated our souls and Lincoln emancipated our bodies, but Franklin D. Roosevelt emancipated the civic side of the Negro."

That was my opening—or sometimes closing—line for almost every campaign speech I had given for Mr. Roosevelt. I said it often because I meant it. Gone were the days of following the Republican Party blindly. Like the president had once stated—whether it was the front or back door, opportunity was slowly beginning to materialize for the Negro.

In these past few years working and living in the White House, I learned that I wasn't a woman who shied away from duty and responsibility. I was a woman who gave with all of her heart, not a Negro maid who just stood back and watched as her people fled their city in search of refuge after unfair persecution and attacks.

Much like I had during the Atlanta riots in 1906.

I had since grown from that terrified twenty-five-year-old woman. And like the president, my life was no longer mine.

Because of my rising "influence" among the Negro community, the president of the Ohio State Democratic League, Thomas J.

Davis, wrote me, asking me to come and help get out the Negro vote for Charles Sawyer as governor. Because Sawyer was a candidate the president also supported, I did. I also spoke during state elections in Illinois, Ohio, and Pennsylvania.

As a token of appreciation for my efforts behind the scenes—as well as on the front lines—of the Democratic Party, Mr. Roosevelt gifted me with something just as precious . . .

A bright yellow canary bird.

Chapter 14

March 2, 1938
White House

Lizzie, are you going to get dressed or not?"

"In a minute . . ." I extended my hand into my pet bird's cage and held out a handful of peas for the small yellow bird hopping wildly inside. "Good evening, Mr. Squeaks."

"So you've settled on Mr. Squeaks?" Mac asked, the exasperation heavy in his tone as he adjusted his shirt collar.

I chuckled, though I could understand Mac's frustration. I had spent the past few months testing out a few names for the energetic canary bird until I had finally settled on a name that fit him perfectly.

"Well, I thought Mr. Butters was a bit too . . . informal," I explained. "Mr. Squeaks just feels right."

Mac shook his head, looping his tie around his neck. "You know it's just a bird, right? No matter what you call it, it's not gonna answer back."

I let out a small laugh and poured the rest of the peas into Mr. Squeaks's small feeding bowl. "Now don't be jealous because he and I share a special bond. Isn't that right, Mr. Squeaks?" I couldn't help but croon.

The small bird hopped around the cage to my outstretched hand, and I ran the backs of my fingers along the curve of his back. Mac stood for a moment, watching me caress the little bird, before he shook his head and continued knotting his tie.

"See how he responds to me?"

When Mr. Squeaks returned his attention to his bowl, I shut the door of the birdcage. The happy little canary began picking at the peas with his tiny beak and I delighted in watching him. Mr. Squeaks was a gift from the president that I didn't know I needed until I had him. The delightful bird had especially kept me company on the days and nights Mac was away, traveling long and far with the president. They had only just recently returned to the White House after some time on the road.

Mac scoffed. "Looks more like he's responding to those peas."

"Not true."

Mr. Squeaks and I had grown quite fond of each other. The tone of his chirping would change to a high pitch whenever he saw me entering our quarters. Then he would hop excitedly around the cage as if he were about to break into a performance. Although Mac would make sly remarks, pretending not to care for the adorable creature, I knew better. Some mornings I would catch him feeding Mr. Squeaks or whistling along with him.

Unfortunately, that was how Mac was.

He was notorious for hiding his emotions as much as he could. His drinking was often his outlet, and whether for emotional or physical comfort, he tended to lean more toward his vice than on me. What wife wouldn't feel resentful?

Even during our time here in the White House, his relationship with alcohol hadn't improved any. He only managed to hide it better, especially in the presence of Mrs. Roosevelt. Though the First Lady no longer sought to dismiss him as she had once advised the president to do, she didn't turn a blind eye to his reckless habit either. Luckily for Mac, it was Mr. Roosevelt who made sure he retained his position.

Yet despite this crippling dependency nearly costing him his job, Mac continued to overindulge. There were still nights he would crawl into bed after a long day smelling harshly of liquor. I didn't know what to say that wouldn't escalate into an argument between us, so I said nothing at all.

And deep down, I knew my silence was only sanctioning this bad behavior.

"Lizzie, you have to hurry or we're going to be late."

Mac studied himself in the mirror, and I studied him from behind. Tonight, he was especially sharp and handsome, dressed in a black drape suit and gleaming dress shoes to match. He picked up his charcoal-gray hat from the top of the table and placed it carefully on his head.

"You look absolutely ravishing, my love."

I caught the smile creeping up his face as he tried to hide his bashfulness. "Why thank you, darling. Now when are you going to finish dressing so we can look stunning together?"

"Ha! If only there was anything even remotely as nice for me to choose from," I said. "Unlike you, who's dressed like he's about to unseat the president himself."

Mac laughed just before he inched closer to me and pulled me into his arms. "Don't be ridiculous. Why would I want the president's job?"

I laughed. "True." In just these past five years at the White House, Mac's dark, neatly trimmed hair had gone from distinguishably salted with gray to completely covered in tufts of white strands.

"And is that a new cologne I'm smelling?" I sniffed around his neck again. "You smell crisp, like fresh banknotes."

Mac laughed again. "It was a gift from the president. This is my first time using it. I thought I'd give it a try for this very special occasion."

I pulled out of his embrace and peered into his eyes. "And what is this special occasion?"

"Well, my love, about thirty years ago I met the woman of my dreams . . . the woman I knew I was going to marry . . . and tonight, I'd like to take her out to dinner. Show her how much I cherish and appreciate our time together."

I looped my arms around him and gave him a long, lingering hug. "Hmm, now that sounds like the perfect occasion."

To my surprised delight, Mac leaned close and placed a warm kiss on my lips.

The kiss was electrifying.

And it transported me back to the time we had first met nearly three decades ago . . .

It was at a small house party. I had just started working for the Inmans that year and it was my first night off. A handsome young man had been eying me from across the room the entire night, but I paid him no mind. Though I found him quite attractive, and wondered all evening who he was, I had found myself too shy to approach or inquire about him. As it turned out, we were the only two at the party who were strangers to each other. Because everyone assumed we had already met, we were never properly introduced that night.

Mac, however, took it upon himself to correct that.

When the party finally broke up, he sauntered across the room to me, took my hand in his, and bowed over it.

"Hello, lovely. My name's Irvin McDuffie." He lifted his head and winked. "But my friends call me Mac."

I was charmed and a little bit flustered. I hadn't realized it then, but it was a case of love at first sight.

"Elizabeth Hall," I managed to reply back.

With my hand still held in his, he smiled and said, "Miss Hall, I have been very favorably impressed with you. I would like to call."

My heart skipped a beat as I returned his smile. "You can start by calling me Lizzie," I teased.

For the next two years after that, he did "call" on me until we eventually got married.

And we have been nearly inseparable since.

"So where are we going?" I asked, pulling out of his arms.

Mac winked just before releasing me. "There's a nice new Negro-owned restaurant I found called Melba's."

"Oh, I've heard of it. Heard they got great cornbread too."

"Yes, and if we hurry we might make it in time to catch their live band playing."

My interest and appetite were further piqued.

"Then what are we waiting for?"

"You!" Mac burst out with a chuckle. "We're waiting for you, my dear. Now finish dressing. I'll wait for you outside."

I began to protest his decision, but I held my tongue as he slipped out of our chambers. I didn't need to fill his mind with worries where there might not be any. These days, the streets were buzzing with undiluted energy over the rising conflict in Europe. It appeared as if all of America was concerned about it, though many certainly had their opinions around it.

Even though the conflict was a world away from our land,

Mr. Roosevelt wasn't taking the growing strife in Europe lightly. There was more security around the White House these days, especially at night.

But like every other colored person in America, I couldn't concern myself with the troubles in Europe. I had enough of my own right here. I worried about the men and women who lived in constant fear of being hunted down like animals because of the color of their skin. Men and women who looked like me. I worried about the lack of protection from the very government I served who refused to do anything about it and rule it an official crime.

I had other more private concerns, as well.

Like Mama's failing health. I knew she was keeping some things from me, not wanting to upset me with how hard things were getting for her. But all I could do was agonize over how she was doing down in Atlanta on her own, unable to do the things she was used to doing. Then there was Mac and his increasing drinking habit. He too kept a lot from me, yet I knew his leg was paining him more than usual these days, which led to more drinking on his part. And when I wasn't brooding over Mama and Mac, I was dwelling on the people I had tried to help but failed.

People like Louise Little.

My heart was broken when I had learned that she had been committed to Michigan's Kalamazoo Mental Hospital late last year. From what I had managed to gather from my own inquiries, the poor woman had suffered a mental breakdown, and all of her young children—including her new baby—had been separated and sent to foster homes.

I couldn't help but feel as if I'd failed her. She had reached out to me a number of times, desperate for assistance, yet I had prioritized other matters over her. The weight of feeling as if I hadn't done enough lay heavy on my heart.

But instead of letting that weight bring me down, I used it to fuel my fire. I wouldn't let another woman who sought out my assistance suffer like Louise. Not if I could help it.

Mr. Squeaks began jumping around in his cage again, pulling me out of my gloomy thoughts.

"Yes, I hear you, little one."

I glanced at the clock and let out a little squeak myself. I had wasted enough time in my head and left Mac waiting long enough. I went to our wardrobe closet and stood there in just my undergarments, confused as to what to wear. I wanted to look just as nice as he did. Mac had apparently put a lot of thought into our rendezvous tonight, and for a man who kept busy, working under the most powerful figure in the country, I was touched by the care and attention he put into making our only night off together special.

I ran my hand through the rows of hanging clothing before I pulled out a black and white floral dress with a slouch hat and pair of black kitten heels. I quickly dressed, then slipped on my smoky gray stroller coat and grabbed my matching handbag before I stepped out of the room.

As promised, Mac stood outside waiting for me. To my surprise, he wasn't as annoyed at my tardiness as I imagined. There was a charming twinkle in his eyes as I approached him, and in that moment, my heart melted all over again for him. When he looked at me like that, I could forgive him almost anything.

Including his occasional overindulgence with alcohol.

With a warm smile, Mac held out his hand. "Shall we?"

I slipped my hand into his, and together we walked down to our awaiting cab.

FIVE YEARS AFTER moving to the White House, I received my first slap on the wrist.

I didn't see it coming and quite frankly, I didn't believe it was warranted.

The resulting incident had involved Mrs. Roosevelt, who had just come back to the White House at six thirty that Sunday morning after a long trip. I was acting as her maid in the absence of her new personal maid, Mabel Haley. Sadly, her long-time maid, Mary Foster, had passed on shortly after the Roosevelts had taken up residency at the White House in '33. At seven fifteen, I was called upon by John Mays, the head doorman, who had been there since the Taft administration.

Though I had been a few minutes late, I didn't expect the outrage from him. It wasn't until I was standing before the man that I understood why he was falling all to pieces.

"Lizzie!" Mr. Mays thundered out. "Where the hell have you been?"

"I—"

"Get to Mrs. Roosevelt immediately!" he interrupted. "She's hurt."

Terrified, I raced up to her room, not even waiting to get into uniform. When I entered her quarters, I could hear water running in the bath.

"Mrs. Roosevelt?" I called as I stood outside her closed door. "May I come in? I was told you might be hurt?"

"No, Lizzie, nothing's the matter," Mrs. Roosevelt shouted back to me above the sound of running water.

I hesitated for a heartbeat, but concern made me persist. "Are you sure there's nothing I can do for you?"

"No! There is nothing you can do, Lizzie. Now please leave me be."

I was taken aback by the harshness in her voice, as I had never seen her lose her cool, much less her temper. Even the opinionated columnist Westbrook Pegler couldn't make the First Lady angry. Once Miss Anna had been complaining about the man and Mrs. Roosevelt shrugged, remarking gracefully to her only daughter, "*A person has stopped growing when she can't take criticism.*"

Whatever had become of Mrs. Roosevelt, she didn't want me or anyone else to be privy to it.

I eventually conceded. "Yes, ma'am. Please send for me if you need anything."

Pushing away from the closed door, I made my way back to Mr. Mays, who seemed to be much worse off than the First Lady.

"Mrs. Roosevelt is currently in the bath," I told the head doorman. "She insists that she's all right and doesn't need my help."

He shook his head as he regarded me with disapproval. "While you are assigned to wait on the First Lady, you need to make yourself available to her at all times. Understood?"

My cheeks burned hotly. "Understood."

That small reprimand did little for my confidence—and served as a harsh reminder that my primary position in the White House was, and always would be, as a maid.

Later that day, I found out from Kathy that Mrs. Roosevelt had tried to throw open a window, lost her balance, and fallen against the glass. It broke, cutting her nose ever so slightly. A few of the servicemen had seen it from outside and told the ushers, who then told Mr. Mays, and of course it was now my fault for not being there to open said window in the first place.

But I didn't argue with the man—nor did I take the First Lady's harshness personally, as I remember Miss Anna had once said, "*The only time you'll ever see Mother get angry is when she hurts herself.*"

She was right.

The First Lady's accidental, self-inflicted injury that morning had made me witness a side of her I had never gotten to experience until that morning.

And one I hoped to never experience again.

As time went on, the sting of that moment began to fade. Besides, I didn't have time to dwell on or take offense at unfair scoldings. At the White House there were always endless rooms to be cleaned, dinners to serve, events to prepare for, and children to tend to.

And, of course, there were the occasional royals to oblige.

Though I had gotten the opportunity to be of service to many world-renowned individuals and serve at many high-class events, the red letter event for me while working at the White House was the visit of the king and queen of England.

Not because of the pomp and excitement either. Just last year, the three sisters of Zog had visited, wearing the most amazingly colorful robes that ever came across the White House threshold. Prime Minister Mackenzie, of Canada, was another frequent guest. He once called me to find out who had cooked a certain dinner and told me to tell Mrs. Roosevelt that it was the *best food I ever ate in my life.*" Elizabeth Riake was the cook in charge that Sunday and the capon was cooked to the guests' taste—or rather, the prime minister's. Then there was the time when Mrs. Somoza, the wife of the president of Nicaragua, had come to visit and left me a delicate gold filigree necklace after her stay. It made me happy to be remembered like that.

Though we were used to having royals visit the White House, it was the visit from the king and queen of England that I would never forget. Their visit that summer was the most significant I had witnessed at the White House—and it was during their visit that I made a faux pas that was about as royal as they were.

Days before their arrival, the servants dining room was buzzing as to whether or not we should curtsy if introduced to King George and Queen Elizabeth. Royal problems had not caused such a controversy among the White House workers since the abdication of Edward VIII. Mac told me then that he had asked the president what he thought of the former king's resignation from the throne over a woman.

Mr. Roosevelt had simply said, *"Why shouldn't he give up a throne for love if he wishes to?"*

My own opinion was that Wallis Warfield Simpson, being an American woman and divorcée, was probably the only woman except his mother who bossed him around—and the former king probably liked it.

But with the current king and queen, things were different.

We all looked forward to getting a peek at the couple, and when they were luncheon guests at the White House we did. But now we had a problem.

To curtsy or not to curtsy?

I asked the chief, who smiled and said, *"No. That would be the custom in England, but here I expect we just do United States."*

But if Mr. Roosevelt was calm about their visit, he was the only one. The prospect of such a royal visit rocked the White House to its foundations. The kitchen girls broke dishes. Fluffy scolded the maids. The hallmen waxed the same floors repeatedly.

When the much-anticipated royal couple finally arrived with their own servants, the whole place had the air of a Sanhedrin court. Despite the gravity of the occasion, there was still an excited charge in the air. I was further delighted to learn that Marian Anderson, who had been presented with the NAACP's Spingarn Medal just this summer—by Mrs. Roosevelt herself!—had been asked to return and sing with Kate Smith and Lawrence Tibbett for the royals.

Later, when the royal party went to New York, the atmosphere changed further. And by my estimation, it changed for the better.

Some of us were sent to Hyde Park early to help get it shined up for the king and queen. When everything was set and waiting for them, the president's mother called me over and said that the carpet on the porch and steps was still too dusty.

"Can you get someone to sweep it again, Lizzie?" Mrs. Delano asked anxiously.

I took a broom and went over it myself, and not long after King George and Queen Elizabeth were walking on my freshly swept carpet!

It was also at Hyde Park that a group of the service staff had a chance to meet the king and queen personally. The queen's maid announced just before dinner that the Hyde Park servants would be received in a moment on the second floor. I hunted down Mac, and a number of us started upstairs. But as luck would have it, we were all caught in an area near the queen's room where we couldn't move because we saw the king standing in the doorway. The queen appeared from the bedroom beside his. The only place we could have gone was through the floor.

And man, did I feel like it.

The king thought we had all assembled for him and began to address us.

"Our visit to your country has been a great opportunity," the king began stiffly. "We have enjoyed every moment and hope we can return again."

Silence.

There our little huddle of servants stood, rooted to the spot, and almost at attention. I felt that someone should reply, but I did not know whether one replied to a king or not. After a long empty pause, I set my shoulders, swallowed, and tried to sound dignified.

"Your Majesties, we are happy that you have been pleased with our country. We have been happy to serve you." Then I began introducing the group. "This is Kate Jennings, Mrs. James Roosevelt's personal maid, who was born in England."

The king visibly relaxed and smiled. "That's great!"

We all relaxed.

"Next is Robert McGaughey from Ireland."

"What part of Ireland?" the king asked the senior butler.

"The north," Robert answered proudly.

"My name is McDuffie," I continued. "And this is my husband, Irvin McDuffie, Mr. Roosevelt's valet. We are from Atlanta, Georgia, a southern state."

"Sounds like Scotland to me," the king teased.

I smiled. And so were the McDuffies "presented" to the king and queen of England. And it was his lightheartedness that helped me to relax in their presence.

"Next is Mary Campbell, Mrs. James Roosevelt's cook, who is also Irish."

"The Campbells are coming, eh?"

I introduced Anna McGowan, the Roosevelts' longtime housekeeper at Hyde Park, along with her sister Frieda and daughter Linnea, who had come down from Campobello in Canada to see the king and queen.

Just then, Franklin Jr. and his younger brother John ran up the stairway to escort the king and queen to dinner. When Franklin Jr. realized we had been in the middle of introductions, he finished them himself and called out the names of the other five servants.

After the introductions, and my ability to speak up when no

one else did, I gained a confidence that nothing else had ever given me, not even speaking to large crowds for President Roosevelt. I was poised and well-spoken and felt completely invincible.

After the formality of the White House, I believed the royal couple and other guests enjoyed their weekend at Hyde Park the most. They ate hot dogs, were entertained by Native American artists, and rode around the estate with Mr. Roosevelt driving them in his own car. The queen shook hands with everybody when she said goodbye, including some state troopers and Monty Snyder, the president's chauffeur. And as for a tip, the king and queen gave a lump sum to be divided among all of the servants.

My unfortunate faux pas, however, could not go ignored.

And as innocent as it had been, it had earned me a second slap on the wrist.

It all began at the White House, when a messenger brought over a beautiful drawing of the king and queen that he was very anxious to have autographed. He knew that I frequently collected autographs and asked me to help him obtain theirs. I gave the pictures to the maid of the lady-in-waiting. The queen's maid suggested I leave it with a note, which I did.

Then I was off to Hyde Park.

Unbeknownst to me, however, the king and queen simply did not autograph anything. Such a fact was supposed to be understood, only I didn't understand it.

The request for an autograph got back to the ushers, then to Mrs. Nesbitt, and ultimately to Mrs. Roosevelt. The chief usher, Mr. Howell Crim, called me onto the floor and I was gently reminded that people have been fired for less.

I was mortified.

Having worked for over twenty-three years for the Inmans

in Atlanta, I was not in the habit of being fired. So, when faced with that prospect over my blunder with the king and queen, I told Mr. Crim that it would not be necessary. If I had committed a grave breach of etiquette, I would willingly resign. I did not want my hobby placing a strain on international relations, now or ever.

I immediately wrote a letter of resignation to Mrs. Roosevelt, who was still at Hyde Park. She, however, did not accept it.

I later learned that Mrs. Roosevelt had also run into trouble with British custom. She had arranged a press conference for the queen to meet the ladies of the press. However, the whole thing had to be called off because the British Embassy notified her that *"the Queen does not submit to questioning."*

Needless to say, I managed to keep my position.

But after that summer, my autograph days had come to an end.

PART 3:

The Back Door
(1939)

Chapter 15

Texas, May 6, 1939:

Tomorrow makes twelve years on this job. I cannot realize the years have flown so fast. The job has been confining and trying, and it has meant personal sacrifices. But anything I have given up I would do all over again for his success and happiness. Because I have learned to love him.

—Your Loving Husband

W elcome to Melba's. May I start you off with a beverage?"

"Yes," Mac began, glancing up from the menu card he'd been studying. "Can you bring me—"

"Can we have some water to start," I interjected, staring pointedly at my husband.

Mac glanced over at me, then back at the thin young waiter. "Yes, two waters to start please."

The waiter nodded. "Very well. Shall I give you both a few minutes to look over the menu?"

"Yes, thank you," I rushed out, though I didn't really need to look over the selection of delicacies offered.

Melba's had become one of our favorite places to dine since our first time here. Typically, I ordered the same thing every time—roasted potatoes with smothered pork chops and yams. Despite the smell of spices and fried chicken, and other savory delicacies that wafted through the air, I decided to stick with my usual.

As the waiter left our table, I stared at the man I had been married to for several decades now, who I shared an incredible life with. This high-yellow, good-looking man could have had any woman of his choosing, yet he had chosen me. Tonight made me realize that, even with thirty years together, there were still issues between us that were polarizing and could quickly turn what should have been a lovely evening into a sour one.

"Mac, can I ask one favor from you?"

"Yes, dear?"

I fiddled with the menu card before me as I tried to choose my next words carefully. "Can we have a dry evening tonight? No spirits. No drink. Just us, the ambience, and some good eating."

Mac put his menu on the table and regarded me quietly for a moment. I couldn't tell what he was thinking, but I hoped he could appreciate my concern and understand why I made this request.

Evidently he did, because suddenly he smiled warmly at me and said, "Why, I was thinking the same thing."

The tension I didn't realize I was holding eased off my shoulders, and I returned his smile.

"So, what are you having tonight?"

He picked up the menu again. "I don't know . . . I was thinking maybe the fried chicken again. You?"

"My usual," I answered.

Mac nodded and flagged down the waiter. As the young man came carrying our waters, I couldn't help but notice how busy the restaurant had gotten since we arrived. The place was practically filled to capacity, and I wondered if it had to do with Miss Marian Anderson's recent patronage just last month.

The famous opera singer's powerful performance at the Lincoln Memorial this past Easter was all anyone could talk about these days. Just remembering how historic that moment had been brought goose pimples up my arms. Thousands of people had turned out for the occasion, making the Daughters of the American Revolution's sad attempt to keep Miss Anderson from singing onstage at their Constitution Hall seem pitiful. It was a shame that just because the years were advancing didn't mean that people's minds or hearts were progressing with the times.

After our waiter quickly took our food order and disappeared in the back, I reached across the table and took Mac's hand. He had just returned to Washington after weeks on the road with the president. I was glad that despite his exhaustion after all the traveling, he still made time for us tonight.

"Thank you for taking me out to dinner," I said with a grin. "Honestly, I don't think I would have been able to stomach another night of Miss Ida's cooking."

Mac threw his head back and let out a shout of laughter. "Anything for you, my dear."

Suddenly he sat back and regarded me closely. I waited for him to say something, but after a while of his silent staring, I began to shift uncomfortably in my seat.

"What?" I asked stiffly.

"Nothing. You look beautiful tonight, is all."

I smiled, relieved, glad he had noticed the care I took in looking my best for him tonight. I was even wearing the new dress that I had purchased while he'd been away, and I had taken extra care with the pin curls in my hair.

"Have I not been looking beautiful before tonight?" I teased.

He chuckled. "That sounds like a trick question. Of course, you look beautiful to me every day. It's just that tonight you look extraordinarily lovely."

I laughed and shook my head. "Irvin Henry McDuffie, you are such a flirt."

He winked, and his next reply brought out a giggle and blush from me.

Eventually our playful banter came to a halt when the waiter arrived with our tray of food. He gently placed the dishes before us, and Mac rubbed his hands together in anticipation.

After saying grace over the food, we picked up our forks and dug into our meal. The potatoes were roasted to a crusted brown, and when I bit into one, my teeth sank right into it. It was heaven. I glanced up to find Mac staring at me, this time gauging my reaction to the food.

"How is it?" Mac asked, his fork still hovering over his plate.

"Hmm . . . I don't know . . . I think I might have preferred Miss Ida's cooking tonight after all." At his horrified expression, I let out a small laugh. "I'm pulling your leg, honey. It's good. It's real good."

Mac shook his head ruefully, though a grin tugged at the corner of his lips. "Glad to hear, 'cause this place ain't cheap."

As he dug into his own meal, he let out a satisfied groan. I smiled, thinking how the simple things in life could bring such pleasure. Just sitting across from my husband tonight, away from the White House and our responsibilities, was a treat, an indulgence we sadly didn't get to experience often. It was moments like this that made me miss our old life in Atlanta.

"Good evening, Mr. McDuffie. Mrs. McDuffie."

A tall Negro man with a heavy beard had suddenly materialized beside our table. Dressed in a fine suit and wide-brimmed hat, the man was clearly not part of the waitstaff.

"Pardon my intrusion, but I had to stop by and say hello," he said, taking off his hat.

Mac nodded and offered the man a tight smile. "Good evening," he returned, his strained smile still in place.

It took me a moment, but I finally recognized Mr. Albert Jackson, the reporter from the Allied Negro Papers. It was years since we'd last seen the man, and it appeared that time had not been too kind to his waistline.

"It's nice to see you again, Mr. Jackson," I lied.

"The pleasure is truly mine," he said, placing a hand over his chest. "I have to say, I didn't expect to find you two here. May I join you for a moment?"

"Uh—" Mac began.

"Why of course," I said with a forced smile, ignoring Mac's reproachful glare. I was willing to spare a few minutes of our time now to avoid the man's vicious criticism of us in the papers later.

Mr. Jackson brought up a chair from nearby and took a seat at our table.

"Nothing like southern hospitality," Mr. Jackson said with a wide grin. "You don't get that a lot around here, and I sure do miss it."

"You're a southern man?" Mac asked.

"Yes, sir. Born and raised. My parents grew up on a cotton field in Texas," Mr. Jackson began just as our waiter returned to our table.

"Good evening, sir. Would you like me to bring you a menu?"

"No, thank you, Silas," Mr. Jackson said to the young waiter. "I'm just stopping by to say hello to some old friends of mine."

I knew I shouldn't have been surprised that Mr. Jackson was a frequent patron of such an upscale Negro restaurant as Melba's, and yet I was. The man evidently got around and apparently knew everyone.

The waiter nodded before turning to me and Mac. "Is there anything else I can bring out for you?"

"Why don't you bring us some champagne," Mr. Jackson interjected as he glanced at our water glasses. "And put it on my tab."

"No, thank you, Mr. Jackson," Mac said stiffly. "We're quite fine."

"But I insist," the reporter said. "Just a small token of my appreciation for what you and Mrs. McDuffie have been doing for the community over the years."

I arched a brow, my memory not as short as his. I would never forget how he considered us "house Negroes" who were out of touch with the issues that affected our community. Despite my barely contained resentment, I held my tongue. The quicker he was gone from our table, the better I would feel.

"Could you just bring us some lemon-lime soda with a splash of ginger ale and grenadine," I said to the confused waiter. It was a drink recipe I had overheard one of the kitchen staff mixing together for little Miss Shirley Temple when she had come to visit the president last year.

Mr. Jackson waited until the waiter left before he continued his story. "As I was saying, my parents were born on a cotton field in Texas but moved to Mississippi after it all ended. They both died when I was nine."

"Oh, how awful," I said, thinking how young nine was to lose the most important people in one's life. "I'm sorry to hear that."

Mr. Jackson shrugged. "It was a long time ago. I came back from playing with my friends out in the farm when I found them both hanging from a noose in the barn. Side by side."

I gasped. "Oh, my Lord."

Mac's eyes rounded in shock, both of us speechless. How could anyone tell such a tale in an oddly detached and casual manner? At least that's what it appeared to be. But maybe after all these years, the cynical reporter had gotten accustomed to what he'd had to witness at an early age. Maybe it was a story he had gotten used to telling a thousand times and had come to accept that this was unfortunately one of the harsh realities of the Negro life.

I couldn't help but think of Louise Little's children and what they must be enduring having lost their father so brutally and then losing their mother to her own mental illness. As I thought of the Little children and what was to become of them, I couldn't help but think of the many letters Mac and I had received at the White House with similar stories—stories that had left many Negro children alone to deal with the aftermath of their trauma. Would they grow to become as detached and critical of the world as Mr. Jackson?

"That's one hell of a story," Mac finally said, blowing out a heavy breath.

Mr. Jackson shrugged. "We all have a story, I'm sure. Mine, luckily, didn't end all that badly. I was adopted by a white Canadian couple who couldn't have children of their own. They found me while I was digging in their trash for food. A couple of years after my parents' murder, we moved up to New York City, where I was able to get a proper education."

Jesus.

I shook my head, astounded and equally disgusted by how

much trauma and pain we had to endure as a group. It was a wonder many more of us hadn't succumbed to mental sickness.

Mr. Jackson grunted as if he could read my thoughts and was in agreement. "For the so-called emancipation we have been given, we're still not truly free. We won't ever be until every Negro takes a stand and does their part. Like you both have. Your lives are an example to all colored folks of what activism, no matter how small, can look like."

My lips tightened as I processed his words, wondering if his sentiment was that of genuine praise for our efforts—or a sly undercut despite them.

"Are you here on or off the record?" I asked the reporter carefully.

"Well, I am a journalist, Mrs. McDuffie," Mr. Jackson said. "Everything is on the record."

I stared at the reporter, wondering when he had taken that approach. Funny how just a few years ago he had a different outlook during that first interview with Mac. Apparently, time had changed more than just his appearance.

I decided to choose my words with him carefully.

"Mr. Jackson, it's easy to say that we must all stand up and protest, but the reality is that it's not possible for the single mother who is worried about how she will feed her kids on her own or the husband who is too busy working two, maybe three jobs to care for his family. We, the fortunate few, are in a position to do more for our people, so we must do so with grace and understanding. There are not many Negroes who are in our privileged position."

Mr. Jackson cocked a brow. "What makes you think I'm in a position of privilege?"

"You're sitting here, aren't you?" Mac said.

"With the means to order champagne for us," I added. I hadn't finished making that pointed observation before the waiter appeared with our sparkling red drinks. For added fun and flare, there were a few bright red cherries inside each glass—a stark contrast to the grim atmosphere surrounding our table.

I waited for the waiter to deposit our drinks and depart before I spoke again. "Mr. Jackson, you are apparently in a position to do a lot for yourself *and* for our people. Why don't you use your platform to encourage and inspire?"

Instead of criticize and make baseless commentary.

Of course, I kept those last words to myself.

"Inspiration is subjective, Mrs. McDuffie," Mr. Jackson said with a slight incline of his head. "But I understand your position. I do have one serious question to ask you, though this time off the record."

"And that is . . . ?" Mac asked, sitting back in his seat, and clearly annoyed by the man's lingering presence.

"Did you know that the Negro only makes up about 10 percent of the American population, yet we make up about 30 percent of the unemployed? How does President Roosevelt truly have the interest of the Negro at heart when the Negro continues to get the short end of his New Deal programs?"

"Well, since we can't confirm or deny your statistical claims," I countered, "I can only say that I know for a fact that the WPA, the NYA, and the CCC have provided and protected a lot of jobs for Negroes."

"I'm sorry, Mrs. McDuffie, but from where I'm sitting it only appears that the president hired you and your husband, along with a slew of colored staff, just to pander to the American Negro vote. Evidently it worked."

"Nonsense!" Mac retorted. The sharpness in his tone startled a few diners who sat close by. "I've been with the Roosevelts since before they came up to the White House. The president sees people as people. I've never met any white man so interested in the struggles of the Negro as the president. Accusing him of pandering to the Negro for votes is ridiculous."

I reached over and gently touched Mac's hand. Mac tended to take others' criticism of the president to heart because he cared so deeply for the man with whom he had spent the last twelve years of his life.

"As you know, Mac here had been working with the president for a little while before his presidency," I began, keeping my attention directed at Mr. Jackson. "And it was Mrs. Roosevelt who hired me and insisted on hiring an all-Negro staff at the White House. White or Black, President Roosevelt sees us all as Americans. He has always been a president for the people."

Mr. Jackson shrugged. "Just not our people."

I could feel the tension radiating from Mac but luckily he didn't take the reporter's bait.

"With all due respect, Mrs. McDuffie," Mr. Jackson continued, "your President Roosevelt has been in office for almost two terms now and he has ignored the anti-lynching bill. While he has never come out to endorse lynching or racial discrimination, he has never publicly come out to condemn them either. He asks for our peoples' support, and you have personally campaigned for him, yet—"

"Which I would gladly do again, if given the opportunity." I wasn't sorry for interrupting the man.

"*Yet*," the reporter continued, "he doesn't care that just last year a total of two hundred Negroes were lynched. And that's just the ones we know about. Not only do the Democrats look the other way, many of them have a front-row seat to these atrocities. How could you support a president who is part of a party that would filibuster a bill that could protect our people from such crimes? How could *you* support such a party, much less ask our people to?"

I couldn't help but feel a sense of uneasiness and uncertainty rise in me. I could argue that it was the southern Democrats who were holding this bill over the flames, but that still didn't excuse the northern Democrats for their silence over the issue.

It certainly didn't excuse the president's.

"Mr. Jackson," Mac interjected, "I'm trying to have a nice dinner out with my wife. Not rally around politics all night. We've had enough of this conversation."

I glanced at Mac, then at Mr. Jackson, who held his hard gaze for some seconds. Both men were silent, staring at each other. Suddenly, Mr. Jackson inclined his head, then rose to his feet.

"My apologies. I didn't mean to dominate your evening. I will just say this before I go . . . The Negro community has learned to trust the president because of you two. There's a war brewing over in Europe, ethnic discrimination against the Jews by the Germans. Everyone is talking about it, many are up in arms over it, but no one wants to talk about how America is still the only country where a Negro man can simply be *accused* of a crime, then tied to a tree, burned, and mutilated. No one wants to admit that America has done more to the Negro than the Germans are doing to the Jews. Who will go to war for us?"

At our silence, Mr. Jackson rose to his feet and placed his hat back on his head.

"Well, Mr. and Mrs. McDuffie, it's been a pleasure. My opinions of the president in no way change how I feel about everything you both have managed to do for our community." He gave a small salute. "Until we meet again."

With that, Mr. Jackson strode away from our table, walking with an air of false importance.

"The nerve of that pompous ass." Daggers shot from Mac's eyes as he watched the man leave. "He's like the devil himself. Ruining our evening, then having the nerve to thank us for it."

I let out a small, shaky breath, my heart still heavy over Mr. Jackson's parting words. How could I be outraged at the man when some of what he said had some validity behind it?

"Don't let him get to you." My feelings didn't match my words.

Mac shook his head. "I don't know what he's up to, but I wouldn't be surprised if he's being sponsored by the Republican Party to sow discord among our community so Mr. Roosevelt can lose the Negro support. That man's trying to confuse us while turning our people against the president, undoing everything we've accomplished."

"To what end?" I asked, as I took a small sip of my sweet sparkling drink, absently aware of how Mac hadn't even touched his glass.

"There are rumors that the president might run for a third term," Mac murmured, then paused. "If that happens, the Republicans are prepared to strike him hard. If he doesn't, they will try their hardest to knock down any Democrat at the next election."

I frowned. "How sure are you of that?"

"Can't you tell? What that man Jackson is doing is trying to build resentment in our hearts. Until we become conflicted and don't know what we believe in anymore."

"No, Mac. I mean, how sure are you that the president will run again?"

He was silent for a moment, then said, "I'm pretty certain he will . . . He didn't outright say it, but he made mention this morning that there's still much work to be done."

I shook my head as I processed what I'd just heard. As much as I enjoyed working with the Roosevelts, and the opportunity to work beside my husband every day, I didn't know if I had another four years in me to remain at the White House. I was pretty certain Mac didn't have it in him either. The job was getting more strenuous for him, and his last letter to me, during his trip in Texas, hinted at that. And unfortunately, his method of coping with his increasing pain was becoming problematic.

Yet I knew it would take a lot for Mac to leave the president's side.

"It's getting late, Mac. We should probably start heading home."

Home . . .

Where was that, exactly?

Mac glanced at his watch before nodding his head in agreement. There was a solemnness in the small action that made me sad. And angry. I had only myself to blame for letting that reporter sit with us and ruin what should have been a beautiful evening.

The streetlights in front of the restaurant did little to illuminate the concrete pathways. I locked my arm around Mac's as we stood right outside of Melba's, waiting to flag down any passing cab. The air was cold and brisk, much chillier than I was used to for this late in May. There were fewer cars on the road compared to the earlier hour when Mac and I had arrived at the bustling restaurant.

"Sometimes I miss Atlanta," Mac blurted out.

"Sometimes?" I murmured, trying to ignore the crisp bite of the cool air. "I *always* miss Atlanta. Especially on nights like this. What I would give to have one of Mama's hot cocoas right now."

"Me too," Mac said with a chuckle. "When was the last time you spoke with her?"

"Hmm, I don't remember . . ."

I tried to think hard about it but couldn't recall if it had been four days or four weeks ago. My shoulders sagged at the realization that I hadn't checked in on her for that long. Things had only recently slowed down for us at the White House, and I made a mental note to call her tomorrow.

"Come on. Let's take a walk down this way," Mac said, leading us down the other end of the street. "We might find better luck getting into a cab there."

The movement of our legs was synchronized as we strolled through the street. We were quite a distance away from the restaurant when we passed a Negro man dressed in rags and clutching an old Bible to his chest. Under the low lights, I could see just how worn his shoes were and how dusty and tattered his clothes were.

Mac increased his pace, his arm locked firmly around mine as we passed the disheveled man. There was no mistaking the man's presence, but Mac carried on as if he wasn't even aware of him. His grip, however, further tightened as we walked arm-in-arm along the desolate road.

A few feet ahead, a small group of white men ambled toward us. They were too old to be regarded as young men, yet not old enough to be considered our age.

And there was no denying the stench of alcohol that lingered around them.

There were four of them in total, and as they neared, it was clear they were all very drunk. As we passed them, the men began singing a drunken, incoherent mesh of sounds—too loose to be called harmony, yet too unholy to be considered music. I ran my tongue over the roof of my mouth as my nerves became unsettled. They were just a bunch of drunken white men, yet they made me nervous.

"Ho, there!" the last man from the group called out to us as we passed them.

"Just ignore them," Mac whispered to me.

We ignored the strange man and continued walking in long, hurried strides.

"Wait, now! I'm talking to you dirty animals!"

The words came out in a belligerent shout as the sound pierced through the quiet night, echoing against the still air and sending a shiver down my spine.

Nothing about this moment felt right, especially around a group of drunken white men at this hour.

Mac and I kept our pace, ignoring the man.

Suddenly we heard the shuffle of several feet as the group of men joined their friend in trying to gain our attention. That was when Mac stopped.

The men surrounded us as their friend stood face-to-face with Mac. In that moment, I was extremely proud of my nonconfrontational husband for standing his ground. He appeared unfazed by the hostile men while I was a terrified mess inside.

"May I help you gentlemen?" Mac asked, his voice strong and steady.

"Filthy nigger lover!" one of the men barked at us. He had a flat cap on with no jacket, and he held a bottle of gin in his hand. "What are you doing with that monkey?"

"Excuse me?" Mac was just as confused as I was.

But what followed Mac's confusion was a heavy backhand across his face. The man standing directly in front of him had struck him. I stood there, too stunned for words or action.

I was too afraid to even breathe.

"You're a disgrace," the man who had struck him sneered as he spat at his feet. Then he struck Mac again. This time the blow knocked him to his knees.

"Stop it!"

I didn't know where those words came from, but I knew they had come from me.

"Shut up, nigger!" One of the men shoved me aside and I nearly lost my footing. "We'll get to you after we teach this nigger lover a lesson."

I managed to steady myself as I watched the four men drag Mac by the collar into the street.

My heart sank.

It dawned on me that the drunken, foolish men had mistaken Mac for a white man. Clearly, their eyesight was as impaired as their judgment. The oversight seemed unfathomable to me, yet here these ignorant drunks were, surrounding my colored husband because of a misunderstanding.

As the men taunted and continued to harass him, Mac struggled to his feet.

"Listen," Mac began as he held out his hand. "You've mistaken me for—"

"Shut up, race traitor!"

The man holding the bottle of gin rushed toward Mac and swung it across the back of his head. There was a loud thunk as Mac grunted and crashed to the ground.

Oh, dear God!

"Mac!" I shrieked, rushing forward. But one of the men grabbed my arm and held me back. "Please stop this! He's not a white man!"

But they ignored me as they laughed and jeered. I noticed Mac was still conscious but there was blood slowly pooling from the back of his head. Ice ran through my veins at the sight of so much blood.

"Please!"

My voice wasn't mine anymore, and I felt as if I was no longer present in that moment, as if my soul had detached itself from my body and I watched helplessly as the men pounced on my husband. They all gathered around him, throwing blow after blow until blood covered his face and stained his clothes.

"Why are you doing this?" I sobbed, no longer recognizing my voice. "He's not white!"

Suddenly a booming voice came intruding into the melee. "Enough! The man's had enough."

I turned to the voice and realized it was the stranger we had passed earlier. The men stopped their attack, surprised at the man's audacity.

"Get the hell out of here, nigger, or you're next!"

"No weapon formed against thee shall prosper," the man said.

One of the men got in his face and raised his fist but didn't strike him. "I said get the hell out of here before we do you like we did this nigger lover."

The stranger laughed in the drunk man's face. "That's a colored man y'all beatin' on."

The drunk man's eyes squinted. "What did you say?"

"Look closely at him," the stranger said. "That man there is a Negro. Just look at his nose, his eyes." He laughed again. "Hell, you can see it just by lookin' at the waves in his hair. He may be as pale as you, but he's no white man."

The drunk men slowly staggered back, away from Mac. As if realizing the extent of their stupidity, they turned and fled into the night. Without another word, the man holding my arm shoved me toward Mac and chased after his friends.

"Mac?" I rushed over to his side. He was still conscious but not fully alert. His head lolled to the side as I tried desperately to wipe the blood from his face. "Please, Mac, talk to me. Tell me you're all right!"

He nodded his head, and though the action wasn't very convincing, I was grateful that he was capable of giving me that small reassurance. The stranger helped me get Mac to his feet, and we hobbled back over to where we had passed him earlier. I had never in my life been more grateful for a stranger's presence.

"Thank you, sir, thank you. We are forever in your debt."

"It's not me you owe, miss. It's the Lord for putting me in your path."

I stared at the man, not feeling very grateful to the Lord in that moment. My husband was badly hurt, all because he had been mistaken for a white man. How fair was that?

But he was still alive, a small voice reminded me.

As the stranger helped me flag down a cab, we helped Mac into the back seat. One thing was certain: I couldn't fathom what I would have done if this stranger hadn't stepped in to help us.

"God bless you, sir."

The man placed his hand over his heart. "Peace be with you, sister."

I nodded, but deep down I knew there was no peace to be had.

Chapter 16

Three arduous weeks had passed since the attack.

Yet it felt more like three days.

I still couldn't wrap my mind around why it had happened.

Mac and I had never been victims of racial violence the way other Negroes had been in this country. During our time inside the White House, we had forgotten what life was like for the common Negro who experienced the pain and shame of being treated as less than a person every day.

But that night, we were served a harsh reminder that we weren't as untouchable as we believed. We were still Negroes living in white America, and not even the high walls of the White House could save us from the violence colored people faced in our very own country. We were no more immune to racism than the train porter or the laundress who faced it on a daily basis.

"Mac?"

I watched his hands quiver over the tie he was attempting to knot around his collar. "Let me help you with that," I offered, slowly approaching him.

"No, no, I'm fine," Mac said, turning away from me.

I locked my brow, disappointed that he didn't want to accept my help but not at all surprised by it. He had been that way since that night—detached, withdrawn, and deeply gutted by emotions. For a man who once smiled and laughed freely, he didn't laugh much since that night. Even with his back turned, I could still see how his hands trembled while he worked on securing his necktie.

We hadn't spoken about the incident that night—not then or since. Once we had gotten safely to our quarters—thankfully through the back door where few people would see us—I cleaned up the blood on his face and head. He was lucky that the cuts to his head were not as deep or serious as the bleeding made it appear. People had inquired about the bruising to his face, but we had managed to explain it away and no one had probed further. Not that they would have gotten much out of him if they tried.

That night wasn't a topic Mac wanted to discuss. Not even with me.

I had hoped that time would allow him to open up to me a bit more about what he was feeling, but unfortunately it didn't look like that moment would come any time soon.

Mr. Squeaks hopped around in his cage, chirping away, as Mac continued to struggle into his uniform.

Mac muttered a curse as he snatched the tie from around his neck and threw it to the ground.

I went to pick it up and carefully placed it around his neck, gently folding it in the proper sequence under his collar. Periodically, I would glance at his face. He looked like a man on the verge of tears.

It destroyed my spirit to see him like this.

"You know," I began cautiously, "it wouldn't be the end of the world if you took a leave from work today."

Mac shook his head. "The boss is expecting me to show up today, and it's important that I do my job to the best of my ability."

He clasped his trembling hands together before cracking a tired smile. "Don't worry about me. It's just nerves from too many long nights and not enough sleep."

I looked at him for a moment, then pulled him into a long, tight hug. It wasn't work that was keeping him from having a restful night. It was the nightmares that I knew he kept from me.

Just last night, he had been muttering words in his sleep that I couldn't make out. Quiet, incoherent whispers of a disturbed man. Before I could reach out to wake him, he would jerk up violently in bed, covered in sweat. It didn't help that after a long day, he would come back staggering through the door of our living quarters reeking of alcohol.

"All right," I finally muttered, releasing him. "Just don't tire yourself out today."

But I knew that was easier said than done. Mac was the first person the president saw when he woke up and the last person he saw when he went to bed. Even now, with his nerves strung so tight, Mac had to go wake the president so they could start his day.

For Mac, there was no time to deal with or process what had happened to him. Not when he had important duties to attend to.

But he wasn't the only one traumatized by that senseless attack the other night.

Watching those men beat him had unlocked a terror in me that I had not felt since Sunny Boy Smith, a neighborhood kid I'd known back in Atlanta. He'd been an innocent Western Union boy who was killed during the 1906 race riot that had turned all of Atlanta upside down.

Despite growing up in the South, I had never been personally faced with such brutal racism until that moment. While I found myself safe inside the Hillyer home when the death and destruction began to rage around us, many had not been so lucky.

I was a twenty-five-year-old live-in nursemaid for William Hillyer's daughter Elinor. Although their home was on the edge of where much of the rioting had occurred, I knew nothing about it until some of the worst was over.

It wasn't until that Sunday morning that I noticed the streets were unusually quiet. Mr. Hillyer had rushed out of the house to buy a paper, which was unusual given that the Hillyers were very religious and would not even buy Sunday newspapers. But at that time I thought nothing of it as I started down the street to pick up little Elinor and bring her home from Sunday school. Just before I arrived at the church, I was met by one of the other maids on the block.

"How do you feel this morning?" she asked, a strained look on her face.

"Fine, I guess . . ." I replied, perplexed by the stiffness in her tone.

She continued to stare at me oddly. "You didn't hear about Sunny Boy Smith?"

The bottom of my stomach dropped as she told me how he had been killed the night before in the riot—a riot I had not known was even occurring.

In that moment, I didn't know what to say . . . or think.

As soon as I got little Elinor home, I looked for the newspaper, but Mr. Hillyer had hidden it. That day I stayed inside the house, afraid to go out, even to check on my own family and friends.

On Monday night, more were reported killed, including one of my best friends. By Tuesday morning, I stood behind the Hillyers' wide windows, watching as Negro families streamed by their home from south Atlanta on Capitol Avenue. They were loaded down with their meager bundles of household items and clothing, fleeing from the riot-torn section of the city to the homes of relatives and friends in other parts of Atlanta.

When I shut my eyes, I could see the crowds of displaced Negroes walking the streets, leaving with nothing but what they could carry. I could see the faces of the people with whom I had interacted just before their lives had been altered or taken by senseless violence. I remembered my sense of helplessness and fear of what would come next.

That moment was the closest I had come to bearing witness to such violence—innocent men, women, and children fearful for their lives as they were hunted down and chased out of their homes.

Those memories plagued me then—and they added to my nightmares now.

I was still that terrified twenty-five-year-old who felt the same helplessness and fear even after all these years. The fact of the matter was that, no matter our position or station, we still lived in a world where a group of drunken white men could physically attack us simply because we were colored.

That ugly fact shook my reality.

Mac and I were not the "house Negroes"—those protected by the confines of their master's home—many thought us to be. We were just like every Negro in America who was at risk of getting lynched, raped, or displaced by white supremacists.

And while Mac found it difficult to sleep, I was afraid to even shut my eyes because every time I did, I would get flashes of blood covering his face and dripping down his shirt until it smeared down my dress. I would dream of a body hanging from a lamppost right in the middle of a quiet street in Washington. The body would sway in the wind, and as I inched closer, I would find it to be that of my beloved husband.

Those were the nightmares I lived through silently since that night.

Worry for my husband had me suggesting that he take a break from work, perhaps even a short sick leave. But he would crack a weak smile and assure me that he was fine enough to do his job.

But I knew he wasn't.

His drinking was getting increasingly out of control. He tried to hide it, but he was not doing a very good job of it. The intense smell of spirits on him proved that he was letting his habit get the best of him. And if I noticed how obvious it was becoming, I was certain others did too.

Did the president?

Worst yet, did Mrs. Roosevelt?

I HAD YET another dream about Mac last night.

It was always the same dream. One minute he was standing by my side. The next he was hanging from a lamppost. And when I moved closer to him, I saw how bloodied and bruised he was.

After every dream like that one, I would jump out of my sleep and stare long and hard at Mac, to make sure I was no longer trapped in that nightmare.

Every night it was the same thing, until I became afraid to lay my head down. But I didn't tell Mac about my dreams. There was no point to it. He was still struggling with his own demons. I could see it on his face every day.

Each morning, I would watch him move mechanically, as if he was just a shell of his former self. He would head out the door and return to our quarters late at night, reeking of booze. His abnormal behavior left a rigid strain between us. Our interactions as of late were almost that of strangers. It put our marriage in a dark place, and I couldn't see a way out.

It also left our relationship with those around us strained.

Including our relationship with the president.

"Lizzie," the president called out one morning as I was cleaning an antique on the shelf of his study. "How's the bird faring?"

I turned toward Mr. Roosevelt, who sat in his wheelchair behind his desk, and flashed him a weak smile. "Mr. Squeaks is doing great, Mr. President. He's doing just fine."

Though some days, I would forget to feed the poor bird. But considering he was trapped in a cage all day, he appeared to be in good shape the last time I'd seen him. At least he was still alive from what I could tell that morning. Yet I couldn't remember if I had fed him.

"I'm glad to hear that. It's not easy caring for a caged bird. As fascinated as I am by the little creatures, I much prefer to watch them in their habitat, in the wild. They are as free as we'd all like to be."

"Yes, Mr. President," I murmured. "But no one, not even birds, are truly ever free."

I hadn't meant to say that last part out loud, but I realized it had spilled out when the president stared pointedly at me through his spectacles.

"Perhaps you're right," the president finally said before he gestured to an empty seat in front of him. "Here. Come have a seat."

He waited for me to settle into the chair before he spoke again.

"You're right, Lizzie. There is no true sense of freedom for any of us. Not even those winged creatures I admire so much. They are limited by their environment and nature as much as we are limited by society and our duties to others. We are all a prisoner to something—or someone. Whether it be to work, our family, or ourselves."

I stared at the president as he spoke. A lot of what he said had some truth in it, and I realized how much a prisoner I was to my own pain and fear.

"You haven't been yourself these past few days, Lizzie," the president continued. "I gather a lot must be on your mind."

I heaved out a sigh and shifted my gaze from him down to my clasped hands, which held the overused duster tightly. I would soon need a new one, I thought vaguely.

"The mouth was made to share the things that are too heavy for the heart to bear," the president recited, urging me to speak.

I couldn't help the grin that quickly kicked up the corner of my lips. I didn't know where Mr. Roosevelt had quoted that line from, but it did resonate with me, and the words began to pour out of me.

"Three weeks ago, Mac and I were attacked on the street by a group of white men." I paused, allowing the president to process what I'd just said. Or maybe it was more for me to come to terms with what we had endured. "It happened while we were coming back from a lovely night out at dinner," I continued. "These men were clearly drunk and had mistaken Mac for a white man out with a Negro woman. They beat Mac up so bad I was afraid they would kill him."

I waited for the president to react to what I had just told him, but there was no dramatic exclamation, shock, or outrage. He only stared back at me, then sighed and took off his glasses before rubbing his eyes.

"So Mac didn't take an unfortunate trip down the stairway?"

"No."

"Eleanor told me that his bruises were from a nasty fall, and knowing how sensitive he is about his leg injury, I avoided asking him about it outright."

"Don't blame her, Mr. President. I told her that lie. I didn't have the courage to tell her what really happened. In fact, I haven't told anyone about that night. Until now."

"Why didn't you tell us about this sooner, Lizzie?"

I let out a wry laugh. "I guess I didn't want to admit the truth for the same reason we don't talk much about his leg injury. It's such a tender topic for him, and I don't think he likes to appear weak or frail in front of others."

Mr. Roosevelt nodded stiffly in full understanding. Although it was the carelessness of another barber that had caused Mac's legs to be badly scalded, the near-crippling injury had limited him in certain areas of his career. I knew that as much as he enjoyed his position as valet, his true passion was barbering.

I also knew how much he despised wearing those rubber stockings.

"You make a valid point there, Lizzie. But perhaps we could have done something about those men."

"I would love to believe that, Mr. President, but I knew there was nothing you could do. We say it's a new day in America, but for many of us it's the same old journey. We say God bless America, the land of the free, but there's only so much freedom the Negro is allowed in this country. We may have been emancipated from slavery, but many of us are still chained by hate and held prisoner by violence."

The president was silent as he listened to me, but from his pursed lips and wary regard he was not too happy with my words. It may have been a harsh truth, but it was a truth I lived every day.

"Centuries ago, a wise Frenchman once said, 'It's difficult to free fools from the chains they revere,'" Mr. Roosevelt finally said. "Those words couldn't be any truer than they are today."

I cocked my head to the side, confused. The corners of his lips kicked up.

"You are so well-read, Lizzie, I'm surprised you're not familiar with Voltaire."

"I am not, sir."

He nodded. "No matter. I'll be sure to get you a copy of his work. I'm just sorry that you and Mac were subjected to the ignorance and violence of those men. In fact, it bothers me more than you know."

I pursed my lips together to keep them from trembling. That night's incident had opened up a portal of truth and pain I had tried for many years to keep buried. Hearing just those simple words of sympathy made the emotions come flooding to the surface once again. Try as I did, I couldn't hold back the tears that began to pool in my eyes. They grew until the president became just a blur.

Mortified, I quickly dropped my head down and dashed the tears away. When I glanced back up again, the president was silently holding out a handkerchief to me.

"Thank you," I murmured as I dabbed at my eyes and nose with it.

According to Mac, Mr. Roosevelt was a man who seldom got angry. On one of those rare occasions, Mac had overheard a quarrel between the president and Al Smith. During that time, their relationship had broken up over Mr. Roosevelt's appointment of Ed Flynn as secretary of state in New York.

Another time was on a trip to South America, and unfortunately his anger was directed toward Mac. Mac had gone ashore to see Buenos Aires and been delayed returning to the ship. Officials did not understand his travel pass and none of them could speak English. Mac was held at the dock while the president's ship sailed away. Mr. Roosevelt had to arrange for a boat to go pick up his missing valet. It was only when Mac finally found someone in the crowd who spoke English that he was rushed to the waiting boat and brought to the president's ship.

"I *had to climb a rope ladder like a sailor*," Mac had told me.

Mac forever regretted that incident because he knew the chief was terribly angry with him, although all the president had said when Mac finally arrived was, *"What on earth took you so long, McDuffie?"*

However, this was the first time I got to witness the president's outrage.

"Lizzie, I'm sorry for what happened to you and Mac the other night. And as much as I hate to admit it, you're probably right. Short of us catching those men in the act, there's probably not much we could have done about the assault. But still . . . I'm glad you felt comfortable enough to share the truth with me."

I nodded. "Thank you for listening to me, Mr. President. I didn't realize how much better I would feel letting it all out."

"The longer we dwell on our misfortunes, the greater is their power to harm us," he said. "Voltaire again."

I cracked my first genuine smile of the day. "And here I thought I was the one known for recitations."

The president laughed. "No one can best you, my dear. Not even me." He quickly sobered up and gave me a look that was filled with concern. "Why don't you retire for the rest of the day. I'll speak to Mrs. Nesbitt about it."

"Oh, no. I couldn't do that. Besides, I'm all right now and quite capable to finish my work."

He regarded me for a few seconds before nodding. "Well, then, I won't keep you any longer."

I finished my cleaning of his study before I went to complete the rest of my tasks.

It was early when I was finally able to retire to my quarters. The large room was quiet, save for the excited chirps coming from Mr. Squeaks's cage. I took a good look at him, then fed him a good heaping of seeds and lettuce. He hopped around the cage, nibbling here and there at his meal. As I changed out of my uniform, I hummed songs he couldn't understand. After my talk with Mr. Roosevelt, I somehow felt lighter . . . uninhibited . . . almost at peace.

When the sun rolled out of sight, the blue sky turned into a dark wide canvas speckled with starlight. Moving without thinking, I picked up Mr. Squeaks's cage and carried him outside to the White House lawn. I opened the small gate of his cage but he simply stood there, the gentle evening wind gently ruffling his feathers.

"I'm going to miss you, little one," I said to the confused bird. "But you're too full of life to be trapped in here. No one deserves to be locked in a cage, least of all a beautiful creature like you."

Gingerly, Mr. Squeaks hopped to the edge of the cage. He slowly flapped his wings before he suddenly soared off. I watched as he glided and circled above me for a few seconds before spreading his wings wide and darting farther into the distance until I could no longer see him.

A small wave of bittersweet joy swept over me as I freed Mr. Squeaks. It felt freeing to know I had done the right thing to let him out of his prison. He was a bird, not a slave or criminal. He deserved to live on his own terms, out there among the trees and clouds.

And in a way, the small act helped me to feel as if I'd been released from my past and present pain and trauma.

Yet even though I felt free, I could see that Mac was still suffering . . . still trapped in his own mental and emotional prison.

I couldn't stand watching him go through his own inner turmoil. With each passing day, Mac's method of dealing with his hurt turned him into someone I barely recognized. He was steadily declining, and I knew he was headed toward an inevitable crash.

And there was nothing I could do to stop it.

Chapter 17

Unfortunately, the crash came sooner than I expected . . .

"Lizzie! You have to come quick!"

Kathy barged into my quarters, and my head jerked up at the other maid's agitated tone. Her face was twisted in panic, and I dropped the book by Voltaire the president had loaned me.

"Why?" I demanded, jumping up to my feet. "What is it?"

"It's Mac."

"What?" My heart jumped to my throat. "What's wrong with him?"

"The First Lady asked me to come find you. He's . . . he's not acting like himself."

"What do you mean?" I asked as I darted past her and out of my quarters. I was determined to find my husband and see for myself what Kathy was talking about.

"I don't quite know," Kathy said, following close behind me. "I heard he may have had a meltdown after he dropped the president and—"

My hand flew to my throat. *What?*

Kathy nodded fervently. "Mr. Fredericks was explaining

everything to Mrs. Roosevelt. They're in the president's chambers. Dr. McIntire is with them now."

I didn't realize how fast I could move until I found myself half running, half walking down the long corridor to the president's suite. Kathy was right at my heels. When I couldn't contain my anxiety any longer, I fully ran the rest of the way to the president's chambers.

The First Lady stood outside her husband's door with Mr. Fredericks and another Secret Service man. She looked just as anxious as I felt.

"Lizzie, thank goodness. I don't know what's gotten into Mac, but he's behaving completely out of character."

"What do you mean?"

"One minute he's shouting at Franklin that there are people out to kill him, that none of us care about whether he lives or dies. Then the next, he's crying uncontrollably. At one point he was babbling on about the pain he's had to endure all his life. I was hoping you could make sense of all this."

I shook my head faintly, though I had a slight inclination as to what he might be rambling about. Mrs. Roosevelt led me into the very dim room. The president sat in his bed, already clad in his pajamas. He appeared a bit disheveled but otherwise fine.

In the corner of the large bedroom, I found Mac slouched in an armchair with Mr. Roosevelt's personal physician, Dr. Ross McIntire, bent over him. As I moved in closer, I saw that Mac's eyes were glassy and red-rimmed. I briefly wondered if it was a result of too much crying—or too much drink.

"Is everything all right with him, Doctor?" I asked.

The highly ranked naval physician straightened and turned to me. "He'll be fine, Mrs. McDuffie. He just suffered a minor mental break, is all."

I frowned, not liking the sound of that. I thought of Louise Little and her current confinement at the Kalamazoo Mental Hospital in Michigan. I didn't think I could handle it if Mac met with a similar fate.

I turned to the doctor. "What will happen to him now?"

"Well, his mind has been under some heavy duress," Dr. McIntire began. "He's clearly been under a lot of stress, and the heavy drinking doesn't help. But, all in all, he should be fine. Nothing a bit of rest and water won't cure. There's nothing to worry about."

"Mac?" I moved closer to where he sat, his eyes shut as if he was too ashamed to face anyone in the room. I understood it because I too was ashamed. "Mac, how are you feeling?"

Please talk to me.

My silent plea was answered when Mac slowly opened his eyes.

"I'm sorry, Lizzie," was all he said.

"It's all right, honey," I said gently. "Though you had us all worried there. How do you feel now?"

"I'm fine now. I think I'd like to head to my quarters now." Mac slowly rose to his feet and turned to the president. "I'm sorry, Boss. I didn't mean to cause so much trouble tonight."

"I thought you had slowed down on the drinking," President Roosevelt said. "If it's your leg, let Dr. McIntire take a look at it and see what we can do about your pain."

"No, no, it's not my leg, sir. It's . . . it's . . ."

"It's a personal family matter," I finished for him. "But we're working through it."

I glanced at Mac, and the look of relief in his glassy eyes made me glad I had interjected.

"Well, whatever the issue, we're all worried about you, Mac," Mrs. Roosevelt said. "You're damaging your health with all this heavy drinking."

"I understand, Mrs. Roosevelt," Mac said. "And I'm sorry. It won't happen again."

His hands were trembling, and I was afraid he would begin crying uncontrollably again.

"It's been a long night for us all. I'll get Mac into bed and we'll let you all get on with your evening." I took Mac's arm and led him toward the door. "Good night, Mr. President. Good night, Mrs. Roosevelt."

"Good night, Lizzie," the president said. "I trust you'll take good care of our Mac."

I nodded toward the couple and Dr. McIntire before slipping through the door with Mac in tow. Kathy was still waiting outside the bedroom when we walked out. She pushed away from the wall she had been leaning against when she saw us. Her dark, worried eyes darted between Mac and me.

"Is everything all right now?" she asked.

"For the most part," I said, feeling more weary by the minute. "I'll explain everything tomorrow. Right now, I need to get Mac into bed."

"Yes, of course."

We all started down the long corridor until we heard the First Lady call after me.

"Lizzie, may I have a word?"

I nodded. "Yes, of course."

I turned to Kathy and asked her to escort Mac to our room. As I made my way back to the First Lady, my heart was pounding in my chest.

"I'm very concerned about Mac's drinking," Mrs. Roosevelt began when I reached her side. "I know it's a problem he's struggled with for years, but I simply can't tolerate this lack of self-control.

Not any longer. My husband may not see it, but Mac is proving to be a danger to him. And to himself."

"Mrs. Roosevelt, I hope I'm not speaking out of turn, but Mac loves working for your husband. He would never intentionally do anything to put him in harm's way, and I can't let you think that. Mac may have made some mistakes in life, but he's not a threat to anyone."

The First Lady pursed her lips, and for a moment I wondered if this might be my and Mac's last night working for the Roosevelts.

"Lizzie, I don't question Mac's loyalty to my husband but as of late, he's proven not to be a good fit for the job any longer. Perhaps he should consider taking a break to gather himself and his senses."

I released a heavy breath and clasped my hands together, not all that surprised by her words.

"I wish a break was an option for us, Mrs. Roosevelt, but it simply is not. A good job for a Black man in this country is hard to come by. Mac's from Elbert County, Georgia, a country man to his core and a very hard worker. His mother was a slave and his father some white man who worked on the plantation. He's only received a few years of schooling, including a year of college and a few courses in night school. He's been through a lot to get himself to this position. And despite his leg injury, he has never shirked his duties."

A look of deep sympathy flashed across her eyes. "I understand all of that, Lizzie. I especially understand sacrifice and hard work. But I can't ignore what happened tonight. It's clear his recent incident down the stairs has affected him more than he cares to admit, and I believe those recent injuries are getting the best of him. We simply can't have him putting the president at risk like this."

I released another deep sigh, realizing there was no sense in keeping this from her any longer. "Mrs. Roosevelt, about that accident . . . I'm deeply sorry for having lied to you, but Mac didn't take a fall down the stairs."

The First Lady frowned as her eyes probed into mine. "Then what is the truth, Lizzie?"

"The other night, as we were heading back from dinner, we were attacked by a group of white men who mistook Mac for a white man out together with a Negro woman."

"Oh, dear God!" Mrs. Roosevelt exclaimed.

"They were clearly drunk," I continued. "But that didn't stop them from nearly killing Mac right there on the street. He was beaten badly by these men, had a bottle smashed on his head, until a stranger managed to convince them that he was simply a Negro man with a fair complexion."

The First Lady's lips were a flat, grim line. "I'm so sorry this happened to you both, Lizzie. I truly am. I wish there was something I could do. At the very least have those men arrested."

"I don't know who they were or where they were headed. What I do know is that it has really taken a toll on Mac and he's not been handling it very well."

"I can only imagine," she murmured. "Which makes me that much more concerned for him and his well-being. He's obviously been through a lot, and he is using drink to settle his problems."

"I promise we will get it under control, ma'am."

To my surprise, the First Lady took my hand in hers. "It's been my experience, Lizzie, that alcohol can have a certain hold on some people. My father was a victim to such afflictions, and nothing and no one could release him from its grip. It was up to him to set himself free. Unfortunately, his choices led to me becoming an orphan."

I blinked back the tears that threatened to overwhelm me. I could understand her pain, as I had also lost my father at a young age. Thankfully, though, I didn't have to see him lose himself to drink. But I certainly didn't want my husband's choices to make me a widow. We still had too much life to live and dreams to fulfill.

"Perhaps some time off from work would help him collect himself," Mrs. Roosevelt continued. "He's been working a bit too much, and I know that handling Franklin can be strenuous at times."

I nodded, appreciating her compassion and understanding. This wasn't a termination, and that filled me with great relief.

"I will talk it over with Mac. Help him understand that some time off may be the answer to getting him back on track."

"Absolutely. Every one of us could use a break from it all some days," she said, with a brief squeeze of my hand. "Please take care of him *and* yourself. I'll have Dr. McIntire check in on him tomorrow."

"Thank you, Mrs. Roosevelt."

As I headed back down the long empty corridor with the soft Persian rug stretching down the quiet halls, I thought about my words to Mac and how I would convince him to take some time off. Irvin Henry McDuffie was a proud man who refused to admit he had a problem with alcohol, much less ever admit to needing a mental and physical break from his duties.

By the time I entered our quarters, I could hear Mac in the bath.

"Mac?" I called.

"I'm fine!" he shouted in response.

I frowned. This was not the man I knew, much less the man I had married nearly thirty years ago.

"No, you are not fine, Mac. We need to talk about what happened tonight."

There was silence from the other side of the door. I sat down on the edge of our bed and waited patiently for him to finish his bath and come out.

But there would be no discussion this night.

When Mac finally emerged from the bathroom, he looked as weary as I felt, and he stopped me before I could get a word out.

"Lizzie, I have an awful headache and just want to get to bed. Let's talk tomorrow."

While we lay in bed, I stared up at the high ceiling and said a little prayer for my troubled husband. I prayed for his health and mind. I prayed for resilience and renewed strength. I prayed that he would come out of this dark place stronger than before.

I prayed harder than I ever had in my life.

THE NEXT DAY the president summoned us to his office.

True to her word, Mrs. Roosevelt had Dr. McIntire look in on Mac. I gathered it was the doctor's reporting after his exam that had the president calling for us.

I followed closely behind Mac into the Yellow Oval Office. The president was smoking a cigarette, and he gently blew out the fumes. The office smelled of fine cologne, with the brash scent of burning tobacco.

Mr. Roosevelt flashed us a smile as we walked into the room. "Mac, Lizzie, please have a seat."

"Good afternoon, Boss," Mac said as we took our seats in front of the president's desk. "I'm sorry I wasn't at my post this morning, but Mrs. Roosevelt ordered me to take the day off."

"As you should," the president said, stubbing out his cigarette in a small ashtray on his desk. "How are you feeling today?"

I watched as the small gleaming end of the cigarette dissolved into a dead mass of ashes. I couldn't guess what the president was thinking in that moment, but I knew today would be the day that everything changed between the two of them.

"I feel much better, Chief," Mac answered. "A lot better, even. The doc gave me something that helped me sleep better than I have in weeks."

"That's great to hear," Mr. Roosevelt said before turning his gaze to me. "And what about you, Lizzie?"

I was taken off guard by the question but quickly recovered. "I'm doing fine, sir. Thanks for asking."

"A guard told me he saw you freeing your bird the other night."

"I did . . . Mr. Squeaks was a gift I didn't know I needed at the time, and I thank you for him. But he's a bird. He's meant to fly free, and freeing him from his cage was what I felt I needed to do."

The president smiled and nodded. Then suddenly the smile fell from his lips as he glanced over at Mac.

"Mac, it's become apparent to us that this job is too much for you."

I glanced at Mac, then at the president, fearing what his next words would be.

Mac moved up to the edge of his seat. "But Mr. President, I have never complained about the job. I love working for you. I apologize for not being at my best last night, and for embarrassing you. For embarrassing my wife," he added, as he glanced over at me. "But I can promise you it will never happen again."

"There's no cause for alarm, Mac. I believe you, and I accept your apology. But I'm more concerned about your health. I know what a handful I can be, and I think you've earned a position that doesn't require you to be at my beck and call at every turn."

"But Boss—"

"Don't worry, Mac," the president interjected. "Our relationship hasn't strained and I'm not sending you away. I have arranged a job transfer to a less rigorous department here at the White House. You'll be working for Henry Morgenthau, the secretary of the treasury. He's a good man, and I think you'll come to like that position much better."

I released the breath that I didn't realize I was holding until now. A sense of relief filled me at the president's words. Mac and I would still be living together at the White House, even if we would no longer be working side by side.

Mac, however, did not see the opportunity the president was offering him.

"Please reconsider, Mr. President," Mac urged, shifting in his seat. "It is my utmost pleasure serving beside you. I would not trade that with any other position. I can still carry on with this job. I insist on carrying on with my duties until the end, sir."

I shifted my gaze between the president and Mac. I wanted to voice my own opinion, but I knew this was a decision Mac would have to come to accept himself.

Besides, when Mr. Roosevelt made up his mind, nothing could change it.

"Look, Mac," the president said. "I'm fully aware how demanding this job can be. You've been doing this for a very long time, and you've been doing a great job. But you've been doing it alone. You deserve some rest. For a man your age, it is time that you prioritize your health."

"Sir, if it's about my drinking—"

"No, Mac, this transfer is not connected to your drinking, and there's no need to allude to that. It's about giving you a break and making things easier for you. And if anyone asks, you can tell them you asked for the transfer because of the stress that comes with being my valet."

"I think that sounds like a fine plan," I finally whispered to

Mac, and I meant it. I could see the toll the job was now taking on him and knew it was time that he took a step back. "I've heard Mr. Morgenthau is a fair man, and a position in Washington would allow us to still live together."

Mac looked hesitant for a moment, before he finally nodded. I believed he had finally come to the realization that Mr. Roosevelt wasn't going to change his mind on this matter.

"When is my last day as your valet, sir?"

"I'm relieving you of your duties effective immediately, Mac. I have two men lined up to assume your position. Although I must admit I will miss your barbering skills."

Mac was silent for a moment, and I could only imagine what he was feeling. Relief? Disappointment? It was hard to tell, since he concealed so much of himself, even from me.

Suddenly, Mac rose to his feet and gave the president a mock salute. "It has been a pleasure working for you, sir. In fact, it's been a delightfully exhausting and grueling honor, Mr. President."

The president threw his head back and let out a shout of laughter at Mac's dramatic display of admiration. His amusement was contagious, and we all joined in his mirth.

Mr. Roosevelt extended his hand to Mac for a handshake. Mac took the president's hand in both of his in appreciation for his friendship and his kindness.

"Good luck to you, Mac."

"Thank you, Boss."

Later, Mr. Early finally confirmed for the press that Mac had officially left the service of the president and had obtained a position as a messenger for the Treasury Department. Mac received many letters congratulating him on his fine job with the president and wishing him well. Mrs. Roosevelt wrote him a fine tribute in her column, and the *Washington Herald* sent him flowers. Mac was the first Washington Negro to be cited by the *Herald*, and the story appeared all over the country.

He deserved every bit of praise. No one has ever been as efficient, as dedicated, or as skilled at their job as Irvin "Mac" McDuffie. This was evident when it ultimately took two valets and a barber to fill my husband's shoes.

Though I missed having Mac by my side regularly, I was at peace knowing my husband had finally found peace.

I maintained my position at the White House, as there was still important work to be done. So long as Franklin Delano Roosevelt was president, I intended to use my position—however big or small—to continue my crusade.

Chapter 18

September 3, 1939
White House

> "I am speaking to you from the Cabinet Room at 10 Downing Street."

That opening line sent shivers down my spine.

Kathy and I sat in my living quarters with the radio turned up high. We leaned forward with great interest, though we already suspected what the British wanted to announce to the world.

> "This morning the British ambassador in Berlin handed the German government a final note stating that unless we heard from them by eleven o'clock that they were prepared at once to withdraw their troops from Poland, a state of war would exist between us. I have to tell you now that no such undertaking has been received, and that consequently this country is at war with Germany."

Occasionally, the radio would static, and I would give it a firm tap to bring it back to life.

"You can imagine what a bitter blow it is to me that all my long struggle to win peace has failed . . ."

I glanced at Kathy as Prime Minister Neville Chamberlain continued his address. Aside from the static of the radio, the silence between us was almost impossible to bear. The tension had built inside me, and I could feel a cold sense of fear and uncertainty lodge in my throat.

"If you ask me," Kathy said, finally breaking the silence between us, "white people going to war is none of our business."

I knew better than to think that, so I couldn't necessarily agree or disagree with her. History had shown us that the decisions white people made always affected everyone, especially the Negro.

"It's like the Great War all over again," I said instead. "I just hope they don't pull the country into yet another European war. We have enough going on in this country to keep us occupied for decades."

"Exactly," Kathy said with a brisk nod. "Do you know there were reports of a man who had gone missing for days in New York, only to be found in a sewer with his neck broken, half eaten by rats?"

My hands flew to my throat. "My God!"

"Do you know what the cops did?"

"What?"

"Nothing. They ruled his death an accident. Of course, he was probably lynched," Kathy continued. "But they would never admit that."

I sighed, hating to hear stories like this, but I knew it was a scenario that happened more often than we would ever know. Perhaps this war was the inevitable end that would swallow this world whole.

Over the next few days, the air around the White House became heavy. There were a number of visitors arriving in expensive cars, wearing suits that looked expensive even from afar. They were businessmen, political delegates, and some foreign nationals.

Since the White House had begun to receive so many visitors, my work was never at an end. There were more beds to make, more cleaning to finish, more running around to do. Mrs. Roosevelt would tell Mrs. Nesbitt and us maids that we would be expecting twenty guests for one occasion, only for that number to easily swell to forty or fifty.

Eventually, I began finding myself having trouble keeping up with the pace and schedule of what was required to keep the White House functioning. Having to remember which rooms were clean, which rooms were not, how best to clean a hundred-year-old antique without breaking it, or making the long, strenuous walk down the lengthy corridors that stretched from end to end only added to my stress.

Yet, I had to count my blessings . . .

My troubles were nothing compared to those of the everyday Negro who struggled through Jim Crow America. Young boys who could not have been more than eighteen years old were lynched in Missouri and Texas for no apparent reason. I couldn't understand why the anti-lynching bill couldn't get past Congress, because the savage killing of Negroes didn't seem to be coming to an end any time soon. I couldn't believe how, in 1939, colored men and women could still be hung and burned—and nothing would be done about it.

At the beginning of the war, the president's position was as clear as Easter Sunday: America was neither for nor against England and France.

Every day, I prayed that this war would come to an abrupt end. It wasn't even our war to fight. Yet it appeared to be spreading, like tiny dots of flame on a large expense of dry bush, spreading its embers bit by bit until it reached across the ocean to our land.

I wasn't prepared to have this conversation with the president, but one morning I found myself doing just that. As I cleaned around his study, I found him staring out the window. He looked like a man who hadn't slept in days.

"Uneasy lies the head that wears the crown," I said, as I dusted the bookshelf behind his desk.

Mr. Roosevelt turned his gaze from the window and regarded me curiously. "Let me guess . . . Shakespeare?"

I nodded. "You appear to have a lot on your mind, sir. Is everything all right?"

The president reclined in his seat, then gestured to the available chair in front of his desk. "Why don't you take a break, Lizzie."

"Thank you, sir, but—"

"Please. I insist."

He remained unsmiling, a grim expression plastered on his face, as I moved to take the empty seat before him.

"How's Mac liking his new position with Henry?"

"He's liking it just fine, Mr. President," I assured him. "Though he misses working for you, of course."

The president let out a dry laugh. "I'm sure he doesn't, but thank you for the reassurance, Lizzie."

I didn't know what to say to that, so I chose to say nothing. A brief silence fell between us before he spoke again.

"Change is never easy, but oftentimes it's necessary."

I shrugged. "Yes, and sometimes it's inevitable."

Like the sudden end of the UGE.

That was a change I had reluctantly come to accept. Since the Congress of Industrial Organizations, with the backing of the American Federation of Labor, had begun organizing government workers, the United Government Employees union was no longer needed, and a part of me was sad to see all the hard work wasted that I, Edgar, and many of the other board members had put into it.

Just last summer, nearly ten thousand Negro women took to the streets of Washington to protest against the limitations of the New Deal programs. It was no secret that some of these programs, like the Works Progress Administration and the National Youth Administration, were preventing these women from earning a living wage. In addition, these women had limited access to government relief programs and were being excluded from receiving Social Security benefits. As a board member of the UGE, I had lent my voice in support of these women, and soon we had grown UGE's membership by the thousands and had seen some progress for these women.

That was probably one of my proudest accomplishments, as I could easily see my family and friends in these women. I saw myself in these women. Though I was blessed with the opportunity to work with the Roosevelts and build a relationship with them that offered me certain privileges, I couldn't forget that these were women who looked like me but hadn't been given the same opportunities.

And now that the CIO and AFL had taken over the unionization of government employees, the UGE had been dismantled. But I couldn't forget that during its short existence, we had made huge strides in creating change in the labor force for colored people.

"That is very true," the president said, pulling me back to our current conversation on change. "Next year we are facing yet another election, and yet there is still so much that hasn't been accomplished."

I tilted my head to the side. "Is that what you think, Mr. President? Because from where I'm sitting, you have done more for the country these past two terms than any other president in my lifetime."

The president reclined again in his wheelchair and sighed. "Well, there's more to be done, but I fear I will have to dismantle some of the social programs we've worked hard to create just to make room for this war."

My frown deepened. That couldn't be so. The New Deal programs were still fairly new, and many of them were still not catering to as many Negroes as they should. How could he even consider dismantling them when many Americans were still relying on these programs to get out of the economic crisis?

"But Chief, I thought we were staying out of the war."

Mr. Roosevelt sighed. "Believe me, it is not my desire to get involved in this looming war, but I sincerely do not know how long our neutrality can last if it drags on longer. We have allies in the west of Europe who are turning to us for support."

"You're not wrong for steering clear of this war, Mr. President," I assured him. "We have our own wars right here at home to settle. Like with Congress, for example. They have been at war with the NAACP over this anti-lynching bill."

The president pursed his lips. I knew it was a subject he wasn't a fan of addressing, but to ignore the fact that it was a major issue for our community—and for the country—would be negligent on my part.

"Now, that matter isn't as simple to tackle as you may believe,

Lizzie. No one can deny that lynchings are a stain in our country's legacy. But timing is everything, and right now . . . it's just not the right time to tackle that mammoth of a cause."

"When will be the right time then, sir? Because a lot of colored people are still living in fear of being attacked for no good reason other than the color of their skin. While Congress makes every effort to filibuster any anti-lynching bill that comes before it, our people are in constant danger of being mutilated and murdered."

He looked away and gazed out the large window again. Typically, I tried not to use such vivid imagery when discussing these kinds of matters with the president. But if this was to be his last term in office, I needed to do my best to make him understand how important this issue was to our community.

"I know it may appear that I do not support this bill, Lizzie," he said, turning his gaze back to me. "But that couldn't be farther from the truth. If I could pass this bill without repercussions from my own party, which would put all the other important bills before Congress at risk, I would sign it into law immediately."

I believed him. There was so much conviction in his eyes when he spoke.

"But like the NAACP, I too am at war with Congress. The southern Democrats have not been subtle about where they stand on this bill, and I can't risk losing the southern vote to the Republicans."

"Why would it matter, Mr. President, when you have a lot of support and votes from Negro voters? Like myself, many have left the Republican Party and have become registered Democrats in support of you. You can't simply forget about us."

The corners of his lips turned down as he regarded me with a mixture of dejection and regret. "Believe me, Lizzie, I haven't. I'm quite aware of how your people's political migration has helped me win two terms. And I certainly credit you and Mac for garnering me that much support."

"We wouldn't have done it if we hadn't believed in you, Chief. And we still believe in you, but there's also still a lot of work to be done. Right here at home."

He nodded. "I agree. But there are also certain matters outside of my control that cannot go ignored."

"What do you mean, sir?"

This time he released a heavy sigh. "I mean war, Lizzie. This conflict with Germany may not end the way we want it to. Only time will tell just how far it will spread."

"I think you should hold on to your resolve, sir, and keep the country out of it. There's no need for America to get involved in another senseless foreign war."

"War has always been senseless, Lizzie," Mr. Roosevelt said. "But as you said, sometimes change is inevitable."

I swallowed hard. Although I was too familiar with change and its inevitability, I had to wonder if the president's change of heart toward the war was truly necessary.

More importantly, what else would it change?

Chapter 19

June 29, 1940
White House

Nylon stockings.

They were all the rage these days, but I didn't understand the fanfare.

I stared at my legs in the mirror of the small boutique, not sure if I liked the look of the sheer material on my round and plump legs. The thin material did feel smooth and comfortable against my skin, but I couldn't be sure if they looked at all flattering.

"They look lovely on you, Mrs. McDuffie," the young female clerk said from behind me, as if reading my mind.

I turned to her and smiled, appreciating the small compliment even if it was a lie. "Thank you, dear. I couldn't decide if I like them on me or not."

"Well, they do look flattering," the young woman insisted, reminding me of my goddaughter Hazel, who always had a way of making me feel younger than my now fifty-nine years. "They smooth out your skin and take about ten years off your legs. Would you like me to ring up two pairs for you?"

I hesitated, then shrugged. "Sure, why not."

The shopping trip had been a way for me to treat myself, anyway. It had been a busy past few weeks, and with Mac working in Atlanta currently, it had been a lonely time too. I had finally gotten a day off and was taking the time to spoil myself. Kathy would typically join me on these shopping trips, but she was spending her time off with her family. And though I usually didn't mind the company, I found the solo trip away from the bustle of the White House to be a much-needed break.

As I paid for my things and left the dress shop, I ran into a newsboy selling today's paper. I could see from where I stood that the headline was about the recent Republican Party convention that had just taken place in Philadelphia. Apparently an attorney from New York, one Wendell Willkie, had been nominated by the party to run for president in the upcoming November election, and that was all I cared to hear about the matter.

I didn't want to see or read about anything remotely political today.

As I made my way down the row of shops, trying my best to enjoy the solitude and summer weather, a man in a brown suit ran across the street toward me.

I instantly recognized him and groaned inwardly.

It was Mr. Albert Jackson.

"Mrs. McDuffie! Mrs. Lizzie McDuffie!"

I stopped in my tracks and waited for the approaching man. Coincidentally, I had recently read his column about the brewing war in Europe and the president's decision to not get the United States involved. To my surprise, the column had commended the president's decision—then went on to criticize him about the rumors of a third presidential run.

"Good day, Mr. Jackson."

The journalist raised a dark brow in obvious surprise. "What a delight. And here I thought you would struggle to remember my name."

"My memory is my best feature, Mr. Jackson. I never forget a name or a face."

"I don't doubt it, Mrs. McDuffie. I've heard all about your talent for recitation. I myself, however, can be quite forgetful."

That wasn't much of a surprise. The man tended to forget that every one of our latest encounters ended with some disagreement or debate. Yet he insisted on meeting under these false pleasantries.

"Somehow I find that hard to believe, Mr. Jackson," I said. "Now, how may I help you today?"

The man chuckled. "Straight to the point. I like that." Suddenly he pulled out a notepad and pen. "Is it true that there was a rift between the president and his former valet?"

I frowned. "His former valet?"

"Yes, ma'am. Your husband, Mr. McDuffie."

"Where did you hear that?"

"I have my sources. And according to them, the president fired your husband because of his alleged drinking problem."

My frown deepened. I hated how he stated it so matter-of-factly.

"Well, sir, your *sources* are wrong. There was no rift between my husband and the president. And quite frankly, their relationship is none of your business."

I walked around the man and continued on my way, not bothering to excuse myself. Of course, Mr. Jackson followed right alongside me. He struggled to match my much slower pace so as not to walk ahead of me.

"I mean no disrespect, Mrs. McDuffie. As a concerned Negro who knows how influential you and your husband have been within the White House, I simply just want to get the truth of the matter out to the people. Many are concerned that with your husband's departure and the rise of this European war, the president's interest in the Afro-American struggle for equality will be even more limited."

"Let's get one thing straight, Mr. Jackson," I began. "My husband wasn't fired by the president. He was transferred because of his own personal, health-related matters. The president and my husband's time together ended quite amicably, and while I'm still employed at the White House, I will continue to advocate for the rights of our people."

Mr. Jackson jotted a few things in his notepad, never breaking his stride with mine. "One more question, Mrs. McDuffie, if you don't mind."

I sighed and stopped in my tracks. "Just one, Mr. Jackson. Then I would like to go about my day. Alone."

"There have been rumors of the president running for a third term. Is this true?"

I shrugged. "The president hasn't said a word about it."

"Do you support the idea?"

"Who wouldn't?"

"Myself, for one."

I wasn't at all surprised. "Well, I think the people believe in President Roosevelt enough to support a third run for him. In fact, they may want it more than he does. With all that's going on, he's perhaps the best leader we have right now."

"I was in England not too long ago, Mrs. McDuffie. Things are not so good there. There is a war in Europe that has taken the attention of the world, yet when I returned home, I came back to find that life here was just as I had left it. No one is worried about the struggling American, never mind the downtrodden Negro."

"You strike me as an intelligent man, Mr. Jackson. You and I both know that if America gets involved in this war, there won't be any advantages for us. The Negro will fight for his country, and all we can hope is that he's not forgotten in the process."

"Elbert Williams."

"Pardon?"

"Another forgotten Negro, Mrs. McDuffie. He was one of the five founding members of the NAACP branch out in Brownsville, Tennessee. Nine days ago, he was lynched for trying to register the Negroes of Brownsville to vote. Can you believe the irony? Being lynched for trying to exercise your rights as an American, all the while as your government, your very president, turns his back on you."

The news of the recent lynching turned my stomach. Chills ran down my arms despite the summer weather as I thought back to all the NAACP meetings I had attended over the years and whether I had ever run across Mr. Williams.

"I'm a journalist, Mrs. McDuffie," Mr. Jackson continued, as if recognizing my discomfort. "And I'm also a realist. Despite what President Roosevelt says, he could do more to help us pass this bill. And he should. He owes us that much."

I didn't disagree with him, but I knew better than to verbally agree with him.

"I can't make any promises, Mr. Jackson, but I'll try to find a way to broach the subject with the president. Let him know about the concerns still surrounding our community."

"Please do. Because from what I witnessed in England, time is not on our side, and I believe the president would gladly spur this country into war without a second thought if it meant some kind of gain for the country. And the minute that happens . . . well, I think we both know what that would mean to the welfare of our people."

I knew exactly what it would mean, but it was a scenario I didn't want to think about.

"Well then, Mr. Jackson, be prepared to put down your pen and paper and pick up a tommy gun."

The reporter's eyes squinted down at me as his dark gaze regarded me stoically. "I admire your sense of humor, Mrs. McDuffie. Unfortunately, I can't share in your lightheartedness when there are a lot of issues for us to tackle right now. More specifically, getting this anti-lynching bill passed into law."

I sighed. "You're right, Mr. Jackson. My apologies. As I said, I will try my best . . ."

"I'm sure there are many who would appreciate that. I, for one, most certainly would. You're my closest shot to gaining access to President Roosevelt. I suspect someone in the White House is blocking me from meeting with the man."

And I wouldn't be surprised if that man blocking the reporter's access was Stephen Early. Though his name continued to spring up in more publications aside from the Allied Negro Papers, Mr. Jackson had quickly managed to develop a reputation in Washington as a pushy and over-the-top journalist.

But then again, Mr. Early was fast becoming known for his efforts in keeping the Negro community from gaining access to the president. Whereas Mr. Early was the stumbling block that many couldn't seem to get around, I made it my mission to continue to get as many letters and correspondents to Mr. and Mrs. Roosevelt as I could.

"Anyway, it's been a pleasure, Mrs. McDuffie." Mr. Jackson stretched out his hand. "Now if you'll excuse me, I think I see a hat I'd like to purchase for my fiancée."

I shook his hand weakly then watched as the burly man crossed to the other side of the street and retreated into a small boutique.

I stood there for a moment, resentful at how easy it was for this one journalist to rattle my world and leave me with much to think about. I sighed, deciding to cut my shopping trip short.

So much for my day away from politics.

NOVEMBER 5 HAD finally arrived.

Unlike the last two elections, this one was filled with naysayers regarding the president's decision to run again for a third term. His nomination in July at the Democratic Party convention didn't come without criticism, but Mr. Roosevelt felt it necessary to continue as leader in the face of the growing conflict in Europe.

Many of us supported him; however, Jim Farley—his close friend and adviser for so many years—did oppose his decision to run for a third term. Mac and I both liked Mr. Farley and we were sorry to see his friendship with the boss break up. I believe it was caused by gossips who kept repeating that Farley was not a real friend but was using Mr. Roosevelt to further his own ambitions, and that Farley wanted to be the next president. I can't be sure that was the case. I truly believed Mr. Farley was just a traditionalist who didn't want Mr. Roosevelt to break from the two-term tradition that had been in place since President Washington.

Another in the president's administration who opposed his run for a third term was Vice President John Nance Garner. It was believed that he too wanted to run for the office. Ultimately, Garner was replaced by Henry Wallace, a replacement made personally by Mr. Roosevelt. Mac liked Mr. Wallace especially well, but I could never feel the confidence in him that I felt in Mr. Roosevelt.

During this particular election, which was the most controversial yet, I found myself campaigning for President Roosevelt again, but it did not come without its challenges. I went on to speak in cities in Indiana, Illinois, Ohio, and Pennsylvania. I was asked all sorts of questions. Mundane questions like . . .

> *How many rooms are in the White House?*
> *Can Mr. Roosevelt walk at all?*
> *Is he always as genial as he seems?*
> *Do Mr. and Mrs. Roosevelt get any privacy?*
> *What is Mrs. Roosevelt's favorite flower?*

Now, the flower question had originally been asked of me during the presidential campaign back in '36. This time my reply was that it was the pansy and not the sunflower, as I had led so many to believe.

Then there were others who didn't care one whit about the Roosevelts' personal lives. Those individuals wanted to know why the president felt he deserved a third term. They wanted to know his position on the growing crisis with Nazi Germany and what that would mean to America. Then there were those who still questioned if he had done enough to protect the social, physical, and economic welfare of the Negro.

Once I had a speech interrupted by a man heckling.

"Why has Mr. Roosevelt never publicly denounced lynching?"

Thank goodness I was able to quote a speech by Mr. Roosevelt, in which the president did just that in a broadcast on December 6, 1933, before the Federal Council of Churches.

> "This new generation is not content with preachings against the vile form of collective murder—lynching—which has broken out in our midst anew. We know that it is murder, a deliberate and definite disobedience of the Commandment: 'Thou shalt not

kill.' We do not excuse those in high places or in low who condone lynch law."

I later mailed the man a complete copy of the speech.

Some might argue that this speech had not led to any actionable policies from the president, but I would counter that it at least revealed his position on the horrific crime. He had nothing to gain by sharing his thoughts on the subject, and I believed he deserved some credit for speaking his mind at that moment.

However, I couldn't ignore that even now the anti-lynching bill had been filibustered to death by Congress. Walter White would often speak out against the president and his administration's lack of support for the bill. In many of his speeches at the NAACP meetings, he would often state: *"What the white supremacists are fighting for is the right to continue to terrorize colored people without the government checking them and locking them in jail. It makes no sense!"*

With such a bold statement, it made it hard to garner support for the president's third run. Sometimes all I wanted to do was just melt into the shadows of the crowd and pretend that I was just a regular, everyday Negro woman. I wanted to go back to the time when I was never the Roosevelts' maid and none of this was my responsibility. All I wanted was to go back to Atlanta and be with my husband.

But there was no going back.

The letters didn't stop coming, no matter how much I wanted a break from it all. There were lots of colored people across the country who wrote to me, fully expecting me to tender their letters and concerns to the president. His careful decision to pardon wrongfully jailed Negro men may have angered the southern elite who needed an excuse for keeping colored folks in chains, but it also served to embolden Negro Americans to stand up against inequality and hate. There were thousands of wrongfully detained people across the country whose families would send letters about the injustices they faced. I was the bridge between the president and our people, and so many were counting on that.

So I went out and advocated for him once again.

There were times I spoke in four or five city precincts in one evening. It was as exhausting as it was exciting. Because of my campaigning, the *Afro-American* newspaper was kind enough to name me one of their eight Women of the Year earlier that year.

However, the stress of it all was steadily building around the White House.

Once, after a rally in the Democratic headquarters in Pittsburgh, an elderly white man called me over to say, "*I was born in Virginia. My parents owned slaves. I never thought I would live to see a colored woman campaigning for a Democrat! How I enjoyed your speech.*"

White or Black, I was glad to be able to convince anyone who would listen that President Roosevelt was the leader we needed. These were unprecedented times and there was no question that Franklin Delano Roosevelt would steer us on the right path.

Back from these tours, I would have a conference with the chief, reporting to him the things that I thought would interest him. The report always included the assurance that we would win.

And we did.

On November 5, 1940, President Roosevelt once again won in a landslide.

Chapter 20

December 4, 1941
White House

M r. President, why don't you put Fala where he belongs?" I said as I scratched the back of the black Scottish terrier. "He's too temperamental to be in the White House. He belongs in Hollywood."

Mr. Roosevelt laughed. "Well, he may get there yet."

In response, Fala moved away from me and lay across the president's feet. I shook my head, not taking it personally. Everyone in the White House—as well as those in Hyde Park and Warm Springs—knew just how temperamental the adorable little dog was. He had been since his arrival to the White House shortly after the president's reelection victory last November. Though I suspected Fala especially saved a lot of his sass just for me, and I knew exactly why . . .

One morning while I was quite busy, Fala came up to me and stretched out, inviting me to start scratching him. I had responded, *"Oh, run along, Fala. I'm too busy now."* For a month, the little dog had nothing more to do with me. It wasn't until

Mr. Roosevelt was away from Hyde Park and Fala was put up in a pen that the dog finally capitulated and we became friends again.

So as not to fall behind on my tasks, I continued with my cleaning of the president's bedroom. The air in the large chamber smelled of tobacco and freshly brewed coffee. The unassuming Arthur Prettyman, the president's new valet, remained quiet and discreet as he cleared the chief's breakfast tray. Ever since Mac's replacement came on board, I didn't serve the president the way I did when I was assisting Mac, but I was still allowed into his chambers to clean.

"Lizzie, when will Mac be getting into town?"

I smiled, excited just by the thought. "This weekend, sir."

"Very good. Don't forget to have him stop by my study next week. I'd like to give him his Christmas gift before you both leave for the holiday."

"Yes, I'll remind him."

Usually, that was a task that he would give to Miss LeHand, but ever since her collapse this past summer, she too was forced into taking a leave of absence. Miss Grace Tully had taken over Miss LeHand's duties, but everyone could tell the relationship wasn't the same. The light had dimmed in the president's eyes after Miss LeHand's collapse, and it was clear that her diminishing health had affected him greatly. Many who had originally doubted Mac's "story" were now starting to believe that working for President Roosevelt was as strenuous as he claimed.

Unfortunately, Miss LeHand's stroke left her partially paralyzed and unable to work anywhere. For a woman that young and smart, I could only imagine the frustration of being limited in such a way. Every day I sent a prayer up for her—and every day, I sent up a prayer of thanks that Mac had not suffered a similar fate.

When the weekend finally arrived, my focus was on making up for the days Mac and I had not seen each other, which had been since the president's last trip to Warm Springs for Thanksgiving.

Despite the fact that Mac no longer worked at the White House, we still managed to enjoy the holidays together. This year was no exception.

This past Thanksgiving was also a testament to not only how sharp Mr. Roosevelt's memory was, but how much he was beloved.

It was no secret that the president loved to carve the turkey at their big Thanksgiving dinner. This year, a pretty big gift arrived at Warm Springs. It was a huge turkey delivered to the Little White House, "compliments of Sylvester Harris." Arthur Prettyman and I took the crate in for him to see the turkey. I handed the card to the president and waited to remind him who Sylvester Harris was. But the minute Mr. Roosevelt read the name, his face broke into a smile.

"Why, it's from Sylvester Harris! I wonder how his farm is these days."

Many years before, Mr. Roosevelt had heard of Mr. Harris under rather peculiar circumstances. Mac, who had been in his employ at the time, had rolled the president into his study one evening when the telephone began to ring. Usually Miss LeHand was there to take care of the calls, and of course, it was only the most important ones that she would put through to the president's line. Since Mr. Roosevelt was a little early that time and Miss LeHand had not yet arrived at the Little White House, the president picked up the phone himself.

"Is this President Roosevelt?" asked a voice with a southern drawl. *"My name is Sylvester Harris. I have been calling all day. I thought they never were going to put me through."*

"All right. What can I do for you?"

"It's about a mule. I can't get my crop in unless I have a mule to plow . . ."

The president was in a high good humor by the time he hung up the phone with Mr. Harris. He promised the old Mississippi Negro farmer to "look into it," and soon after, the farmer received a mule. Apparently, this particular Thanksgiving, Sylvester Harris remembered the president's generosity—and so did Mr. Roosevelt.

Unfortunately, these were the small gestures that the everyday American didn't get to witness, much less hear about. We were closing in on a year into Mr. Roosevelt's third term as president, yet many were beginning to forget the progress we'd made as a nation since Mr. Roosevelt came into office. Many were forgetting how the president had pulled the country out of an economic crisis, creating jobs and social programs that helped the everyday American begin to thrive again.

But I also had to remember that most people's memories were short, and if I wanted to help the president continue to succeed, I needed to keep the people from forgetting how far we'd come since 1933.

Earlier that week, Mac and I attended a special meeting held by the NAACP. While Mac never spoke at any NAACP gathering, he had been invited to say a few words. Everyone was curious to know what the president's former valet thought about the chief's unprecedented third term. Because Mac was no longer at the White House, I felt many believed his position and opinions would be the most neutral and honest.

Knowing the bond and loyalty Mac had for the president, I wasn't at all worried about him fumbling before the crowd. I knew Mac would speak from his heart.

I sat there in the front row, watching as he climbed up to the podium and stood behind the lectern. This was the first time he would speak in front of a crowd, and though I was surprised he had agreed to it, I was also very proud of him for stepping outside his comfort zone to express himself.

"As Negroes," Mac began, "we fight wars every day . . ."

The crowd murmured in agreement. Mac may not have been formally educated, but he was extremely well-read, even more so than many men who had received a college degree. Because of the time he had spent with Mr. Roosevelt, he kept his mind sharp with classical literature and philosophy.

Mac went on to move the crowd with a testimony of his own struggles with personal failures and his physical and emotional pain. He didn't necessarily go into detail, and he didn't have to. His short speech moved everyone in the room, and a quick glance around revealed just how much everyone was relating to him. For the first time, I witnessed him opening himself up, being vulnerable, and it left me feeling closer to him than I had in a long time.

"No one can deny that we as a people have suffered a lot," Mac continued. "Not only in this country, but around the world. While there's a war going on in Europe, no one speaks of the Afro-Germans who are also being slaughtered at the hands of the Nazis. Our people are being attacked from all fronts, are being treated as second-class citizens everywhere, but we must continue to exercise our rights as American citizens. We must continue to speak out, march, and protest against injustice. Despite everyone fighting against us, we cannot lose hope. We cannot lose our fire."

The applause in the room was deafening. Tears blurred my eyes at the immense pride I felt in that moment for my husband. No one knew exactly just how much those words were directed to himself as they were to the crowd. But I knew. Mac had battled many demons—literally and figuratively—and had come out stronger for it.

However, the few days following Mac's speech were tense.

The war in Europe was continuing to escalate and it was becoming almost impossible for the president to keep the country from getting involved. The threat of it possibly spreading even farther west left the air around the White House heavy with uncertainty. It left little room for conversation with the president, which meant that left little opportunity for me to raise pressing concerns that mattered most in our community.

I could already sense the shift within the president. His focus and attention centered more around the growing war—and trying to keep the country in a position of neutrality—than it was on anything else. And my fear was that if the country entered this war, so many issues—and so many of our people—would go forgotten.

My fears were confirmed that Sunday afternoon.

Myself and a few of the staff were having lunch in the servants' dining room when Kathy came bursting in, frantic.

"Turn on the radio!" she shouted. "Switch it on, quick!"

Someone rushed over to where a radio sat on the cabinet, accidentally knocking off some pans and cutlery in the process.

"What's going on?" I asked as I made my way closer to the radio.

Kathy didn't answer.

The radio sparked to life and we all stood in stark silence as the gruff voice of the radio announcer came on the air and reported the tragic news.

A U.S. naval base had been attacked by the Japanese.

I covered my mouth in stunned disbelief and fell against the nearest wall. I knew this attack could not go ignored. Nor would it. In that moment, we all knew that the United States had just been violently thrust into this war.

I heaved a deep sigh and stared out the window, as if I could see all the hopes and goals of our people being diminished in the afternoon light. In that moment, I felt my spirit being gutted.

The next day, a little past noon, President Roosevelt went on the radio and his address to Congress was broadcasted live throughout the nation.

I sat in my quarters, this time with Kathy at my side. With Mac back in Atlanta, I hadn't wanted to be alone during such an uncertain time. The younger woman sat across from me, a blank expression on her face as we stared at the radio.

"Yesterday, December 7, 1941, a date which will live in infamy—the United States of America was suddenly and deliberately attacked by the naval and air forces of the Empire of Japan . . ."

I exchanged glances with Kathy as we listened to the president's voice come alive through the speakers. There were no words for what I was feeling in that moment. All I knew for certain was that it was the end of everything. The United States would join the war, and a lot of Negro men would be called to go overseas to fight for their country—a country that wouldn't fight for them.

"With confidence in our armed forces, with the unbounding determination of our people, we will gain the inevitable triumph—so help us God . . ."

When I stared at Kathy, there was a look of helplessness in her eyes that I was certain mirrored my own. I shut off the radio, unable to listen anymore. The biting realization that everything would change after this moment, that everything we had struggled to get the president's attention on would fizzle into obscurity, left me feeling afraid for our country . . . and terrified for our future.

Chapter 21

The bombing of Pearl Harbor continued to shake the country to its core.

It also exposed a side of Mr. Roosevelt that I had never seen before. It was an ugly, retaliatory side that I never would have imagined he possessed. But it finally presented itself when he signed into law Executive Order 9066.

The recent order would force hundreds of thousands of Japanese American men, women, and children into internment camps. And I could not fathom how that was any different than Hitler's concentration camps for the Jews.

I especially couldn't understand how he could move so quickly on a decision that would devastate the lives of so many innocent people, yet ignore the anti-lynching bill—a bill that could potentially protect and save so many others.

Then I would recall what he had done for Miss LeHand and how he had taken responsibility for all of her medical needs while she recovered from her stroke. Miss LeHand had even been brought back to the White House to be watched and cared for, though rumor had it that she was having a hard time adjusting to her life as an invalid.

Then there was the letter from Leroy Commons.

The multilingual war veteran who had written me nearly ten years ago had written again, and this time it was a happier letter. Mr. Commons was in New York doing very well, working in a government office where he was able to use his linguistic ability to translate weather reports. Apparently, the Negro war hero had wanted to let the president know how things had turned out for him, and to tell him how much he had appreciated those earlier efforts on his behalf.

One afternoon, I got a chance to speak to the president about Mr. Commons.

"Chief, do you remember the Negro man in France I mentioned to you several years ago? The one who had been interested in getting a guide job at the memorial cemetery?"

"You mean Leroy Commons?"

I was surprised the president recalled him by name, and that he was interested to learn what his news was. When I told him of his current status, the president was pleased.

"Give him my regards, and more power to him."

It did my heart good to see that the president, despite the time that had passed and the troubles that now occupied his mind, had still remembered the old war vet and our initial efforts to help him secure a job in the memorial cemetery.

Though the president was making a few decisions I didn't necessarily agree with, I believed he was making those decisions for the betterment of the country. A number of those decisions, however, left little room for me to discuss the growing issues in our community, specifically those surrounding the rising number of lynchings throughout the country.

Just last month, a Negro man from Missouri was accused of assaulting a white woman and later abducted from his jail cell by a white mob. The man was dragged behind a car and then set on fire in front of a Black church as service let out.

The man's name was Cleo Wright, and he didn't deserve such an end.

I can't imagine the pain and suffering he had endured by the hands of that white mob, or the terror that had surely consumed the Negro people of Sikeston, Missouri.

But Mr. Wright's murder was just one of many that would go uninvestigated and unprosecuted. That same month, about a year and a half after the lynching of NAACP charter member Elbert Williams, the Justice Department determined that there was not sufficient evidence to warrant prosecution. His murder would also go forgotten.

Though the Brownsville chapter of the NAACP had since dissolved in fear of further attacks, Walter White had called Mr. Williams "the first martyr of the NAACP." I wondered how many more of our fearless men and women we would have to sacrifice in the name of equal rights and justice.

And it wasn't just physical violence or harassment that was on the rise against Negroes. Just a week after the president signed Executive Order 9066, a mob of over a thousand white people rioted outside a public housing project in Detroit to keep Negro families from moving in. This scenario was also one of many happening throughout the country.

While the president kept himself embroiled in war matters, I continued to listen to the endless accounts of injustice, discrimination, and brutality. When the time was right, I would try to get my moment with the president.

In the meantime, I still had a job to do.

Despite the many outside conflicts, there were still guests to tend to, trips to organize, and an endless number of rooms to clean or turn over. We all went on about our daily routines as life moved forward all around us. And there was one happy occasion we were all looking forward to celebrating at the White House.

Harry Hopkins's wedding.

Over the years, I had come to appreciate Mr. Hopkins—though it hadn't started off that way. At first, my initial impression of the president's personal friend and adviser was that he was a cynical, indifferent politician. I even questioned why in thunder Mr. Roosevelt, who had been proven to be a man of the people, would be associated with such a person.

But as I grew to know Mr. Hopkins, it was easy to see that he was really a person of amazing depth and shrewdness, and surprisingly interested in the minute details of any individual and their problems. I got to see that in him as he supervised and directed many of the New Deal programs. He was just as passionate and committed to those programs as Mr. Roosevelt, and he managed to grow the Works Progress Administration, or WPA, into one of the largest relief programs in the country.

Not only was Mr. Hopkins a close confidant of Mr. Roosevelt, but he traveled frequently to Britain and acted as a chief liaison between the United States and the United Kingdom. And he managed all this while not in the best of health. On one occasion, when he had taken a trip to England for the president, he was lying in bed while his suitcases were being packed. He asked me to hand him a pill from his bedside table, which was crowded with medicine, before he eventually got up. His determined spirit to serve the president reminded me so much of Mac's fervor and how he had worked himself into poor health.

Luckily, on the day of his wedding, Mr. Hopkins was operating at his best. It was a quiet little affair held in the president's study, the Yellow Oval Room, and all those invited couldn't have been more excited to be there.

Myself included.

I was delighted when Mr. Hopkins had sent for me and invited me to attend.

"And Duffie, I want you to dress up. Don't you come in that uniform," he had said with a smile.

John Mays, the head doorman, had also been invited. Despite that moment when he had chastised me over that incident with Mrs. Roosevelt, we had managed to work amicably with each other. But I still made it a point to steer clear of the easily flustered man.

Mr. Hopkins's only daughter, little Diana Hopkins, was also in attendance, and I helped out a good deal in taking care of her during the ceremony. The poor child, who had lost her birth mother about five years before, had practically been adopted by the White House staff, and we were all so glad to see her getting a second mother. Luckily, Louise Macy Hopkins made a wonderful mother for little Diana and was a lovely wife to Mr. Hopkins. We all loved her.

Despite Mr. Hopkins's recent nuptials and failing health, he remained at the White House, still very much a loyal confidant to Mr. Roosevelt and his war efforts. And as the president's chief ambassador, Mr. Hopkins made frequent trips to visit with Prime Minister Winston Churchill. Of course, like many other diplomats, the prime minister also made frequent trips to the White House as well. Before his first visit, there was a great hustle and bustle in the air and all the help was wondering who was expected.

One of the kiddies tipped us off by telling me her daddy had said that *"Santa Claus from England is coming."*

I chuckled at that as I was afraid the poor child was in for a disappointment, because later we realized that Santa Claus was in fact Winston Churchill.

Churchill, and most of our other visitors from overseas, ate the White House food as though they never expected to eat a square meal again. I could understand their appreciation and compliments, because I knew they had been under strict rationing throughout the war.

The following year, in 1943, the country was still deep into the war.

It was naive of me to think that the conflict would resolve itself in such a short time. Because the First World War had lasted only four years, I had high hopes that this second one could soon find an end. Many people did.

Unfortunately, that would not be the case.

Instead, what we saw was an end to many of the social programs that the president had created during his first term in office. The so-called New Deal programs had lost a lot of their purpose and allure to the American people.

The first to go was the Civilian Conservation Corps, a program in which Edgar Brown had served as an adviser for the Negro community. It was soon followed by the large and popular WPA, and with that one gone, so went the National Youth Administration. These programs had helped so many young Black women under the leadership of Mrs. Mary McLeod Bethune. My own goddaughter Hazel had managed to receive job training under the NYA. Now with these programs discontinued, there went the opportunities for these young women to thrive.

Many other smaller programs also ceased operation once funds were budgeted toward the war efforts. It saddened me to see so many of these much needed initiatives terminated so abruptly. Though I credited the president's administration for keeping a handful of the New Deal programs active, it was the First Lady's advocacy of them that led to their continued survival: programs like the Federal Housing Administration, the Social Security Administration, and the Federal Deposit Insurance Corp, or FDIC as it was commonly being referred to. These last few surviving programs helped many working-class Americans, including Negro workers, sustain their livelihoods and secure a bit of financial stability. Only time would tell, however, if these programs would continue to exist long after the president's term—or through this unpredictable war.

As debates surrounding the reallocation of government funds continued in Congress, many Americans were steadily being carted off overseas to fight the Nazis and their allies.

Life around us, however, went on.

The White House continued to receive visitors and guests from all over, and that meant more work for us. But I didn't mind it. I enjoyed meeting new people and cultures, which allowed me to take my mind off the problems that continued to plague our country, especially the everyday Negro who didn't have the luxury I had of being protected within these White House walls.

The crown prince and princess of Norway were frequent visitors to the White House and Hyde Park, as they were living in Maryland during the German occupation of their country.

Crown Princess Juliana of the Netherlands also made several visits to the White House and Hyde Park with her children. I frequently babysat her two little girls, so they knew me well.

One day, the girls came running down the hall calling, *"Duffie! Duffie! Come and see!"*

I went with them, and there was Crown Princess Juliana in

a bathroom, down on her knees by the big bathtub, bathing the baby. I felt a little silly standing there, but the crown princess simply said, *"Come right on in, Duffie. The children love to watch me bathe the baby."*

No foolishness about her. She was a real princess and a real mother.

But it was the visit from Madame Chiang Kai-shek that I especially enjoyed. Lots of unkind publicity had been given to her. Rumors swirled around that she had to have her sheets changed on the bed every time she lay down. But I was one of the few assigned to her room, and she was no trouble at all. Madame Chiang was in fact ill and nervous, and she had a right to her whims, if she had any. She brought along a day and night nurse to look after all her needs. I liked her and felt sorry for her—not to mention she paid for any services she enjoyed.

Her nephew looked after her business, and he was generous to those who served Madame Chiang. Her niece was also in the Chinese party. She was an independent little thing who dressed exactly like a boy. One day we all had a good laugh at one of the valets. He had pressed the girl's suit and then delivered it to her room, expecting to find a man. When he knocked, the girl opened the door, and I don't know which one was more surprised. The girl snatched the suit from the valet's arm and slammed the door in his face.

We laughed about that for weeks.

But as the days progressed, and the war continued to spread, there were fewer guests and even fewer laughs around the White House.

The most crushing loss came from watching the joy and humor fade from Mr. Roosevelt's eyes. His once resilient spirit, the driving force behind our nation's rising success, was now forced to endure a world at war and his own failing health. Despite his efforts to mask the reality of his weakened condition, the toll of the presidency was etched all along every aspect of his frame.

Each day, the weight of the world bore its mark across his tired eyes, pinched lips, and stooped shoulders. His once vibrant voice faltered and became just a faint echo of its former timbre. Yet, his sacrifices and steady resolve were a testament to his commitment in rebuilding our great nation. No other president in our history had endured so much strife—nor had they given so much of themselves. For the first time, I understood the unwavering love Mac held for him because I too had come to love him.

But his increasingly weakened frame frightened me.

Beneath the shadows of my worry and fear, I held my breath and asked God to grant our beloved leader the strength to endure these tumultuous times.

All I could do now was pray . . .

It was all any of us could do.

PART 4:

Goin' Home
(1945)

Chapter 22

March 28, 1945
White House

"Good morning, Arthur. How's the president faring today?"

Mr. Roosevelt's main valet pursed his lips and gave a slight shake of his head. Without a word, he continued down the hall.

I glanced over at the president's bedroom door. Usually around this time, I would be in the president's quarters cleaning. But he hadn't left his room since his return home from Yalta. Everyone knew the trip had been exhausting for him, but there were also rumors that he was gravely ill.

Nevertheless, I didn't want to get worked up over servant gossip. We were all getting older and a bit weary of the demands of the White House. If anyone had told me I would still be working at the White House at sixty-three, I would have laughed in their face.

Yet here I was.

I was entering yet another term with the president. His fourth, to be exact. And because we were still embroiled in a long and devastating world war, his inauguration this time around was not at all the fanfare it usually was. In fact, it had been held on the back lawn of the White House, with a few hundred invited guests, with the shortest address the president had ever given. Even the customary parade and other festivities had been canceled.

Sadly, the whole affair had been rather bleak.

But I was happy to remain at the White House and be of service to the president and his family. Truth be told, I was quite concerned about him. Mr. Roosevelt wasn't looking in the best of health these days, and the fact that some of the Secret Service men had been heard to confirm those rumors left me worried. No one carried such a heavy load as our president. He was entering his fourth term in office—something that no other president had done before—while still trying to lead a divided country and navigate through a brutal war.

No one man should be forced to carry such a burden.

"Lizzie, is Father all packed and ready for his trip to Warm Springs?"

The Roosevelts' daughter startled me out of my deep thoughts, but I managed to maintain my composure.

"Yes, Miss Anna. We're all ready to go."

"We" included myself, Arthur Prettyman, Charles Fredericks, and a few other Secret Service men. It was my opinion that the president was doing too much traveling to begin with. How was he supposed to get the rest he needed if he was constantly on the move?

"Excellent," Miss Anna said. "There will be several guests visiting during Papa's stay. Please make sure they are well received."

"Of course."

"But above all, please make sure my father is well taken care of."

"He will be in good hands, Miss Anna. Don't you worry."

She took my hand and gave it a squeeze. "Thank you, Lizzie. I'll try to come down for a visit when I can."

For the rest of the day, I continued with my chores, which mostly consisted of preparing for our trip to Warm Springs. There was no telling how long we would be down there, only that the chief wanted to go. He always felt that a trip to Warm Springs could help solve any problem. He would splash about in the warm pools like a kid or slip away from his Secret Service men and drive the "Queen Mary" over the little red clay roads of Pine Mountain. Warm Springs had a special way of breathing life back into him, and he never gave up his idea of making it a really great institution, available to all.

By noon, I caught a glimpse of the president being wheeled out of his room, two of his Secret Service men keeping a respectable distance away. Fala, as usual, was resting on his lap. The president looked more gaunt and weary than usual. His favorite old gray sweater was draped across his shoulders and he sat slightly hunched over in his chair. He looked so fragile in his chair, the sight was startling.

But when the chief saw me, his eyes lit up. For a moment, he was the same old cheerful and charming Franklin D. Roosevelt.

"Lizzie, I didn't see you this morning."

"We've been preparing for the trip to Warm Springs," I said as the president was wheeled closer to me. Subconsciously, I reached down and scratched Fala on his back. He didn't even stir but I knew he appreciated the attention. "I'll be in your room shortly to straighten up."

Mr. Roosevelt nodded, then placed a gentle hand on my sleeve. "Please accept my sincerest condolences for your goddaughter. She was a very brave young woman."

I placed my hand over his. "Thank you, Mr. President. It's been tough on the family. She was so young."

It had been difficult receiving the news of Hazel's passing in

London last October. She had devoted her young life to making a difference, becoming a Red Cross nurse stationed far from home, from Canada to London, helping out with the war effort. She had made us all proud of her sacrifice and bravery.

Until she had fallen ill.

All the reasons behind her selflessness didn't matter then. She was gone, and it pained me to know that she had died on that operating table alone. It hurt even more to know she was buried so far from home.

"Is there anything we can do for you?"

I took a moment and thought about the president's question. There was in fact one thing that the family had been working on, and his involvement could possibly make a huge difference.

"Right now she is buried in London. We have been petitioning to get her body back home to Atlanta so we can have a proper burial."

"Say no more. I'll reach out to my contacts and see what I can do."

"Thank you, sir."

He patted my arm. "And how's Mac?"

It always warmed my heart to see that even after Mac's troubles had forced him to take a less strenuous job within the government, Mr. Roosevelt never forgot him.

"He's enjoying retirement," I teased, not wanting to mention the recent scare we had suffered earlier that month.

For an instant, anxiety gripped my chest as I reflected on the moment I thought I would lose my husband. Just a few weeks back, Mac had suffered a debilitating headache that led to what the doctors were calling a "minor" seizure. Seeing the bruises on his body from where he had fallen during the episode sent chills down my spine. That fall alone could have been the end for him.

But I told none of this to the chief.

Instead, I swallowed the lump forming in my throat as I plastered a comforting smile on my face, keeping my feelings hidden like a grim secret. He and Mac shared a camaraderie that no one would ever understand. I didn't want to further dampen the president's spirits with such harrowing news of his most loyal aide.

"Well, he deserves it. I too am looking forward to that day." The lightness in his tone didn't quite reach his eyes. "And how is your lovely mother faring?"

I pressed my lips together, trying to keep my sorrow from spilling into my voice. For the last six years, she had been bound to her bed, unable to walk and even barely able to speak. I knew I shouldn't be sad. Mama had lived a long and useful life. I knew her time was near, but I hated the thought of losing her. I especially hated having her suffer this much.

"Sadly, Mama isn't doing very well."

His brows turned down in sympathy. "I'm sorry to hear that, Lizzie. Your mother is a fine woman."

"Yes, she is." I blew out a weary breath, not wanting to think about the day I would eventually lose her. "I'm gonna miss her so."

"I know." His eyes were filled with understanding. "No matter how old we are, we always need our mother. Take peace in knowing that soon she too will find peace."

I nodded stiffly, unable to speak. The emotions I tried so hard to hold back threatened to overwhelm me. There had been so much loss already, it was as if death was lurking to rob me of the remaining time I had left with the people I cared about. I was certain he was thinking of his dear friend Miss LeHand, who had passed away just last summer. She too had been very young, and her death had come as a shock to us all. I think my grief was more so for the president, who had been hit the hardest by the unexpected news.

Suddenly the chief flashed me one of his contagious smiles and turned to his new valet. "Arthur, have the kitchen bring lunch out to the back porch. I'd like to dine outside today."

"Yes, sir." Arthur took the handles of his chair and began to wheel him away.

"And have them prepare enough for two. Lizzie will join me and Fala."

"Now Mr. President," I said, following behind them. "You know Mrs. Nesbitt will have a fit if she knew I was away from my chores."

A twinkle flashed in his blue eyes. "Who's going to tell her? Come along."

"Yes, sir, Mr. President."

I followed him and Arthur to the back porch, which faced the great lawn. I recalled our first stimulating conversation on a similar porch at Hyde Park. About birds, no less. It was nice to see the president, although tired looking, was still very jovial and . . . alive. At that moment, he was every bit the commander in chief, projecting an air of authority and power like none other. But deep in his core, he was the same hardworking man who loved his family and liked nothing better than a good laugh.

The servants' gossip seemed silly now.

Our chief was going to be all right.

April 12, 1945
Warm Springs

The papers were late that morning.

Mr. Roosevelt sat in bed waiting for them, an old blue cape pulled around his shoulders, as I cleaned around his bedchamber. The atmosphere around Warm Springs didn't have the typical lightness that it usually had. Everyone knew the health of the president wasn't improving, and for the first time in over twenty years, not even his beloved Warm Springs could bring the spark back into him.

"How are my boys getting along, Lizzie?" Mr. Roosevelt asked in a tired yet cheerful, friendly tone. Without his papers, he had nothing else to keep his mind occupied. "I haven't heard about them for a long time now."

I smiled and glanced up from my dusting. With his declining health, I refrained from bringing up political conversations with the president these days. Yet I was surprised to learn that he hadn't forgotten about the Houston war veterans and their controversial case that I had brought to his attention. It was actually nice to see that with all his work, Mr. Roosevelt still remembered the three obscure Negroes he had pardoned several years back. Ever since the pardon he always referred to them as his "boys."

"They're getting along quite well, Chief."

I was able to give him a good report on all three, as I still kept in touch with the young men myself, and his eyes lit up as he nodded.

"That's fine news, Lizzie."

He talked on, casually, and I listened as I continued my cleaning. He looked beyond tired, yet he smiled, the same warm smile I had known for so many years. I knew how just a small task like conversing could easily tire him out, but the conversations also seemed to lift his spirits. So I stayed and kept him company.

"By the way, tell Mac I didn't forget his birthday. I was at Yalta, you know . . ."

"Yes, he knows," I assured him.

"I got him a few nice things during my trip."

"I don't know, Chief . . . Mac's a traditionalist. He might be a little disappointed not to get those stockings."

Mr. Roosevelt's eyes twinkled. "Oh, I got him a pair of those too."

The boss whom Mac knew always remembered his birthday. They were the same age, yet Mr. Roosevelt always treated Mac more like his younger brother. He gave him twenty dollars when they went on vacation together and passed down to him all sorts of odds and ends. So far, Mac had accumulated an assortment of gifts, from cowboy hats to canes to a bourbon bottle with Mr. Roosevelt's picture inside. There was even a grain of rice sent to him from India with 310 letters written on it. I chuckled at the memory. That may have been the strangest gift of all.

"What did you think of Graham's performance of 'Goin' Home' the other day?"

The question took me by surprise, as I wasn't prepared for the abrupt change of topic.

"I thought it was lovely," I said. "The way the two of you collaborated on it made it very special."

Mr. Roosevelt smiled. "You're not just saying that because he's a friend, now, are you?"

"No, sir. Honest. It nearly brought tears to my eyes."

"Excellent."

I wasn't certain if he was pleased by the fact that I enjoyed the rendition or that it had made me emotional. It was no secret that Antonín Dvořák's "Goin' Home" song was one of his favorites. Mr. Roosevelt had even requested that it be played at his mother's funeral. However, his current interest in having Graham Jackson produce a special version of the song left me a bit uneasy. While the musical notes were moving, they conjured up thoughts of life, death, and the passing of time—thoughts I would much rather not have while so many around me were being called home . . .

"I telephoned Anna last night," Mr. Roosevelt chatted on. "It's been a while since we spoke, but it appears everyone's in good health, including little Johnnie."

"Oh, that's wonderful news," I said. "I'm glad to hear he's doing better."

"Same. I have been quite worried about him," Mr. Roosevelt mused. He rubbed the back of his head, frowning slightly. "I remember, Lizzie, you always said that even though Johnnie was quick tempered, it's easy for him to forgive."

I nodded. "That is true."

"He doesn't take that from the Roosevelts, does he?"

"Not at all," I said smoothly, not missing a beat from my dusting.

The president laughed. And it was a wonderful sound. It was the kind of carefree joy that made one feel good all over.

Fala waddled in and we talked about him and his latest fan mail. We talked about the furnace and about the weather and about the chocolate waffles Daisy had made for supper the night before, when Henry Morgenthau was a guest.

"You know, Daisy used the waffle irons Mr. Morgenthau gave you for Christmas last year."

"Is that so?"

"Yes, sir. The last time he came to visit, he had a huge hankering for some waffles, but we had no waffle iron."

Mr. Roosevelt chuckled. "We must let him know that. I could see that old Henry really enjoyed them."

The small talk was just that—small and, for the most part, insignificant. But it was small talk with a great man. The greatest man of our time. And I cherished every moment of it.

Eventually, Mr. Roosevelt asked to be taken out of bed. I continued my cleaning in and around the main house. About three hours later, I passed through the hall and caught a glimpse of Mr. Roosevelt. He was writing a letter at his desk, and I wondered if it was yet another to his son John. Over the years, as the war continued to rage, he was the son who wrote most often to his father.

His longtime friend Mrs. Rutherfurd wasn't far from his side. She had even brought a painter friend with her. As Mr. Roosevelt wrote at the table, Miss Elizabeth Shoumatoff painted his portrait. She managed to capture the essence of him splendidly, removing the tired lines and fatigue from his eyes and giving him the vivaciousness we were all accustomed to from him.

His cousins Miss Daisy Suckley and Miss Laura Delano were also in the room, keeping him company. Fala lay resting at his feet. Everything was quiet except for an occasional snap from a small log fire.

I stood there a moment, taking in the scene, wanting to remember him this way. In his eyes, there was no weariness, no defeat.

Suddenly, he sat back from his writing. He caught a glimpse of me and smiled.

"Lizzie, what was all that laughing about earlier?"

"What do you mean, sir?"

"I could hear the lot of you cackling about in the kitchen like some wild hens."

"Oh, it was nothing," I said with a small chuckle, remembering the silly conversation. "Somehow we got to talking about reincarnation and what we would like to come back as," I explained. "I told them that if there was such a thing as reincarnation, I wanted to come back as a canary bird."

He cocked a brow. "A canary?"

"Yes. I want to come back as a little bird, live in a big cage, and nibble lettuce all day."

The president looked thoughtful for a moment, studying my robust, full-bodied frame, then doubled over with laughter.

"I love it!" he exclaimed loudly. "I love it!"

I and everyone else in the room joined in on his laughter, it was that contagious.

"This husky, strapping woman!" he exclaimed, still laughing. "Imagine her confined in a cage, nibbling on lettuce. You gotta love it!"

Suddenly a little red bird came flying into the room and landed on Mr. Roosevelt's desk. It took us all by surprise, and the laughter abruptly stopped.

"What a beautiful cardinal," Mr. Roosevelt whispered, as he stared at the small red bird with much delight. For a moment, I thought about the little red bird that we had spotted in the house just a few days before his mother had died. Rumor had it that it was Mrs. Delano who had come back reincarnated as the small red bird to be near and to watch over her family. Though I knew it was nothing more than foolish superstition, an eerie chill ran along my arm.

Realizing there was an unexpected visitor, Fala stood up and let out a sharp bark. The little bird flew out of the room from the same direction it flew in.

"Hmm, I've always been fond of birds," Mr. Roosevelt said. "Perhaps I'll come back as a red cardinal myself. Will you make room for me in your cage, Lizzie?"

I smiled. "Of course, Mr. President. But I'm not sharing my lettuce."

More laughter erupted.

I eventually excused myself and went to tidy up Mr. Roosevelt's room and bath. I spent the rest of the late morning cleaning Miss Suckley's room before I went on to the guest cottage. The aroma of Daisy's cheese soufflé wafted in the air as I walked past the kitchen. Cheese soufflé was one of the president's favorites, and Daisy planned to surprise him by preparing his most favorite dinner, her popular Country Captain. I had to admit, I was looking forward to it myself.

A little while later, as I was making the beds in the guest room, Mr. Arthur came rushing in.

"Lizzie, I need a hot-water bottle."

His sense of urgency got me moving and I went to fetch one for him. He grabbed it and hurried away, without a word of explanation. I frowned after him, but not out of alarm. Working in the White House—little or big—there was no time for explanations or questions. Yet I still found the request odd. But I gave it no further thought and continued with my cleaning.

Sometime later, Daisy came rushing into the guest house. She appeared surprised to find me shaking out the rugs.

"Lizzie! Why haven't you come down?"

"What do you mean?" I paused in my task and frowned at her. "It's not time for lunch."

"Didn't Arthur tell you?"

"Tell me what?"

She was silent a moment. Then she said, "Lizzie, the president may be dying."

My heart sank in that moment, and the rug slipped from my fingers. I stood there staring at her, not quite understanding her words. It couldn't be. Just earlier that day, he had been in great spirits. We had laughed and joked like old times.

He can't be dying.

Her quiet words left me with a sense of great loss, a loss I had never felt before. I imagined this is what some must feel when they lose their hope because in that moment the future looked bleak. For all of us.

I pushed past Daisy and ran as fast as my body would allow to the main house. I was met by the Secret Service man Charles

Fredericks, who stood in front of the door as stiff as a board. I continued toward the door, but he blocked my access. He clasped and unclasped his hands but never spoke a word. However, it was all in his eyes and in that wordless gesture.

It was over.

President Franklin Delano Roosevelt was dead.

Chapter 23

FDR IS DEAD.

The big bold print left no room for anyone to escape the cold, harsh reality . . .

America had lost her leader.

We had lost our leader.

As I sat in the funeral train heading back to Washington, I couldn't help but be amazed at how fast the news had made headlines. My eyes remained glued to those large simple words that spanned across the top of the newspaper, like an albatross's wings engulfing the page. To the world, President Roosevelt was a formidable figure. But to his fellow countrymen, he was more than just a commander living inside the White House, and certainly more than just a voice behind the radio. He was their adviser, their confidant, and, for so many, their savior.

But for us—the McDuffies—he had been our friend.

I managed to tear my gaze away from the newsprint and stare out the small window. By now, news would have reached Mac about the chief's passing. I could imagine his pain and heartbreak.

I regretted not calling him the night before, but I couldn't bring myself to deliver that news to him. I could barely manage my own grief—how was I to handle his? This news would crush him.

Mrs. Roosevelt had arrived at Warm Springs late last night, joining her cousins in preparing Mr. Roosevelt's body to be brought back to Washington. She, her cousins, and the few of us servants and staff were all on board the Ferdinand Magellan rail car with the president's body.

The crowd at Warm Springs was overwhelming. There were people everywhere, including reporters and photographers. A part of me resented the spectators. We had only lost him yesterday. There was no room for speculation and gossip. But as I looked upon the faces of the people, I realized they too were mourning a great loss.

Soon the entire country would be.

As the procession left Warm Springs, Graham Jackson played the rendition of "Goin' Home" he had practiced in front of the president just a few days before. There was not a dry eye on the platform as the crowds gathered around the train. Despite Graham's own tears, he played the song beautifully.

I knew the chief would have loved the way he played it today.

That thought brought more tears to my eyes, and I blinked them away. Suddenly, a red cardinal flew across my window. I let my gaze follow it until it landed on the arm of the hanging post right outside the train station. The full-breasted little bird let out a series of melodious sounds that were musically enchanting and pierced through the somber air.

I thought about the president's last moments with me as we talked and laughed about reincarnation and birds. I even thought about Mr. Squeaks, the little yellow canary the president had gifted me many years ago. I thought about the many moments and conversations I shared with Franklin Delano Roosevelt and the jovial, free-spirited man that he was. That is the way I chose to remember him . . . talking, smiling, laughing.

"'Til we meet again, old friend," I murmured, watching as the red bird flew and disappeared into the trees.

I stared out the window as the crowd continued to grow along our path. In that moment, it looked as though the whole world had walked down to the railroad tracks. There were no "white" and "colored" waiting rooms in the Georgia stations that day. I looked out at the crowds, all races, all ages, rich and poor.

As daylight began to fade, the lights from the train picked out the sparkle of tears on the onlookers' cheeks. I watched as a jaunty truck driver stopped and offered a salute as the train passed by. Sometimes the crowds simply stood silently with their heads bowed. Other times the crowds sang. In one small town they sang "Home on the Range." In another city they sang "Onward Christian Soldiers."

With the curtains pulled back, I watched the lights and shadows of the sharecroppers' cabins disappear into the night of the passing countryside. They nested like old gray hens in the cotton fields. For some odd reason I couldn't help but think of the very cabin in which I had been born and raised.

I remembered the green gourd vines that grew on our porch and the Chinaberry tree that threw its umbrella of shade over the yard. I remembered the feel of the hot sand against my bare little feet as I ran inside our small farmhouse from the cotton fields for a taste of my mother's cracklin' bread, collards, fried chicken, and biscuits. I remembered washday and the clothes boiling in a black pot in the yard. I also remembered my early years of Christmas on the farm, and the candy mice and tea cakes "Santa" had left in my stocking.

Life had been so simple then.

In my small, young world, there was no violence, no intolerance, no war. In my bubble of innocence, illness and death did not exist, and I had no knowledge of the cruelty and injustices that plagued my people. Now those were recurring themes in my life, concepts I was all too familiar with.

For the first time that day, my heart weighed heavier in my chest for something other than Mr. Roosevelt's passing.

Usually, the ride from Georgia to the capital didn't feel very long, but tonight it felt like an eternity. Sleep eluded me as I lay in my berth of the slow-moving train, my mind drifting to thoughts of my own life. I had lived sixty-four years and had seen and experienced so much. I had met tons of celebrities and royalty. I had traveled around the country and met with lots of important people. I had been written about—and written to—from so many people around the world.

Yet, a small part of me felt as if I hadn't done enough.

Our progress for social justice and economic freedom for the Negro had been cut short because of the war. As age advanced on me, I feared there wouldn't be any more time to do the things I still wanted and needed to do. And now that we'd lost one of our biggest advocates, I feared no more advancement would be made toward our rights for equality.

I stared out the train window and saw a lonely pine tree towering above the rest of the forest. It loomed in the distance with such distinguished power and solitary splendor, much like the man we were bringing back home.

As the train rumbled north, we happened upon a forest fire. I watched as yellow tongues of flame licked up the low underbrush of the distant trees. High over the scene was the torch of a single burning pine. The fire outlined every crook and branch, rushing through the heart of the pine. The flames made a cone of its trunk, breaking through it like melted gold.

I couldn't tear my gaze away.

Just as the train passed, the tree fell. Much like Franklin Delano Roosevelt had gone down.

A giant in life. A glory in death.

As dawn once again crept through the horizon, I caught a glimpse of the flag flying from the engine as we rounded a bend. There were even more people along the tracks now. A bent old farmer stood at his plow, holding a battered straw hat over his heart as our long train rolled past. Mr. Roosevelt was indeed a giant in his time. He was the lonely pine towering above the rest of the forest. He was the chief Mac and I had served and loved. He was the friend of our people.

Because Franklin Delano Roosevelt lived, there had been hope for our future.

Now that hope was gone.

THE WEATHER WAS surprisingly hot in Washington and there was much to be done.

I still found it hard to believe the president was gone. The flag-draped caisson and the six white horses, the dirge of muffled drums, and the half million people lining the streets should have made it real.

But it hadn't.

His casket stood on display in the East Room as hundreds of mourners filed in to pay their respects, while thousands more gathered outside along the iron fences. It felt like I was living a movie, and soon this performance would come to an abrupt end.

But it didn't . . .

Somehow, I managed to convince myself that speaking with

Mac before I officially cleared out our living quarters of twelve years would lift my spirits.

It had not.

"Why didn't you telephone me when it happened, Lizzie?" he had demanded during our last phone conversation. "I was awake all night waiting for your call."

"I'm sorry, Mac. I wanted to, but I just didn't know how to tell you."

He blew out a breath. "I guess I can't blame you. It was the greatest shock I ever had. It was as though part of me had died too."

"Oh, Mac . . ."

"It's true," Mac said, his voice thick with emotion. "I should have been there with him. Maybe I could have convinced him to stop pushing himself so hard."

I clutched the phone to my ear, my heart breaking over my husband's despair. This was the first time that he was openly sharing his pain with me without prompting, yet I couldn't find the right words to help ease his sorrow. There was no reason for me to ask now why he hadn't come to the White House for the funeral service. I knew his heart wouldn't have been able to take it.

"There was nothing anyone could have done, Mac," I eventually said. "Not even you."

They say "No man is a hero to his valet," but I knew that not to be true. No man was any closer than those two. The chief was Mac's hero until the day he died.

"He was only sixty-three, Lizzie. My age. It wasn't his time yet."

Though part of me agreed with him, I knew I couldn't let us both go down that rabbit hole of remorse and regret.

"We can't know that, Mac. Only God can say how long we have left on this earth. We can only live life and walk in our purpose."

He was silent for a moment, and I hoped he was processing my words.

"When my time comes to go," he said quietly, "I'll be ready."

I didn't know what to say to that, so I said nothing. We ended our call and I sat in our quiet living quarters for what seemed like an eternity before I mustered up enough energy to finish my tasks.

Today I would be leaving the White House for good.

After the long, heart-rending service, after the numerous guests had viewed the president's casket and left, after the White House's mountain of flowers had been dispersed to hospitals, I still couldn't wrap my mind around the fact that our chief was gone. I half expected him to roll out in his chair at any time. Even now, I could close my eyes and see him at the dining table at Warm Springs, looking up from his writing, conversing and smiling.

To the American people, Franklin Delano Roosevelt was a radio voice, a newsreel smile, an editorial quip. He was a global leader who had ushered in a new era within the country. It was no wonder the chief had been elected to the highest office four times now. Though he was larger than life, he was also the kind of man who would help one of his former cooks through an expensive illness long after she had left his service. Just as he had helped Miss LeHand.

He had committed his life to his country, for the people, 'til the very end.

I made my way down the long, quiet halls of the White House. I found my way to the State Dining Room. I had served thousands of guests, countless times, in this room, not realizing at those times how important and rare those moments would be. I went to the central mantel and stood staring up at the portrait of Lincoln. It was eighty years ago, almost to the day, that he had been carried across cities and mourned by the country with such depth.

"Nature's first green is gold," I murmured, reciting one of my favorite Robert Frost poems. "Her hardest hue to hold . . ."

It was in that moment, staring at the portrait of Lincoln during this sad time after losing the greatest president of my time, that I fully understood the meaning of the short poem.

Nothing good or precious lasted forever.

As if materializing out of thin air, the head doorman, John Mays, came up beside me and whispered, "They were two of a kind, weren't they?"

I glanced over at him and witnessed the grief etched across his dark, weary face.

"Yes, they were," I agreed. "But Roosevelt was truly one of a kind."

"True enough. It may be another eighty years before this country is blessed with such greatness again."

I nodded in acknowledgment, though secretly praying that for the sake of the country, for the sake of our people, we wouldn't have to wait that long.

"I hear you're leaving today."

I nodded again. "Yes. It's time for me to come home."

I had asked for a leave of absence because of my health. I was truly starting to feel my age. I had spent more time in the White House than I had ever imagined I would. Twelve years may not seem like much when I had spent over twenty years prior working in Atlanta. But no job had challenged me, had exhilarated me, or had exhausted me more than that of being a maid in the White House. Mac had been my motivation for coming here, Mr. Roosevelt had been my reason for staying. Both were no longer here, therefore my purpose in staying was gone.

"Well, let me know when you're ready. I'll have some of the ushers bring your things down to the car."

"Thank you, John."

Arrangements for me to leave for Atlanta tonight had been set. It was still shocking to me how much stuff Mac and I had accumulated during our residency at the White House. So far, I had packed away about two suitcases of souvenirs from our twelve years with the Roosevelts—eighteen years, if I counted the time Mac had spent with Mr. Roosevelt before the White House. There was the chief's fishing hat, his campaign Panama, a tan sweater, a brown sweater, a dress coat, handkerchiefs with "FDR" stitched in the corner. There were two cigarette holders, a shaving brush, a pair of suspenders, a pair of pajamas. There was a donkey and an elephant from his desk, autographed pictures, a White House Bible inscribed *"For Irvin McDuffie, from his friend, Franklin Delano Roosevelt."*

There was also the red tie that Mr. Roosevelt wore in Miami that February day in 1933, when the Chicago mayor Anton Cermak had been struck down by the gunshot that had been intended for the then president-elect. The chief had refused to give up the infamous tie, but Mac made sure he never wore it to another function again. Now it too was part of the many souvenirs we had gathered during our time here at the White House.

"The chief hated throwing anything away."

I didn't realize I had blurted that fleeting memory until John gave me a strange look. I chuckled to hide my embarrassment.

"Sorry. I was just thinking about the president and how . . . frugal he was. Especially with his clothes."

"Is that why he would always be in that tired-looking gray sweater?"

I laughed, remembering the overly worn gray sweater and the time Mrs. Roosevelt, her personal maid Mary Foster, her seamstress Lillian Rogers, and Mac had all conspired to get rid of the patched and mended gray sweater. They had buried it deep in the closet, hoping that after several months Mr. Roosevelt would have forgotten it.

He had not.

I fleetingly wondered what had become of that old thing.

"The president did love that sweater, didn't he?" I mused. "If I'm not mistaken, I think it had been with him since his governorship in New York."

Right before his death, Mr. Roosevelt had twenty-five brand new sweaters on hand, though he continued to wear the same overly mended gray one time and time again. He was reluctant to throw away his things, always thinking he could use them someday.

"Good thing the chief had Mac, else he would have been a laughingstock in the papers."

I nodded. "Mac's philosophy was always that the president was not feeling fit unless his attire reflected it. And he always wanted the chief to feel at his best."

John grunted in what I believed to be agreement. Suddenly, the longtime doorman handed me a large book. On the front was the imprinted title *Roosevelt Omnibus*.

"Mrs. Nesbitt found this in the president's study and wanted to be sure you got this."

I took the book and murmured a quiet "thank you." John nodded and left me standing in the great room. As nostalgic as I felt in that moment, I also began to feel at peace. I was finally going home to be with my husband, to be with my Mac. That was my rightful place. That was where I belonged.

I opened the front flap of the large book and inside was a short inscription:

For McDuffie . . . a very good record of our wanderings together . . .

—*Franklin D. Roosevelt*

I closed the cover and held it close to my chest. Yet another memento the president had passed on to Mac. That was one thing about him: He was always very generous, and he gave as many things to Mac as he gave to others. He would sometimes pass on things for Mac to give to Big Jim Palmer, an old man from Atlanta and big-time Republican, who began to vote Democratic during Mr. Roosevelt's first run for the presidency, in 1932.

I shook away the memory, still finding it hard to believe that our chief was gone. Yet standing in the quiet of the grand house, it became all the more real. There would be no more jokes or teasing or witty remarks. There would be no more laughter or talks of reform. There would be no more trips to Hyde Park or Warm Springs.

An era had ended, and our wanderings were truly over.

The president—our friend—had gone home.

Chapter 24

Ten months later . . .
Atlanta, GA

I had never been comfortable around death.

I didn't know many people who were. For me, I hated the smell and sight of it. The way it held a person in its suffocating grip of pain and misery until all they could think about was their own mortality. I especially couldn't stand the anguish and finality that came with it.

And I never imagined in such a short time, I would find myself yet again in a state of deep sorrow and despair.

On Wednesday, January 30, 1946, Irvin "Mac" McDuffie, my husband of thirty-five years, passed away in his sleep, six weeks before his sixty-fourth birthday. Coincidentally, he had passed on the day of Mr. Roosevelt's sixty-fourth birthday.

The letters and telegrams were endless as they continued to pour in. Articles were written about Mac's great accomplishments as President Roosevelt's most loyal valet. Even Mr. Albert Jackson, one of our few and loudest challengers over the years, had written a touching tribute to Mac. I received condolences from as far away as Canada and Australia, each expressing sympathy for my loss.

But none of it helped to ease my pain.

I still couldn't believe I was burying my beloved husband so soon. Several days before he passed, Mac had complained of being extremely tired. He had only recently retired from his position as a messenger for the Internal Revenue Service here in Atlanta this past summer. We had been in the process of settling back into a normal routine before he had begun experiencing those debilitating headaches again. Several weeks ago, they became more intense and he had spent much of his days in bed. Though he had appeared listless and weak, he had been in such high spirits. Then three days after, he had passed on.

And with his passing came the realization that life for me would never be the same.

With a small sigh, I stuffed the latest batch of telegrams in the small floral box that had now become their keepsake. We had just laid him to rest at South View Cemetery this past Friday, and though the service had been lovely with an unbelievable turnout, it had been the hardest day of my life. It was one that I was eager to put far behind me so that I could concentrate on our happier days.

It was those memories that kept me going.

To others, Irvin Henry McDuffie would mainly be remembered as a faithful servant and friend to Franklin Delano Roosevelt. Mac had been with his boss when he had twice been elected governor of New York and twice been reelected as president of the United States. He had been with him on campaign trains and on vacation yachts, had traveled with him to Europe, South America, and Hawaii.

He was the kind of servant who could stand silently at the side of Mr. Roosevelt in a Paris art gallery for two hours while the chief studied a certain painting. He could romp and joke with him on the way to Pine Mountain in a Model-T Ford to help put out a forest fire.

Mac had even nursed him through two cases of pneumonia. He had cut his hair, helped him dress, rolled his wheelchair, ran his errands, put him to bed, and woke him up in the morning. Whether it had been at Warm Springs, Hyde Park, Albany, or the White House, he had been Mr. Roosevelt's most devoted companion.

As I set aside the small keepsake box, I pulled out another that held all of Mac's letters to me throughout the years. It felt fitting to place his memorial card from his funeral service inside, yet something compelled me to pull out a few of his letters instead. I remembered when Mac would come home to see me in Atlanta during his early days with Mr. Roosevelt, filled and practically running over with stories of people and places he had seen.

One of those letters immediately brought a smile to my lips . . .

Buffalo, N.Y., Oct. 20, 1930:

It is cold and snowing here in Buffalo. I ride with the reporters in a closed car, but the poor governor is in an open car with the curtains up, so he can speak by just standing up and not getting out. We are all wearing our winter underwear.

—Your Devoted Husband

I let out a small chuckle at the memory, remembering how I had to send him more winter underwear and stockings to help guard against the cold.

Another letter caught my attention, and the place and date brought a wave of nostalgia through me.

Paris, May 16, 1931:

Yesterday I rode by auto all over Paris with the Governor and party, and last night we were out again. It reminded me of New Orleans, the way she must have been in the '90s. The beautiful gardens were all lit, with men and women sitting around drinking wine or beer. There were no drunks and no disorder. I will bring home some pictures of the beautiful buildings. I saw plenty of colored people on the Decatur Street of Paris . . . in looks, not conduct. The people here are gay but not immoral the way they are pictured. They are a happy people. Everybody is friendly.

—*Your Devoted Husband*

Try as I might, I couldn't keep the large grin off my face. Of the many letters Mac had sent me of his travels with Mr. Roosevelt, I thoroughly enjoyed this one. He had fallen in love with French culture, and I could practically feel his excitement emanate from the page. I remembered the promise he had made to me shortly after sending this letter . . .

"Next time I go to Paris, I'm taking you along."

Of course, Mac and I never got to see Paris together, but that was okay. Mac's letters managed to transport me to places I knew I would never visit, yet I still got to experience the world through his eyes.

And it was magical.

I would forever have his letters and he would forever live on as my loving, devoted husband.

For twelve years, Irvin McDuffie was the person with whom the chief had started his day, and I think my husband was a pretty good one to start the day with. To me, he was a loving husband, a devoted friend, and overall a wonderful man.

And I would never forget that it took two valets and a barber to fill my husband's shoes.

"Lizzie, more letters came for you today."

"Thank you, Leona," I said as my darling half-sister placed the new stack of letters and telegram cards on the table in front of me.

"I also have your dinner warming on the table," she said. "Do you need anything else?"

I took her hand and gave it a squeeze. We had never been very close, yet she had been such a great help to me during this difficult time. I honestly don't know how I would have gotten through any of this without her help.

"No, dear, I should be fine. But thank you."

She gave my hand a reassuring pat. "I'll check on you again tomorrow."

After Leona left, I sifted through the stack of mail. I needed to keep my mind busy. The quiet, which I had once welcomed, bothered me now. As I sifted through the letters, I stopped on one from Margaret Mitchell. I smiled, remembering that time so long ago when the popular author had invited me to her home. I placed the other letters down and tore hers open.

Dear Lizzie:

I've just now read in a column about how you're going to write a book about the Roosevelts. Go ahead and write that book. Write it your own way. Write it as soon as you can. It will sell well, and you will have done a good service to the people as well as made your own future secure. But write that book.

Wishing you well, I am,

—Margaret Mitchell Marsh

I set the letter down as I replayed her words again in my head. I couldn't even remember giving that interview, much less mentioning writing a book. I had sat through so many interviews and gave comments to so many reporters, I couldn't even remember the last one I had given. But the idea of writing our story had been something Mac and I had once talked about doing together after he had left his position at the bureau. It was yet another goal we wouldn't be able to fulfill together, and a heavy pang thudded in my chest.

Despite the pain and disappointment of that lost achievement, Miss Margaret's encouraging words inspired me. I once again gave it some serious thought. Though my life had been filled with so much loss recently, it had also been filled with tons of adventure and opportunity.

I remembered the visit of the Ethiopian prince and my awe at witnessing such Black excellence. I remembered meeting the first lady of the Republic of China and how she left me a fifty-dollar tip. I remembered the visit of the king and queen of England, and how I swept the carpet they walked on.

I leaned back in my seat and shut my eyes, remembering it all . . .

I remembered Mr. Roosevelt's first inauguration and how it had been one of the happiest yet most nerve-racking days of my life. I remembered that, because of Mac's many responsibilities on those days, he had never been able to witness any of the president's inaugural ceremonies.

I remembered the time I told the president that I was going to serve as his "self-appointed secretary on colored people's affairs," and how he laughed in that boisterous way of his.

In the quiet stillness of my sitting room, I reflected on my twelve years of service to the most magnetic man, and the most enthralling family, I had ever been charged to work for. I remembered one of the last conversations Mr. Roosevelt had with Mac before he'd been transferred out of his position as the president's valet . . .

"After all this is over, Mac, you and I are going to take a trip around the world. Then we'll retire to Hill Top House and I will write books."

Needless to say, Mr. Roosevelt and Mac didn't get to take that trip around the world together, just as Mac and I never got to go to Paris.

As I allowed myself to delve further back into the past, back even to when I first met Mac at that dismal party, I remembered our thirty-five years of marriage. I remembered the day when he had decided to quit his barbershop and take a job with Mr. Roosevelt at Warm Springs. I remembered the dreams and plans we had put on hold so we could live and work in the White House. But in my sixty-plus years of living, I had come to learn that it's what we do that is important, not what we don't do.

Thinking back on my life, there were three pivotal moments that set me on a path where I could do for others. The first was acting as a go-between for my people and the president, connecting our otherwise disconnected communities. This was perhaps my most worthy accomplishment.

The next was when I helped organize the United Government

Employees union. My efforts to lead a labor union and unite the low-earning federally employed domestic workers marked the beginning of an era for me and thousands of Black women. Although the union was eventually joined with another, I held hope that it would continue to give Negro federal workers a space to voice their concerns and demands from their employers.

My third, and perhaps my most notable, achievement was my campaigning for President Roosevelt. I spoke with passionate conviction at every stop and managed to win the support of many Black voters for our former late president. For me, it hadn't been about getting the Negro to leave the party of Lincoln—but to vote for progress and the chance to decide what our future would look like as a people.

These three important moments in my life highlighted the efforts I consistently made in working for my community. My commitment to see our people progress was what kept me going. Even now, change was in the air, and I would continue to do everything in my power to see it take flight.

Mac and I may not have gotten to take those trips he promised, but that didn't mean I couldn't write about all the fun and excitement we shared beforehand. Hell, not many maids, much less a Negro one, could say that they had been in the same room as the king of England. Or that they had poured tea for the queen.

I would make sure that Mac was remembered, and not just for being President Roosevelt's most trusted and loyal servant, because he was more than that. Irvin Henry McDuffie was the backbone of the most powerful man in the world. He was as resilient and tenacious as they came. He was all that was right and flawed about this country. Essentially, he was the everyday American Mr. Roosevelt had worked so hard to serve.

Now Mac and I had a legacy to share.

It hadn't been clear to me then why I had been so determined to help complete strangers, but it was plain to me now. My heart had gone all in for those who had not only shared but entrusted me with their burdens. If I contributed anything to the progress of my race in helping to rally them solidly behind Franklin Delano Roosevelt, if I contributed to them in any personal cases where I was able to intercede with the president, then I believed I had kept faith with those frightened people who had fled Atlanta that morning after the 1906 riot.

And I took solace in knowing that while activism may not have been my initial passion in life, my small crusade had changed the lives of many.

More importantly, it had changed my life.

I refolded Miss Margaret's letter and set it aside. I went to my desk and sat in front of my underused typewriter. With my heart full and my mind drifting into a not-so-distant past, I began to write my story . . .

THE BACK DOOR OF THE WHITE HOUSE

BY

ELIZABETH McDUFFIE

Author's Note

Mrs. Elizabeth "Lizzie" McDuffie was an extraordinary woman, and it is evident from all the letters, correspondences, and articles written about her. Much of my research materials came from the Atlanta University Center Robert W. Woodruff Library archives, which offered me an intimate look into her life and story. Although a large part of her legacy was her activism, I was fortunate enough to read her unfinished memoir and gain a better insight into the multifaceted woman she truly was.

Because this book is meant to be a work of fiction, I took a few creative liberties with the timeline of events for the purposes of this story. While all the letters and notes featured throughout are actual correspondences written to Lizzie, I did alter the author of the final letter for dramatic impact. Though Margaret Mitchell, the notable author of *Gone with the Wind*, had written to Mrs. McDuffie numerous times, that letter encouraging Lizzie to write her memoir was actually written by Augusta Legg Barton.

The only other letter fabricated for dramatic purposes was the one Lizzie reads to Mac from the grieving mother who lost her son in the First World War and pleads for their assistance in gaining an audience with the president. Although the letter is fake, the grieving mother's situation was real and very common at that time. Admittedly, it is also a nod to my next novel about the African American Gold Star mothers and widows who protested the segregation of the U.S.-sponsored pilgrimage to France to honor their loved ones who died in the war and were buried overseas.

In crafting this work of fiction, I tried to retain the essence of Mrs. McDuffie's unique life. However, it's important to note several elements within the story that have been fictionalized or embellished for creative purposes. Like the meeting with FDR's son Franklin Jr. in April 1966. Although their meeting did take place, I embellished his motive, using his political ambitions to gain an endorsement from Lizzie. Similarly, her friendship with Kathuran "Kathy" Brooks, a fellow maid referenced in her memoir, was also embellished to add depth to Lizzie's narrative and character growth.

Lizzie's imagined encounters with Louise Little, the mother of Malcolm X, and young Thurgood Marshall were dramatized to explore the social and cultural dynamics of these famed activists. Even her recurring encounters with the fictionalized reporter Albert Jackson were written to further examine the complexity of political beliefs, social responsibilities, and Lizzie's internal conflict.

Additionally, the Allied Negro Papers referenced in this story is a fictional journal inspired by the real-life Associated Negro Press (ANP), a popular media source for African American news during that time. It was only after the writing of this book that I learned about James Albert "Billboard" Jackson, a reporter for the ANP. Any resemblance to the fictional Albert Jackson in this narrative is completely coincidental.

Further, there has been contradictory information regarding

whether a television set was first made available in the White
House during President Hoover's term (1931) or FDR's (1939). For
the purposes of this story, I featured one early in FDR's second
term in office (1937).

While Irvin McDuffie's drinking problem has been referenced
in several historical reports, his physical attack in this story, and
any incidents related to his nervous breakdown and subsequent
retirement, were purely from my imagination. Although Eleanor
Roosevelt took exception to his drinking and it was reported that
she wanted to dismiss him from his position, FDR remained committed to his valet. The resulting conflict featured in the story
because of his drinking should not be taken as historical fact.

Despite Mac's personal struggles, Lizzie also remained devoted
to her husband. She was a true unsung hero, and together they
spearheaded a lot of policies for the civil rights movement. Although
her work in and out of the White House may be overshadowed by
many who came before and after her, she was a true activist of her
time and her small victories managed to change thousands of lives.
She is a figure still worth exploring and at the time of this writing, I'm excited to mention that the Atlanta University Center has
digitized the McDuffie collection and made it available online on
their website.

Lastly, it is important to note that the conflict between Lizzie
and FDR in this story over the signing of the anti-lynching bill was
also exaggerated. Although lynchings were a controversial topic
during his presidency, Lizzie barely makes any mention of them
in her memoir. I used this subject matter not only as a source of
conflict between Lizzie and President Roosevelt but also to shed
light on the longest yet most disregarded civil rights issue America has faced. Reportedly, attempts to pass an anti-lynching law
date back to 1900 with scores of activists, scholars, politicians,

and organizations working diligently for decades to get this violent act of terror recognized as a federal hate crime.

On March 29, 2022, the Emmett Till Antilynching Act was signed into law.

It took **122** years.

Acknowledgments

To say that this book was a labor of love is an understatement. In February 2021, one phone call changed my life—and took my writing career to a place I could only imagine. Yet in the time it took me to write and publish this book, I managed to make it through a pandemic, overcome multiple high-risk pregnancies, write my second book, and birth three beautiful babies.

But I couldn't have done this all without the support of my writing tribe and my ever-faithful village . . .

First, a very heartfelt thanks to my incredible agent, Kevan Lyon—your advocacy, tireless efforts, and belief in my stories gave me the motivation to see this project to "The End." Another big thank-you to my brilliant editor, Tessa Woodward, whose guidance, keen insight, and constructive feedback played an instrumental part in refining this story. I am extremely grateful to you both for making my publishing dream a reality.

A very special thank-you to the archivists and staff at the Atlanta University Center Robert W. Woodruff Library for taking such great care with the McDuffie collection. Thanks for making it possible for me to carefully sift through each artifact and letter while the world was still healing. Additionally, I want to thank my copy editor for the meticulous attention to detail, my cover designer for bringing my vision to life, and assistant editor Madelyn Blaney for keeping the production wheels turning.

As for my writing tribes—my Divas and Lyonesses—thank you for your camaraderie and unwavering support. Your encouragement and shared experiences have been a source of inspiration and motivation for me throughout this journey. I want to especially thank Kaia Alderson for providing the seeds that helped produce this idea; to K.D. King for those much-needed brainstorming sessions early on; to Piper Huguley for being an invaluable resource and friend; and to Kate Quinn—your insight and guidance have led to my immense learning and growth as a writer.

To my sister-friends: Alyssa Cole, PennyMaria Jackson, and Darling Deligent—thank you for your support, enthusiasm, acceptance, and for just checking in, especially when I needed it the most.

Lastly, my utmost and profound gratitude to my mother, husband, and sisters. You all make up my small but steadfast village, and it's your unconditional love, support, and understanding that keep me writing.

To my amazing mother, Josette, for being an exceptional mom and grandma—thank you for your unwavering belief in my dreams and for pushing me to my peak potential.

To my devoted husband, Jeffrey—thank you for taking this journey with me and loving me through all the highs and lows of this writing life.

To my sister Mita—thank you for consistently reminding me of who I am.

And to Sandra—the greatest sister of all time. It's with all my heart that I thank you for being my sounding board, my harshest critic, and my biggest fan. Thanks for always challenging me, believing in me, dreaming with me, and geeking out with me no matter the story idea. You take the crown for the world's best sister *and* auntie!

Finally, to my first born, my "Son-shine." Thank you for helping me recognize my purpose. You may have missed the best parts of me while I worked hard to finish this book, but we now have forever together.

To each and every one of you, I say thank you. I am truly fortunate to have such an incredible group of people in my corner.